SOMETHING I'VE BEEN MEANING TO TELL YOU

Alice Munro was born in 1931 and is the author of twelve collections of stories, most recently *Dear Life*, and a novel, *Lives of Girls and Women*. She has received many awards and prizes, including three of Canada's Governor General's Literary Awards and two Giller Prizes, the REA Award for the Short Story, the Lannan Literary Award, the WHSmith Book Award in the UK, the National Book Critics Circle Award in the US, was shortlisted for the Booker Prize for *The Beggar Maid*, has been awarded the Man Booker International Prize 2009 for her overall contribution to fiction on the world stage and in 2013 won the Nobel Prize in Literature. Her stories have appeared in the *New Yorker*, *Atlantic Monthly*, *Paris Review* and other publications, and her collections have been translated into thirteen languages.

She lives with her husband in Clinton, Ontario, near Lake Huron in Canada.

ALSO BY ALICE MUNRO

Lying Under the Apple Tree
Dear Life
Too Much Happiness
The View from Castle Rock
Runaway
Hateship, Friendship, Courtship, Loveship, Marriage
The Love of a Good Woman
Selected Stories
Open Secrets
Friend of My Youth
The Progress of Love
The Moons of Jupiter
The Beggar Maid
Lives of Girls and Women
Dance of the Happy Shades

ALICE MUNRO

Something I've Been Meaning To Tell You

VINTAGE BOOKS
London

Published by Vintage 2014

2 4 6 8 10 9 7 5 3 1

Copyright © Alice Munro 1974

Alice Munro has asserted her right under the Copyright, Designs and
Patents Act 1988 to be identified as the author of this work

First published in 1974 by
McGraw-Hill Ryerson

First published in Great Britain in 1985 by
Penguin Books

Random House, 20 Vauxhall Bridge Road,
London SW1V 2SA

A Penguin Random House Company

Penguin
Random House
UK

www.vintage-books.co.uk

global.penguinrandomhouse.com

A CIP catalogue record for this book
is available from the British Library

ISBN 9781784700898

Penguin Random House supports the Forest Stewardship Council®
(FSC®), the leading international forest-certification organisation.
Our books carrying the FSC label are printed on FSC®-certified
paper. FSC is the only forest-certification scheme supported by the
leading environmental organisations, including Greenpeace. Our
paper procurement policy can be found at:
www.randomhouse.co.uk/environment

Printed and bound in Great Britain by
CPI Group (UK) Ltd, Croydon, CR0 4YY

FOR SHEILA, JENNY, ANDREA

CONTENTS

SOMETHING I'VE BEEN MEANING TO TELL YOU · 1

MATERIAL · 28

HOW I MET MY HUSBAND · 53

WALKING ON WATER · 78

FORGIVENESS IN FAMILIES · 108

TELL ME YES OR NO · 124

THE FOUND BOAT · 147

EXECUTIONERS · 162

MARRAKESH · 182

THE SPANISH LADY · 204

WINTER WIND · 223

MEMORIAL · 240

THE OTTAWA VALLEY · 264

SOMETHING I'VE BEEN
MEANING TO TELL YOU

'Anyway he knows how to fascinate the women,' said Et to Char. She could not tell if Char went paler, hearing this, because Char was pale in the first place as anybody could get. She was like a ghost now, with her hair gone white. But still beautiful, she couldn't lose it.

'No matter to him the age or the size,' Et pressed on. 'It's natural to him as breathing, I guess. I only hope the poor things aren't taken in by it.'

'I wouldn't worry,' Char said.

The day before, Et had taken Blaikie Noble up on his invitation to go along on one of his tours and listen to his spiel. Char was asked too, but of course she didn't go. Blaikie Noble ran a bus. The bottom part of it was painted red and the top part was striped, to give the effect of an awning. On the side was painted: LAKESHORE TOURS, INDIAN GRAVES, LIMESTONE GARDENS, MILLIONAIRE'S MANSION, BLAIKIE NOBLE, DRIVER, GUIDE. Blaikie had a room at the hotel, and he also worked on the grounds, with one helper, cutting grass and clipping hedges and digging the borders. What a comedown, Et had said at the beginning of the summer when they first found out he was back. She and Char had known him in the old days.

So Et found herself squeezed into his bus with a lot of strangers, though before the afternoon was over she had made friends with a number of them and had a couple of promises of jackets needing letting out, as if she didn't have enough to do already. That was beside the point, the thing on her mind was watching Blaikie.

And what did he have to show? A few mounds with grass growing on them, covering dead Indians, a plot full of odd-shaped, greyish-white, dismal-looking limestone things – far-fetched imitations of plants (there could be the cemetery, if that was what you wanted) – and an old monstrosity of a house built with liquor money. He made the most of it. A historical discourse on the Indians, then a scientific discourse on the Limestone. Et had no way of knowing how much of it was true. Arthur would know. But Arthur wasn't there; there was nobody there but silly women, hoping to walk beside Blaikie to and from the sights, chat with him over their tea in the Limestone Pavilion, looking forward to having his strong hand under their elbows, the other hand brushing somewhere around the waist, when he helped them down off the bus ('I'm not a tourist,' Et whispered sharply when he tried it on her).

He told them the house was haunted. The first Et had

ever heard of it, living ten miles away all her life. A woman had killed her husband, the son of the millionaire, at least it was believed she had killed him.

'How?' cried some lady, thrilled out of her wits.

'Ah, the ladies are always anxious to know the means,' said Blaikie, in a voice like cream, scornful and loving. 'It was a slow – poison. Or that's what they said. This is all hearsay, all local gossip.' (*Local my foot*, said Et to herself.) 'She didn't appreciate his lady friends. The wife didn't. No.'

He told them the ghost walked up and down in the garden, between two rows of blue spruce. It was not the murdered man who walked, but the wife, regretting. Blaikie smiled ruefully at the busload. At first Et had thought his attentions were all false, an ordinary commercial flirtation, to give them their money's worth. But gradually she was getting a different notion. He bent to each woman he talked to – it didn't matter how fat or scrawny or silly she was – as if there was one thing in her he would like to find. He had a gentle and laughing but ultimately serious, narrowing look (was that the look men finally had when they made love, that Et would never see?) that made him seem to want to be a deep-sea diver diving down, down through all the emptiness and cold and wreckage to discover the one thing he had set his heart on, something small and precious, hard to locate, as a ruby maybe on the ocean floor. That was a look she would like to have described to Char. No doubt Char had seen it. But did she know how freely it was being distributed?

Char and Arthur had been planning a trip that summer to see Yellowstone Park and the Grand Canyon, but they did not go. Arthur suffered a series of dizzy spells just at the end of school, and the doctor put him to bed. Several things were the matter with him. He was anaemic, he had an irregular heartbeat, there was trouble with his kidneys. Et worried about leukaemia. She woke at night, worrying.

'Don't be silly,' said Char serenely. 'He's overtired.'

Arthur got up in the evenings and sat in his dressing gown. Blaikie Noble came to visit. He said his room at the hotel was a hole above the kitchen, they were trying to steam-cook him. It made him appreciate the cool of the porch. They played the games that Arthur loved, schoolteacher's games. They played a geography game, and they tried to see who could make the most words out of the name Beethoven. Arthur won. He got thirty-four. He was immensely delighted.

'You'd think you'd found the Holy Grail,' Char said.

They played 'Who Am I?' Each of them had to choose somebody to be – real or imaginary, living or dead, human or animal – and the others had to try to guess it in twenty questions. Et got who Arthur was on the thirteenth question, Sir Galahad.

'I never thought you'd get it so soon.'

'I thought back to Char saying about the Holy Grail.'

'*My strength is as the strength of ten*,' said Blaikie Noble, '*Because my heart is pure.* I didn't know I remembered that.'

'You should have been King Arthur,' Et said. 'King Arthur is your namesake.'

'I should have. King Arthur was married to the most beautiful woman in the world.'

'Ha,' said Et. 'We all know the end of that story.'

Char went into the living room and played the piano in the dark.

The flowers that bloom in the spring, tra-la,
Have nothing to do with the case . . .

When Et arrived, out of breath, that past June, and said, 'Guess who I saw downtown on the street?' Char, who was on her knees picking strawberries, said, 'Blaikie Noble.'

'You've seen him.'

'No,' said Char. 'I just knew. I think I knew by your voice.'

A name that had not been mentioned between them for thirty years. Et was too amazed then to think of the explanation that came to her later. Why did it need to be a surprise to Char? There was a postal service in this country, there had been all along.

'I asked him about his wife,' she said. 'The one with the dolls.' (As if Char wouldn't remember.) 'He says she died a long time ago. Not only that. He married another one and she's dead. Neither could have been rich. And where is all the Nobles' money, from the hotel?'

'We'll never know,' said Char, and ate a strawberry.

The hotel had just recently been opened up again. The Nobles had given it up in the twenties and the town had operated it for a while as a hospital. Now some people from Toronto had bought it, renovated the dining room, put in a cocktail lounge, reclaimed the lawns and garden, though the tennis court seemed to be beyond repair. There was a croquet set put out again. People came to stay in the summers, but they were not the sort of people who used to come. Retired couples. Many widows and single ladies. Nobody would have walked a block to see them get off the boat, Et thought. Not that there was a boat any more.

That first time she met Blaikie Noble on the street she had made a point of not being taken aback. He was wearing a creamy suit and his hair, that had always been bleached by the sun, was bleached for good now, white.

'Blaikie. I knew either it was you or a vanilla ice-cream cone. I bet you don't know who I am.'

'You're Et Desmond and the only thing different about you is you cut off your braids.' He kissed her forehead, nervy as always.

'So you're back visiting old haunts,' said Et, wondering who had seen that.

'Not visiting. Haunting.' He told her then how he had got wind of the hotel opening up again, and how he had been doing this sort of thing, driving tour buses, in various places, in Florida and Banff. And when she asked he told her about his two wives. He never asked was she married, taking for granted she wasn't. He never asked if Char was, till she told him.

Et remembered the first time she understood that Char was beautiful. She was looking at a picture taken of them, of Char and herself and their brother who was drowned. Et was ten in the picture, Char fourteen and Sandy seven, just a couple of weeks short of all he would ever be. Et was sitting in an armless chair and Char was behind her, arms folded on the chair-back, with Sandy in his sailor suit cross-legged on the floor – or marble terrace, you would think, with the effect made by what had been nothing but a dusty, yellowing screen, but came out in the picture a pillar and draped curtain, a scene of receding poplars and fountains. Char had pinned her front hair up for the picture and was wearing a bright blue, ankle-length silk dress – of course the colour did not show – with complicated black velvet piping. She was smiling slightly, with great composure. She could have been eighteen, she could have been twenty-two. Her beauty was not of the fresh timid sort most often featured on calendars and cigar boxes of the period, but was sharp and delicate, intolerant, challenging.

Et took a long look at this picture and then went and looked at Char, who was in the kitchen. It was washday. The woman who came to help was pulling clothes through the wringer, and their mother was sitting down resting and staring through the screen door (she never got over Sandy, nobody expected her to). Char was starching their father's collars. He had a tobacco and candy store on the Square and wore a fresh collar every day. Et was prepared to find that some metamorphosis had taken place, as in the background, but it was not so. Char, bending over the starch basin, silent and bad-humoured (she hated washday, the heat and steam and flapping sheets and chugging commotion of the machine – in fact, she was not fond of any kind of housework), showed in her real face the same almost disdainful harmony as in the photograph. This made Et understand, in some not entirely welcome way, that the qualities of legend were real, that they surfaced where and when you least expected. She had almost thought beautiful women were a fictional invention. She and Char would go down to watch the people get off the excursion boat, on Sundays, walking up to the Hotel. So much white it hurt your eyes, the ladies' dresses and parasols and the men's summer suits and Panama hats, not to speak of the sun dazzling on the water and the band playing. But looking closely at those ladies, Et found fault. Coarse skin or fat behind or chicken necks or dull nests of hair, probably ratted. Et did not let anything get by her, young as she was. At school she was respected for her self-possession and her sharp tongue. She was the one to tell you if you had been at the blackboard with a hole in your stocking or a ripped hem. She was the one who imitated (but in a safe corner of the schoolyard, out of earshot, always) the teacher reading 'The Burial of Sir John Moore'.

All the same it would have suited her better to have found one of those ladies beautiful, not Char. It would have been more appropriate. More suitable than Char in her wet apron with her cross expression, bent over the starch basin. Et was a person who didn't like mysteries or extremes.

She didn't like the bleak notoriety of having Sandy's drowning attached to her, didn't like the memory people kept of her father carrying the body up from the beach. She could be seen at twilight, in her gym bloomers, turning cartwheels on the lawn of the stricken house. She made a wry mouth, which nobody saw, one day in the park when Char said, 'That was my little brother who was drowned.'

The park overlooked the beach. They were standing there with Blaikie Noble, the hotel owner's son, who said, 'Those waves can be dangerous. Three or four years ago there was a kid drowned.'

And Char said – to give her credit, she didn't say it

tragically, but almost with amusement, that he should know so little about Mock Hill people – 'That was my little brother who was drowned.'

Blaikie Noble was not any older than Char – if he had been, he would have been fighting in France – but he had not had to live all his life in Mock Hill. He did not know the real people there as well as he knew the regular guests at his father's hotel. Every winter he went with his parents to California, on the train. He had seen the Pacific surf. He had pledged allegiance to their flag. His manners were democratic, his skin was tanned. This was at a time when people were not usually tanned as a result of leisure, only work. His hair was bleached by the sun. His good looks were almost as notable as Char's but his were corrupted by charm, as hers were not.

It was the heyday of Mock Hill and all the other towns around the lakes, of all the hotels which in later years would become Sunshine Camps for city children, T.B. sanatoriums, barracks, for R.A.F. training pilots in World War II. The white paint on the hotel was renewed every spring, hollowed-out logs filled with flowers were set on the railings, pots and flowers swung on chains above them. Croquet sets and wooden swings were set out on the lawns, the tennis court rolled. People who could not afford the hotel, young workingmen, shop clerks and factory girls from the city, stayed in a row of tiny cottages, joined by latticework that hid their garbage pails and communal outhouses, stretching far up the beach. Girls from Mock Hill, if they had mothers to tell them what to do, were told not to walk out there. Nobody told Char what to do, so she walked along the boardwalk in front of them in the glaring afternoon, taking Et with her for company. The cottages had no glass in their windows, they had only propped-up wooden shutters that were closed at night. From the dark holes came one or two indistinct, sad or drunk invitations, that was all. Char's looks and style did not attract men, perhaps intimidated them. All through high school in Mock Hill she had not one boy friend. Blaikie Noble was her first, if that was what he was.

What did this affair of Char's and Blaikie Noble's amount to, in the summer of 1918? Et was never sure. He did not call at the house, at least not more than once or twice. He was kept busy, working at the hotel. Every afternoon he drove an open excursion wagon, with an awning on top of it, up the lakeshore road, taking people to look at the Indian graves and the limestone garden and to glimpse through the trees the Gothic stone mansion, built by a Toronto distiller and known locally as Grog Castle. He was also in charge of the variety show the hotel put on once a week, with a mixture of local talent, recruited guests, and singers and comedians brought in especially for the performance.

Late mornings seemed to be the time he and Char had. 'Come on,' Char would say, 'I have to go downtown,' and she would in fact pick up the mail and walk part way round the Square before veering off into the park. Soon Blaikie Noble would appear from the side door of the hotel and come bounding up the steep path. Sometimes he would not even bother with the path but jump over the back fence, to amaze them. None of this, the bounding or jumping, was done the way some boy from Mock Hill High School might have done it, awkwardly yet naturally. Blaikie Noble behaved like a man imitating a boy; he mocked himself but was graceful, like an actor.

'Isn't he stuck on himself?' said Et to Char, watching. The position she had taken up right away on Blaikie was that she didn't like him.

'Of course he is,' said Char.

She told Blaikie. 'Et says you're stuck on yourself.'

'What did you say?'

'I told her you had to be, nobody else is.'

Blaikie didn't mind. He had taken the position that he liked Et. He would with a quick tug loosen and destroy the arrangement of looped-up braids she wore. He told them things about the concert artists. He told them the Scottish ballad singer was a drunk and wore corsets, that the female impersonator even in his hotel room donned a blue nightgown with feathers, that the lady ventriloquist talked to her dolls – they were named Alphonse and Alicia – as if they were real people, and had them sitting up in bed one on each side of her.

'How would you know that?' Char said.

'I took her up her breakfast.'

'I thought you had maids to do that.'

'The morning after the show I do it. That's when I hand them their pay envelope and give them their walking papers. Some of them would stay all week if you didn't inform them. She sits up in bed trying to feed them bits of bacon and talking to them and doing them answering back, you'd have a fit if you could see.'

'She's cracked I guess,' Char said peacefully.

One night that summer Et woke up and remembered she had left her pink organdy dress on the line, after handwashing it. She thought she heard rain, just the first few drops. She didn't, it was just leaves rustling, but she was confused, waking up like that. She thought it was far on in the night, too, but thinking about it later she decided it might have been only around midnight. She got up and went downstairs, turned on the back kitchen light, and let herself out the back door, and standing on the stoop pulled the clothesline towards her. Then almost under her feet, from the grass right beside the stoop, where there was a big lilac bush that had grown and spread, untended, to the size of a tree, two figures lifted themselves, didn't stand or even sit up, just roused their heads as if from bed, still tangled together some way. The back kitchen light didn't shine directly out but lit the yard enough to her to see their faces. Blaikie and Char.

She never did get a look at what state their clothes were in, to see how far they had gone or were going. She wouldn't have wanted to. To see their faces was enough for her. Their mouths were big and swollen, their cheeks flattened, coarsened, their eyes holes. Et left her dress, she fled into the house and into her bed where she surprised herself by falling asleep. Char never said a word about it to her next day. All she said was, 'I brought your dress in, Et. I thought it might rain.' As if she had never seen Et out there pulling on the clothesline. Et wondered. She knew if she said, 'You saw me,' Char would probably tell her it had been a dream. She let Char think she had been fooled into believing that, if that was what Char was thinking. That way, Et was left knowing more; she was left knowing what Char looked like when she lost her powers, abdicated. Sandy drowned, with green stuff clogging his nostrils, couldn't look more lost than that.

Before Christmas the news came to Mock Hill that Blaikie Noble was married. He had married the lady ventriloquist, the one with Alphonse and Alicia. Those dolls, who wore evening dress and had sleek hairdos in the style of Vernon and Irene Castle, were more clearly remembered than the lady herself. The only thing people recalled for sure about her was that she could not have been under forty. A nineteen-year-old boy. It was because he had not been brought up like other boys, had been allowed the run of the hotel, taken to California, let mix with all sorts of people. The result was depravity, and could have been predicted.

Char swallowed poison. Or what she thought was poison. It was laundry blueing. The first thing she could reach down from the shelf in the back kitchen. Et came home after school – she had heard the news at noon, from Char herself in fact, who had laughed and said, 'Wouldn't that kill you?' – and she found Char vomiting into the toilet. 'Go get the Medical Book,' Char said to her. A terrible involuntary groan came out of her. 'Read what it says about poison.' Et went instead to phone the doctor. Char came staggering out of the bathroom holding the bottle of bleach they kept behind the tub. 'If you don't put up the phone I'll drink the whole bottle,' she said in a harsh whisper. Their mother was presumably asleep behind her closed door.

Et had to hang up the phone and look in the ugly old book where she had read long ago about childbirth and signs of death, and had learned about holding a mirror to the mouth. She was under the mistaken impression that Char had been drinking from the bleach bottle already, so she read all about that. Then she found it was the blueing. Blueing was not in the book, but it seemed the best thing to do would be to induce vomiting, as the book advised for most poisons – Char was at it already, didn't need to have it induced – and then drink a quart of milk. When Char got the milk down she was sick again.

'I didn't do this on account of Blaikie Noble,' she said between spasms. 'Don't you ever think that. I wouldn't be such a fool. A pervert like him. I did it because I'm sick of living.'

'What are you sick of about living?' said Et sensibly when Char had wiped her face.

'I'm sick of this town and all the stupid people in it and Mother and her dropsy and keeping house and washing sheets every day. I don't think I'm going to vomit any more. I think I could drink some coffee. It says coffee.'

Et made a pot and Char got out two of the best cups. They began to giggle as they drank.

'I'm sick of Latin,' Et said. 'I'm sick of Algebra. I think I'll take blueing.'

'Life is a burden,' Char said. '*O Life, where is thy sting?*'

'*O Death. O Death, where is thy sting?*'

'Did I say Life? I meant Death. *O Death, where is thy sting?* Pardon me.'

One afternoon Et was staying with Arthur while Char shopped and changed books at the Library. She wanted to make him an eggnog, and she went searching in Char's cupboard for the nutmeg. In with the vanilla and the almond extract and the artificial rum she found a small bottle of a strange liquid. *Zinc phosphide.* She read the label and turned it around in her hands. A rodenticide. Rat poison, that must mean. She had not known Char and Arthur were troubled with rats. They kept a cat, old Tom, asleep now around Arthur's feet. She unscrewed the top and sniffed at it, to know what it smelled like. Like nothing. Of course. It must taste like nothing too, or it wouldn't fool the rats.

She put it back where she had found it. She made Arthur his eggnog and took it in and watched him drink it. A slow poison. She remembered that from Blaikie's foolish story. Arthur drank with an eager noise, like a child, more to please her, she thought, than because he was so pleased himself. He would drink anything you handed him. Naturally.

'How are you these days, Arthur?'

'Oh, Et. Some days a bit stronger, and then I seem to slip back. It takes time.'

But there was none gone, the bottle seemed full. What awful nonsense. Like something you read about, Agatha Christie. She would mention it to Char and Char would tell her the reason.

'Do you want me to read to you?' she asked Arthur, and he said yes. She sat by the bed and read to him from a book about the Duke of Wellington. He had been reading it by himself but his arms got tired holding it. All those battles, and wars, and terrible things, what did Arthur know about such affairs, why was he so interested? He knew nothing. He did not know why things happened, why people could not behave sensibly. He was too good. He knew about history but not about what went on, in front of his eyes, in his house, anywhere. Et differed from Arthur in knowing that something went on, even if she could not understand why; she differed from him in knowing there were those you could not trust.

She did not say anything to Char after all. Every time she was in the house she tried to make some excuse to be alone in the kitchen, so that she could open the cupboard and stand on tiptoe and look in, to see it over the tops of the other bottles, to see that the level had not gone down. She did think maybe she was going a little strange, as old maids did; this fear of hers was like the absurd and harmless fears young girls sometimes have, that they will jump out a window, or strangle a baby, sitting in its buggy. Though it was not her own acts she was frightened of.

Et looked at Char and Blaikie and Arthur, sitting on the porch, trying to decide if they wanted to go in and put the light on and play cards. She wanted to convince herself of her silliness. Char's hair, and Blaikie's too, shone in the dark. Arthur was almost bald now and Et's own hair was thin and dark. Char and Blaikie seemed to her the same kind of animal – tall, light, powerful, with a dangerous luxuriance. They sat apart but shone out together. *Lovers.* Not a soft word, as people thought, but cruel and tearing. There was Arthur in the rocker with a quilt over his knees, foolish as something that hasn't grown its final, most necessary, skin. Yet in a way the people like Arthur were the most trouble-making of all.

'I love my love with an R, because he is ruthless. His name is Rex, and he lives in a – restaurant.'

'I love my love with an A, because he is absent-minded. His name is Arthur, and he lives in an ashcan.'

'Why Et,' Arthur said. 'I never suspected. But I don't know if I like about the ashcan.'

'You would think we were all twelve years old,' said Char.

After the blueing episode Char became popular. She became involved in the productions of the Amateur Dramatic Society and the Oratorio Society, although she was never much of an actress or a singer. She was always the cold and beautiful heroine in the plays, or the brittle exquisite young society woman. She learned to smoke, because of having to do it on stage. In one play Et never forgot, she was a statue. Or rather, she played a girl who had to pretend to be a statue, so that a young man fell in love with her and later discovered, to his confusion and perhaps disappointment, that she was only human. Char had to stand for eight minutes perfectly still on stage, draped in white crepe and showing the audience her fine indifferent profile. Everybody marvelled at how she did it.

The moving spirit behind the Amateur Dramatic Society and the Oratorio Society was a high school teacher new to Mock Hill, Arthur Comber. He taught Et history in her last year. Everybody said he gave her A's because he was in love with her sister, but Et knew it was because she worked harder than she ever had before; she learned the History of North America as she had never learned anything in her life. Missouri Compromise. Mackenzie to the Pacific, 1793. She never forgot.

Arthur Comber was thirty or so, with a high bald forehead, a red face in spite of not drinking (that later paled) and a clumsy, excited manner. He knocked a bottle of ink off his desk and permanently stained the History Room floor. 'Oh dear, oh dear,' he said, crouching down to the spreading ink, flapping at it with his handkerchief. Et imitated that. 'Oh dear, oh dear!' 'Oh good heavens!' All his flustery exclamations and miscalculated gestures. Then, when he took her essay at the door, his red face shining with eagerness, giving her work and herself such a welcome, she felt sorry. That was why she worked so hard, she thought, to make up for mocking him.

He had a black scholar's gown he wore over his suit, to teach in. Even when he wasn't wearing it, Et could see it on him. Hurrying along the street to one of his innumerable, joyfully undertaken obligations, flapping away at the Oratorio singers, jumping on stage – so the whole floor trembled – to demonstrate something to the actors in a play, he seemed to her to have those long ridiculous crow's wings flapping after him, to be as different from other men, as absurd yet intriguing, as the priest from Holy Cross. Char made him give up the gown altogether, after they were married. She had heard that he tripped in it, running up the steps of the school. He had gone sprawling. That finished it, she ripped it up.

'I was afraid one of these days you'd really get hurt.'

But Arthur said, 'Ah. You thought I looked like a fool.'

Char didn't deny it, though his eyes on her, his wide smile, were begging her to. Her mouth twitched at the corners, in spite of herself. Contempt. Fury. Et saw, they both saw, a great wave of that go over her before she could smile at him and say, 'Don't be silly.' Then her smile and her eyes were trying to hold on to him, trying to clutch into his goodness (which she saw, as much as anybody else did, but which finally only enraged her, Et believed, like everything else about him, like his sweaty forehead and his galloping optimism), before that boiling wave could come back again, altogether carry her away.

Char had a miscarriage during the first year of her marriage and was sick for a long time afterwards. She was never pregnant again. Et by this time was not living in the house; she had her own place on the Square, but she was there one time on washday, helping Char haul the sheets off the line. Their parents were both dead by that time – their mother had died before and their father after the wedding – but it looked to Et like sheets for two beds.

'It gives you plenty of wash.'

'What does?'

'Changing sheets like you do.'

Et was often there in the evening, playing rummy with Arthur while Char, in the other room, picked at the piano in the dark. Or talking and reading library books with Char, while Arthur marked his papers. Arthur walked her home. 'Why do you have to go off and live by yourself anyway?' he scolded her. 'You ought to come back and live with us.'

'Three's a crowd.'

'It wouldn't be for long. Some man is going to come along some day and fall hard.'

'If he was such a fool as to do that I'd never fall for him, we'd be back where we started.'

'I was a fool that fell for Char, and she ended up having me.'

Just the way he said her name indicated that Char was above, outside, all ordinary considerations – a marvel, a mystery. No one could hope to solve her, they were lucky just being allowed to contemplate her. Et was on the verge of saying, 'She swallowed blueing once over a man that wouldn't have her,' but she thought what would be the good of it, Char would only seem more splendid to him, like a heroine out of Shakespeare. He squeezed Et's waist as if to stress their companionable puzzlement, involuntary obeisance, before her sister. She felt afterwards the bumpy pressure of his fingers as if they had left dents just above where her skirt fastened. It had felt like somebody absent-mindedly trying out the keys of a piano.

Et had set up in the dressmaking business. She had a long narrow room on the Square, once a shop, where she did all her fitting, sewing, cutting, pressing and, behind a curtain, her sleeping and cooking. She could lie in bed and look at the squares of pressed tin on her ceiling, their flower pattern, all her own. Arthur had not liked her taking up dressmaking because he thought she was too smart for it. All the hard work she had done in History had given him an exaggerated idea of her brains. 'Besides,' she told him, 'it takes more brains to cut and fit, if you do it right, than to teach people about the War of 1812. Because, once you learn that, it's learned and isn't going to change you. Whereas every article of clothing you make is an entirely new proposition.'

'Still it's a surprise,' said Arthur, 'to see the way you settle down.'

It surprised everybody, but not Et herself. She made the change easily, from a girl turning cartwheels to a town fixture. She drove the other dressmakers out of business.

They had been meek, unimportant creatures anyway, going around to people's houses, sewing in back rooms and being grateful for meals. Only one serious rival appeared in all Et's years, and that was a Finnish woman who called herself a designer. Some people gave her a try, because people are never satisfied, but it soon came out she was all style and no fit. Et never mentioned her, she let people find out for themselves; but afterwards, when this woman had left town and gone to Toronto – where, from what Et had seen on the streets, nobody knew a good fit from a bad – Et did not restrain herself. She would say to a customer she was fitting, 'I see you're still wearing that herringbone my foreigner friend tacked together for you. I saw you on the street.'

'Oh, I know,' the woman would say. 'But I do have to wear it out.'

'You can't see yourself from behind anyway, what's the difference.'

Customers took this kind of thing from Et, came to expect it, even. She's a terror, they said about her, Et's a terror. She had them at a disadvantage, she had them in their slips and corsets. Ladies who looked quite firm and powerful, outside, were here immobilized, apologetic, exposing such trembly, meek-looking thighs squeezed together by corsets, such long sad breast creases, bellies blown up and torn by children and operations.

Et always closed her front curtains tight, pinning the crack.

'That's to keep the men from peeking.'

Ladies laughed nervously.

'That's to keep Jimmy Saunders from stumping over to get an eyeful.'

Jimmy Saunders was a World War I veteran who had a little shop next to Et's, harness and leather goods.

'Oh, Et. Jimmy Saunders has a wooden leg.'

'He hasn't got wooden eyes. Or anything else that I know of.'

'Et you're terrible.'

Et kept Char beautifully dressed. The two steadiest criticisms of Char, in Mock Hill, were that she dressed too elegantly, and that she smoked. It was because she was a teacher's wife that she should have refrained from doing either of these things, but Arthur of course let her do anything she liked, even buying her a cigarette holder so she could look like a lady in a magazine. She smoked at a high school dance, and wore a backless satin evening dress, and danced with a boy who had got a high school girl pregnant, and it was all the same to Arthur. He did not get to be Principal. Twice the school board passed him over and brought in somebody from outside, and when they finally gave him the job, in 1942, it was only temporarily and because so many teachers were away at war.

Char fought hard all these years to keep her figure. Nobody but Et and Arthur knew what effort that cost her. Nobody but Et knew it all. Both of their parents had been heavy, and Char had inherited the tendency, though Et was always as thin as a stick. Char did exercises and drank a glass of warm water before every meal. But sometimes she went on eating binges. Et had known her to eat a dozen cream puffs one after the other, a pound of peanut brittle, or a whole lemon meringue pie. Then pale and horrified she took down Epsom salts, three or four or five times the prescribed amount. For two or three days she would be sick, dehydrated, purging her sins, as Et said. During these periods she could not look at food. Et would have to come and cook Arthur's supper. Arthur did not know about the pie or the peanut brittle or whatever it was, or about the Epsom salts. He thought she had gained a pound or two and was going through a fanatical phase of dieting. He worried about her.

'What is the difference, what does it matter?' he would say to Et. 'She would still be beautiful.'

'She won't do herself any harm,' said Et, enjoying her food, and glad to see that worry hadn't put him off his. She always made him good suppers.

It was the week before the Labour Day weekend. Blaikie had gone to Toronto, for a day or two he said.

'It's quiet without him,' said Arthur.

'I never noticed he was such a conversationalist,' Et said.

'I only mean in the way that you get used to somebody.'

'Maybe we ought to get unused to him,' said Et.

Arthur was unhappy. He was not going back to the school; he had obtained a leave of absence until after Christmas. Nobody believed he would go back then.

'I suppose he has his own plans for the winter,' he said.

'He may have his own plans for right now. You know I have my customers from the hotel. I have my friends. Ever since I went on that excursion, I hear things.'

She never knew where she got the inspiration to say what she said, where it came from. She had not planned it at all, yet it came so easily, believably.

'I hear he's taken up with a well-to-do woman down at the hotel.'

Arthur was the one to take an interest, not Char.

'A widow?'

'Twice, I believe. The same as he is. And she has the money from both. It's been suspected for some time and she was talking about it openly. He never said anything, though. He never said anything to you, did he, Char?'

'No,' said Char.

'I heard this afternoon that now he's gone, and she's gone. It wouldn't be the first time he pulled something like this. Char and I remember.'

Then Arthur wanted to know what she meant and she told him the story of the lady ventriloquist, remembering even the names of the dolls, though of course she left out all about Char. Char sat through this, even contributing a bit.

'They might come back but my guess is they'd be embarrassed. He'd be embarrassed. He'd be embarrassed to come here, anyway.'

'Why?' said Arthur, who had cheered up a little through the ventriloquist story. 'We never set down any rule against a man getting married.'

Char got up and went into the house. After a while they heard the sound of the piano.

The question often crossed Et's mind in later years – what did she mean to do about this story when Blaikie got back? For she had no reason to believe he would not come back. The answer was that she had not made any plans at all. She had not planned anything. She supposed she might have wanted to make trouble between him and Char – make Char pick a fight with him, her suspicions roused even if rumours had not been borne out, make Char read what he might do again in the light of what he had done before. She did not know what she wanted. Only to throw things into confusion, for she believed then that somebody had to, before it was too late.

Arthur made as good a recovery as could be expected at his age, he went back to teaching History to the senior classes, working half-days until it was time for him to retire. Et kept up her own place on the Square and tried to get up and do some cooking and cleaning for Arthur, as well. Finally, after he retired, she moved back into the house, keeping the other place only for business purposes. 'Let people jaw all they like,' she said. 'At our age.'

Arthur lived on and on, though he was frail and slow. He walked down to the Square once a day, dropped in on Et, went and sat in the park. The hotel closed down and was sold again. There was a story that it was going to be opened up and used as a rehabilitation centre for drug addicts, but the town got up a petition and that fell through. Eventually it was torn down.

Et's eyesight was not as good as it used to be, she had to slow down. She had to turn people away. Still she worked, every day. In the evenings Arthur watched television or read, but she sat out on the porch, in the warm weather, or in the dining room in winter, rocking and resting her eyes. She came and watched the news with him, and made him his hot drink, cocoa or tea.

There was no trace of the bottle. Et went and looked in the cupboard as soon as she could – having run to the house in response to Arthur's early morning call, and found the doctor, old McClain, coming in at the same time. She ran out and looked in the garbage, but she never found it. Could Char have found the time to bury it? She was lying on the bed, fully and nicely dressed, her hair piled up. There was no fuss about the cause of death as there is in stories. She had complained of weakness to Arthur the night before, after Et had gone, she had said she thought she was getting the flu. So the old doctor said heart, and let it go. Nor could Et ever know. Would what was in that bottle leave a body undisfigured, as Char's was? Perhaps what was in the bottle was not what it said. She was not even sure that it had been there that last evening, she had been too carried away with what she was saying to go and look, as she usually did. Perhaps it had been thrown out earlier and Char had taken something else, pills maybe. Perhaps it really was her heart. All that purging would have weakened anybody's heart.

Her funeral was on Labour Day and Blaikie Noble came, cutting out his bus tour. Arthur in his grief had forgotten about Et's story, was not surprised to see Blaikie there. He had come back to Mock Hill on the same day Char was found. A few hours too late, like some story. Et in her natural confusion could not remember what it was. Romeo and Juliet, she thought later. But Blaikie of course did not do away with himself afterwards, he went back to Toronto. For a year or two he sent Christmas cards, then was not heard of any more. Et would not be surprised if her story of his marrying had not come true in the end. Only her timing was mistaken.

Sometimes Et had it on the tip of her tongue to say to

Arthur, 'There's something I've been meaning to tell you.' She didn't believe she was going to let him die without knowing. He shouldn't be allowed. He kept a picture of Char on his bureau. It was the one taken of her in her costume for that play, where she played the statue-girl. But Et let it go, day to day. She and Arthur still played rummy and kept up a bit of garden, along with raspberry canes. If they had been married, people would have said they were very happy.

MATERIAL

I don't keep up with Hugo's writing. Sometimes I see his name, in the library, on the cover of some literary journal that I don't open – I haven't opened a literary journal in a dozen years, praise God. Or I read in the paper or see on a poster – this would be in the library, too, or in a book-store – an announcement of a panel discussion at the University, with Hugo flown in to discuss the state of the novel today, or the contemporary short story, or the new nationalism in our literature. Then I think, will people really go, will people who could be swimming or drinking or going for a walk really take themselves out to the campus to find the room and sit in rows listening to those vain quarrelsome men? Bloated, opinionated, untidy men, that is how I see them, cosseted by the academic life, the literary life, by women. People will go to hear them say that such and such a writer is not worth reading any more, and that some writer must be read; to hear them dismiss and glorify and argue and chuckle and shock. People, I say, but I mean women, middle-aged women like me, alert and trembling, hoping to ask intelligent questions and not be ridiculous; soft-haired young girls awash in adoration, hoping to lock eyes with one of the men on the platform. Girls, and women too, fall in love with such men, they imagine there is a power in them.

The wives of the men on the platform are not in that audience. They are buying groceries or cleaning up messes or having a drink. Their lives are concerned with food and mess and houses and cars and money. They have to remember to get the snow tyres on and go to the bank and take back the beer bottles, because their husbands are such brilliant, such talented incapable men, who must be looked after for the sake of the words that will come from them. The women in the audience are married to engineers or doctors or businessmen. I know them, they are my friends. Some of them have turned to literature frivolously, it is true, but most come shyly, and with enormous transitory hope. They absorb the contempt of the men on the platform as if they deserved it; they half-believe they do deserve it, because of their houses and expensive shoes, and their husbands who read Arthur Hailey.

I am married to an engineer myself. His name is Gabriel, but he prefers the name Gabe. In this country he prefers the name Gabe. He was born in Romania, he lived there until the end of the war, when he was sixteen. He has forgotten how to speak Romanian. How can you forget, how can you forget the language of your childhood? I used to think he was pretending to forget, because the things he had seen and lived through when he spoke that language were too terrible to remember. He told me this was not so. He told me his experience of the war was not so bad. He described the holiday uproar at school when the air raid sirens sounded. I did not quite believe him. I required him to be an ambassador from bad times as well as distant countries. Then I thought he might not be Romanian at all, but an impostor.

This was before we were married, when he used to come and see me in the apartment on Clark Road where I lived with my little daughter, Clea, Hugo's daughter too, of course, but he had to let go of her. Hugo had grants, he travelled, he married again and his wife had three children; he divorced and married again, and his next wife, who had been his student, had three more children, the first born to her while he was still living with his second wife. In such circumstances a man can't hang on to everything. Gabriel used to stay all night sometimes on the pull-out couch I had for a bed in this tiny, shabby apartment; and I would look at him sleeping and think that for all I knew he might be a German or a Russian or even of all things a Canadian faking a past and an accent to make himself interesting. He was mysterious to me. Long after he became my lover and after he became my husband he remained, remains, mysterious to me. In spite of all the things I know about him, daily and physical things. His face curves out smoothly and his eyes, set shallowly in his head, curve out too under the smooth pink lids. The wrinkles he has are traced on top of this smoothness, this impenetrable surface; they are of no consequence. His body is substantial, calm. He used to be a fine, rather lazy-looking, skater. I cannot describe him. I could describe Hugo, if anybody asked me, in great detail – Hugo as he was eighteen, twenty years ago, crew-cut and skinny, with the bones of his body and even of his skull casually, precariously, joined and knitted together, so that there was something uncoordinated, unexpected about the shifting planes of his face as well as the movements, often dangerous, of his limbs. He's held together by nerves, a friend of mine at college said when I first brought him around, and it was true; after that I could almost see the fiery strings.

Gabriel told me when I first knew him that he enjoyed life. He did not say that he believed in enjoying it; he said that he did. I was embarrassed for him. I never believed people who said such things and anyway, I associated this statement with gross, self-advertising, secretly unpleasantly restless men. But it seems to be the truth. He is not curious. He is able to take pleasure and give off smiles and caresses and say softly, 'Why do you worry about that? It is not a problem of yours.' He has forgotten the language of his childhood. His lovemaking was strange to me at first, because it was lacking in desperation. He made love without emphasis, so to speak, with no memory of sin or hope of depravity. He does not watch himself. He will never write a poem about it, never, and indeed may have forgotten it in half an hour. Such men are commonplace, perhaps. It was only that I had not known any. I used to wonder if I would have fallen in love with him if his accent and his forgotten, nearly forgotten, past had been taken away; if he had been, say, an engineering student in my own year at college. I don't know, I can't tell. What holds anybody in a man or a woman maybe something as flimsy as a Romanian accent or the calm curve of an eyelid, some half-fraudulent mystery.

No mystery of this sort about Hugo. I did not miss it, did not know about it, maybe would not have believed in it. I believed in something else, then. Not that I knew him, all the way through, but the part I knew was in my blood and from time to time would give me a poison rash. None of that with Gabriel, he does not disturb me, any more than he is disturbed himself.

It was Gabriel who found me Hugo's story. We were in a bookstore, and he came to me with a large, expensive paperback, a collection of short stories. There was Hugo's name on the cover. I wondered how Gabriel had found it, what he had been doing in the fiction section of the store anyway, he never reads fiction. I wondered if he sometimes went and looked for things by Hugo. He is interested in Hugo's career as he would be interested in the career of a magician or popular singer or politician with whom he had, through me, a plausible connection, a proof of reality. I think it is because he does such anonymous work himself, work intelligible only to his own kind. He is fascinated by people who work daringly out in the public eye, without the protection of any special discipline – it must seem so, to an engineer – just trying to trust themselves, and elaborating their bag of tricks, and hoping to catch on.

'Buy it for Clea,' he said.

'Isn't it a lot of money for a paperback?'

He smiled.

'There's your father's picture, your real father, and he has written this story you might like to read,' I said to Clea, who was in the kitchen making toast. She is seventeen. Some days she eats toast and honey and peanut butter and Oreos and creamed cheese and chicken sandwiches and fried potatoes. If anybody comments on what she is eating or not eating, she may run upstairs and slam the door of her room.

'He looks overweight,' said Clea and put the book down. 'You always said he was skinny.' Her interest in her father is all from the point of view of heredity, and what genes he might have passed on to herself. Did he have a bad complexion, did he have a high I.Q., did the women in his family have big breasts?

'He was when I knew him,' I said. 'How was I to know what had happened to him since?'

He looked, however, very much as I would have thought he would look by now. When I saw his name in the newspaper or on a poster I had pictured somebody much like this; I had foreseen the ways in which time and his life would have changed him. It did not surprise me that he had got fat but not bald, that he had let his hair grow wild and had grown a full, curly beard. Pouches under his eyes, a dragged-down look to his cheeks even when he is laughing. He is laughing, into the camera. His teeth have gone from bad to worse. He hated dentists, said his father died of a heart attack in the dentist's chair. A lie, like so much else, or at least an exaggeration. He used to smile crookedly for photographs to hide the right top incisor, dead since somebody at high school pushed him into a drinking fountain. Now he doesn't care, he laughs, he bares those rotting stumps. He looks, at the same time, woebegone and cheerful. A Rabelaisian writer. Checked wool shirt open at the top to show his undershirt, he didn't use to wear one. Do you wash, Hugo? Do you have bad breath, with those teeth? Do you call your girl students fond exasperated dirty names, are there phone calls from insulted parents, does the Dean or somebody have to explain that no harm is meant, that writers are not as other men are? Probably not, probably no one minds. Outrageous writers may bounce from one blessing to another nowadays, bewildered, as permissively reared children are said to be, by excess of approval.

I have no proof. I construct somebody from this one smudgy picture, I am content with such clichés. I have not the imagination or good will to proceed differently; and I have noticed anyway, everybody must have noticed as we go further into middle age, how shopworn and simple, really, are the disguises, the identities if you like, that people take up. In fiction, in Hugo's business, such disguises would not do, but in life they are all we seem to want, all anybody can manage. Look at Hugo's picture, look at the undershirt, listen to what it says about him.

Hugo Johnson was born and semi-educated in the bush, and in the mining and lumbering towns of Northern Ontario. He has worked as a lumberjack, beer-slinger, counter-man, telephone lineman and sawmill foreman, and has been sporadically affiliated with various academic communities. He lives now most of the time on the side of a mountain above Vancouver, with his wife and six children.

The student wife, it seems, got stuck with all the children. What happened to Mary Frances, did she die, is she liberated, did he drive her crazy? But listen to the lies, the half-lies, the absurdities. *He lives on the side of a mountain above Vancouver.* It sounds as if he lives in a wilderness cabin, and all it means, I'm willing to bet, is that he lives in an ordinary comfortable house in North or West Vancouver, which now stretch far up the mountain. He has been *sporadically affiliated with various academic communities.* What does that mean? If it means he has taught for years, most of his adult life, at universities, that teaching at universities has been the only steady well-paid job he has ever had, why doesn't it say so? You would think he came out of the bush now and then to fling them scraps of wisdom, to give them a demonstration of what a real male *writer*, a creative *artist*, is like; you would never think he was a practising *academic*. I don't know if he was a lumberjack or a beer-slinger or a counter-man, but I do know that he was not a telephone lineman. He had a job painting telephone poles. He quit that job in the middle of the second week because the heat and the climbing made him sick. It was a broiling June, just after we had both graduated. Fair enough. The run really did make him sick, twice he came home and vomited. I have quit jobs myself that I could not stand. The same summer I quit my job folding bandages at Victoria Hospital, because I was going mad with boredom. But if I was a writer, and was listing all my varied and colourful occupations, I don't think I would put down *bandage folder*, I don't think I would find that entirely honest.

After he quit, Hugo found a job marking Grade Twelve examination papers. Why didn't he put that down? Examination marker. He liked marking examination papers better than he liked climbing telephone poles, and probably better than he liked lumberjacking or beer-slinging or any of those other things if he ever did them; why couldn't he put it down? *Examination marker.*

Nor has he, to my knowledge, ever been the foreman in a sawmill. He worked in his uncle's mill the summer before I met him. What he did all day was load lumber and get sworn at by the real foreman, who didn't like him because of his uncle being the boss. In the evenings, if he was not too tired, he used to walk half a mile to a little creek and play his recorder. Black flies bothered him, but he did it anyway. He could play 'Morning', from *Peer Gynt*, and some Elizabethan airs whose names I have forgotten. Except for one: 'Wolsey's Wilde'. I learned to play it on the piano so we could play a duet. Was that meant for Cardinal Wolsey, and what was a *wilde*, a dance? Put that down, Hugo. *Recorder player.* That would be quite all right, quite in fashion now: as I understand things, recorder playing and such fey activities are not out of favour, now, quite the contrary. Indeed, they may be more acceptable than all that lumberjacking and beer-slinging. Look at you, Hugo, your image is not only fake but out-of-date. You should have said you'd meditated for a year in the mountains of Uttar Pradesh; you should have said you'd taught Creative Drama to autistic children; you should have shaved your head, shaved your beard, put on a monk's cowl; you should have shut up, Hugo.

When I was pregnant with Clea we lived in a house on Argyle Street in Vancouver. It was such a sad grey stucco house on the outside, in the rainy winter, that we painted the inside, all the rooms, vivid ill-chosen colours. Three walls of the bedrooms were Wedgwood blue, one was magenta. We said it was an experiment to see if colour could drive anybody mad. The bathroom was a deep orange-yellow. 'It's like being inside a cheese,' Hugo said when we finished it. 'That's right, it is,' I said. 'That's very good, phrase-maker.' He was pleased but not as pleased as if he'd written it. After that he said, every time he showed anybody the bathroom, 'See the colour? It's like being inside a cheese.' Or, 'It's like peeing inside a cheese.' Not that I didn't do the same thing, save things up and say them over and over. Maybe I said that about peeing inside a cheese. We had many phrases in common. We both called the landlady the Green Hornet, because she had worn, the only time we had seen her, a poison-green outfit with bits of rat fur and a clutch of violets, and had given off a venomous sort of buzz. She was over seventy and she ran a downtown boarding house for men. Her daughter Dotty we called the harlot-in-residence. I wonder why we chose to say *harlot*; that was not, is not, a word in general use. I suppose it had a classy sound, a classy depraved sound, contrasting ironically – we were strong on irony – with Dotty herself.

She lived in a two-room apartment in the basement of the house. She was supposed to pay her mother forty-five dollars monthly rent and she told me she meant to try to make the money baby-sitting.

'I can't go out to work,' she said, 'on account of my nerves. My last husband, I had him six months dying down at Mother's, dying with his kidney disease, and I owe her three hundred dollars board still on that. She made me make him his eggnog with skim milk. I'm broke every day of my life. They say it's all right not having wealth if you got health, but what if you never had either one? Bronchial pneumonia from the time I was three years old. Rheumatic fever at twelve. Sixteen I married my first husband, he was killed in a logging accident. Three miscarriages. My womb is in shreds. I use up three packs of Kotex every month. I married a dairy farmer out in the Valley and his herd got the fever. Wiped us out. That was the one who died with his kidneys. No wonder. No wonder my nerves are shot.'

I am condensing. This came out at greater length and by no means dolefully, indeed with some amazement and pride, at Dotty's table. She asked me down for cups of tea, then for beer. This is life, I thought, fresh from books, classes, essays, discussions. Unlike her mother, Dotty was flat-faced, soft, doughy, fashioned for defeat, the kind of colourless puzzled woman you see carrying a shopping bag, waiting for the bus. In fact, I had seen her once on a bus downtown, and not recognized her at first in her dull blue winter coat. Her rooms were full of heavy furniture salvaged from her marriage – an upright piano, overstuffed chesterfield and chairs, walnut veneer china cabinet and dining room table, where we sat. In the middle of the table was a tremendous lamp, with a painted china base and a pleated, dark red silk shade, held out at an extravagant angle, like a hoop skirt.

I described it to Hugo. 'That is a whorehouse lamp,' I said. Afterwards I wanted to be congratulated on the accuracy of this description. I told Hugo he ought to pay more attention to Dotty if he wanted to be a writer. I told him about her husbands and her womb and her collection of souvenir spoons, and he said I was welcome to look at them all by myself. He was writing a verse play.

Once when I went down to put coal on the furnace, I found Dotty in her pink chenille dressing gown saying good-bye to a man in a uniform, some sort of delivery man or gas station attendant. It was the middle of the afternoon. She and this man were not parting in any way that suggested either lechery or affection and I would not have understood anything about it, I would probably have thought he was some relative, if she had not begun at once a long complicated slightly drunk story about how she had got wet in the rain and had to leave her clothes at her mother's house and worn home her mother's dress which was too tight and that was why she was now in her dressing gown. She said that first Larry had caught her in it delivering some sewing he wanted her to do for his wife, and now me, and she didn't know what we would think of her. This was strange, as I had seen her in her dressing gown many times before. In the middle of her laughing and explaining, the man, who had not looked at me, not smiled or said a word or in any way backed up her story, simply ducked out the door.

'Dotty has a lover,' I said to Hugo.

'You don't get out enough. You're trying to make life interesting.'

The next week I watched to see if this man came back. He did not. But three other men came, and one of them came twice. They walked with their heads down, quickly, and did not have to wait at the basement door. Hugo couldn't deny it. He said it was life imitating art again, it was bound to happen, after all the fat varicose-veined whores he'd met in books. It was then we named her the harlot-in-residence and began to brag about her to our friends. They stood behind the curtains to catch a glimpse of her going in or out.

'That's not her!' they said. 'Is that her? Isn't she disappointing? Doesn't she have any professional clothes?'

'Don't be so naive,' we said. 'Did you think they all wore spangles and boas?'

Everybody hushed to hear her play the piano. She sang or hummed along with her playing, not steadily, but loudly, in the rather defiant, self-parodying voice people use when they are alone, or think they are alone. She sang 'Yellow Rose of Texas', and 'You Can't Be True, Dear'.

'Whores should sing hymns.'

'We'll get her to learn some.'

'You're all such voyeurs. You're all so mean,' said a girl named Mary Frances Shrecker, a big-boned, calm-faced girl with black braids down her back. She was married to a former mathematical prodigy, Elsworth Shrecker, who had had a breakdown. She worked as a dietician. Hugo said he could not look at her without thinking of the word *lumpen*, but he supposed she might be nourishing, like oatmeal porridge. She became his second wife. I thought she was the right wife for him, I thought she would stay forever, nourishing him, but the student evicted her.

The piano-playing was an entertainment for our friends, but disastrous on the days when Hugo was home trying to work. He was supposed to be working on his thesis but he really was writing his play. He worked in our bedroom, at a card table in front of the window, facing a board fence. When Dotty had been playing for a bit, he might come out to the kitchen and stick his face into mine and say in low, even tones of self-consciously controlled rage, 'You go down and tell her to cut that out.'

'You go.'

'Bloody hell. She's your friend. You cultivate her. You encourage her.'

'I never told her to play the piano.'

'I arranged so that I could have this afternoon free. That did not just happen. I arranged it. I am at a crucial point, I am at the point where this play *lives or dies*. If I go down there I'm afraid I might strangle her.'

'Well don't look at *me*. Don't strangle *me*. Excuse my breathing and everything.'

I always did go down to the basement, of course, and knock on Dotty's door and ask her if she would mind not playing the piano now, because my husband was at home and was trying to work. I never said the word *write*, Hugo had trained me not to, that word was like a bare wire to us. Dotty apologized every time, she was scared of Hugo and respectful of his work and his intelligence. She left off playing but the trouble was she might forget, she might start again in an hour, half an hour. The possibility made me nervous and miserable. Because I was pregnant I always wanted to eat, and I would sit at the kitchen table greedily, unhappily, eating something like a warmed-up plateful of Spanish rice. Hugo felt the world was hostile to his writing, he felt not only all its human inhabitants but its noises and diversions and ordinary clutter were linked against him, maliciously, purposefully, diabolically thwarting and maiming him and keeping him from his work. And I, whose business it was to throw myself between him and the world, was failing to do so, by choice perhaps as much as ineptitude for the job. I did not believe in him. I had not understood how it would be necessary to believe in him. I believed that he was clever and talented, whatever that might mean, but I was not sure he would turn out to be a writer. He did not have the authority I thought a writer should have. He was too nervous, too touchy with everybody, too much of a showoff. I believed that writers were calm, sad people, knowing too much. I believed that there was a difference about them, some hard and shining, rare intimidating quality they had from the beginning, and Hugo didn't have it. I thought that someday he would recognize this. Meanwhile, he lived in a world whose rewards and punishments were as strange, as hidden from me, as if he had been a lunatic. He would sit at supper, pale and disgusted; he would clench himself over the typewriter in furious paralysis when I had to get something from the bedroom, or he would leap around the living room asking me what he was (a rhinoceros who thinks he is a gazelle, Chairman Mao dancing a war dance in a dream dreamt by John Foster Dulles) and then kiss me all over the neck and throat with hungry gobbling noises. I was cut off from the source of these glad or bad moods, I did not affect them. I teased him sourly:

'Suppose after we have the baby the house is on fire and the baby and the play are both in there, which would you save?'

'Both.'

'But supposing you can just save one? Never mind the baby, suppose *I* am in there, no, suppose I am drowning *here* and you are *here* and cannot possibly reach us both –'

'You're making it tough for me.'

'I know I am. I know I am. Don't you hate me?'

'Of course I hate you.' After this we might go to bed, playful, squealing, mock-fighting, excited. All our life together, the successful part of our life together, was games. We made up conversations to startle people on the bus. Once we sat in a beer parlour and he berated me for going out with other men and leaving the children alone while he was off in the bush working to support us. He pleaded with me to remember my duty as a wife and as a mother. I blew smoke in his face. People around us were looking stern and gratified. When we got outside we laughed till we had to hold each other up, against the wall. We played in bed that I was Lady Chatterley and he was Mellors.

'Where be that little rascal John Thomas?' he asked thickly. 'I canna find John Thomas!'

'Frightfully sorry, I think I must have swallowed him,' I said, ladylike.

There was a water pump in the basement. It made a steady, thumping noise. The house was on fairly low-lying ground not far from the Fraser River, and during the rainy weather the pump had to work most of the time to keep the basement from being flooded. We had a dark rainy January, as is usual in Vancouver, and this was followed by a dark rainy February. Hugo and I felt gloomy. I slept a lot of the time. Hugo couldn't sleep. He claimed it was the pump that kept him awake. He couldn't work because of it in the daytime and he couldn't sleep because of it at night. The pump had replaced Dotty's piano-playing as the thing that most enraged and depressed him in our house. Not only because of its noise, but because of the money it was costing us. Its entire cost went into our electricity bill, though it was Dotty who lived in the basement and reaped the benefits of not being flooded. He said I should speak to Dotty and I said Dotty could not pay the expenses she already had. He said she could turn more tricks. I told him to shut up. As I became more pregnant, slower and heavier and more confined to the house, I got fonder of Dotty, used to her, less likely to store up and repeat what she said. I felt more at home with her than I did sometimes with Hugo and our friends.

All right, Hugo said, I ought to phone the landlady. I said he ought. He said he had far too much to do. The truth was we both shrank from a confrontation with the landlady, knowing in advance how she would confuse and defeat us with shrill evasive prattle.

In the middle of the night in the middle of a rainy week I woke up and wondered what had wakened me. It was the silence.

'Hugo, wake up. The pump's broken. I can't hear the pump.'

'I am awake,' Hugo said.

'It's still raining and the pump isn't going. It must be broken.'

'No, it isn't. It's shut off. I shut it off.'

I sat up and turned on the light. He was lying on his back, squinting and trying to give me a hard look at the same time.

'You didn't turn it off.'

'All right, I didn't.'

'You did.'

'I could not stand the goddamn expense any more. I could not stand thinking about it. I could not stand the noise either. I haven't had any sleep in a week.'

'The basement will flood.'

'I'll turn it on in the morning. A few hours' peace is all I want.'

'That'll be too late, it's raining torrents.'

'It is not.'

'You go to the window.'

'It's raining. It's not raining torrents.'

I turned out the light and lay down and said in a calm stern voice, 'Listen to me, Hugo, you have to go and turn it on, Dotty will be flooded out.'

'In the morning.'

'You have to go and turn it on *now*.'

'Well I'm not.'

'If you're not, I am.'

'No, you're not.'

'I am.'

But I didn't move.

'Don't be such an alarmist.'

'*Hugo?*'

'Don't *cry*.'

'Her stuff will be ruined.'

'Best thing could happen to it. Anyway, it won't.' He lay beside me stiff and wary, waiting, I suppose, for me to get out of bed, go down to the basement and figure out how to turn the pump on. Then what would he have done? He could not have hit me, I was too pregnant. He never did hit me, unless I hit him first. He could have gone and turned it off again, and I could have turned it on, and so on, how long could that last? He could have held me down, but if I struggled he would have been afraid of hurting me. He could have sworn at me and left the house, but we had no car, and it was raining too hard for him to stay out very long. He would probably just have raged and sulked, alternately, and I could have taken a blanket and gone to sleep on the living room couch for the rest of the night. I think that is what a woman of firm character would have done. I think that is what a woman who wanted that marriage to last would have done. But I did not do it. Instead, I said to myself that I did not know how the pump worked, I did not know where to turn it on. I said to myself that I was afraid of Hugo. I entertained the possibility that Hugo might be right, nothing would happen. But I wanted something to happen, I wanted Hugo to crash.

When I woke up, Hugo was gone and the pump was thumping as usual. Dotty was pounding on the door at the top of the basement stairs.

'You won't believe your eyes what's down here. I'm up to my knees in water. I just put my feet out of bed and up to my knees in water. What happened? You hear the pump go off?'

'No,' I said.

'I don't know what could've gone wrong. I guess it could've got overworked. I had a couple of beers before I went to bed else I would've known there was something wrong. I usually sleep light. But I was sleeping like the dead and I put my feet out of bed and Jesus, it's a good thing I didn't pull on the light switch at the same time, I would have been electrocuted. Everything's floating.'

Nothing was floating and the water would not have come to any grown person's knees. It was about five inches deep in some places, only one or two in others, the floor being so uneven. It had soaked and stained the bottom of her chesterfield and chairs and got into the bottom drawers and cupboards and warped the bottom of her piano. The floor tiles were loosened, the rugs soggy, the edges of her bedspread dripping, her floor heater ruined.

I got dressed and put on a pair of Hugo's boots and took a broom downstairs. I started sweeping the water towards the drain outside the door. Dotty made herself a cup of coffee in my kitchen and sat for a while on the top step watching me, going over the same monologue about having a couple of beers and sleeping more soundly than usual, not hearing the pump go off, not understanding why it should go off, if it had gone off, not knowing how she was going to explain to her mother who would certainly make it out to be her fault and charge her. We were in luck, I saw. (*We* were?) Dotty's expectation and thrifty relish of misfortune made her less likely than almost anyone else would have been to investigate just what had gone wrong. After the water level went down a bit, she went into her bedroom, put on some clothes and some boots which she had to drain first, got her broom and helped me.

'The things that don't happen to me, eh? I never get my fortune told. I've got these girl friends that are always getting their fortune told and I say, never mind me, there's one thing I know and I know it ain't good.'

I went upstairs and phoned the University, trying to get Hugo. I told them it was an emergency and they found him in the library.

'It did flood.'

'What?'

'It did flood. Dotty's place is under water.'.

'I turned the pump on.'

'Like hell you did. This morning you turned it on.'

'This morning there was a downpour and the pump couldn't handle it. That was after I turned it on.'

'The pump couldn't handle it last night because the pump wasn't on last night and don't talk to me about any downpour.'

'Well there was one. You were asleep.'

'You have no idea what you've done, do you? You don't even stick around to look at it. I have to look. I have to cope. I have to listen to that poor woman.'

'Plug your ears.'

'Shut up, you filthy moral idiot.'

'I'm sorry. I was kidding. I'm sorry.'

'Sorry. You're bloody sorry. This is the mess you made and I told you you'd make and you're bloody sorry.'

'I have to go to a seminar. I am sorry. I can't talk now, it's no good talking to you now, I don't know what you're trying to get me to say.'

'I'm just trying to get you to *realize*.'

'All right, I realize. Though I still think it happened this morning.'

'You don't realize. You never realize.'

'You dramatize.'

'*I* dramatize!'

Our luck held. Dotty's mother was not so likely as Dotty to do without explanations and it was, after all, her floor tiles and wallboard that were ruined. But Dotty's mother was sick, the cold wet weather had undermined her too, and she was taken to hospital with pneumonia that very morning. Dotty went to live in her mother's house, to look after the boarders. The basement had a disgusting, mouldy smell. We moved out too, a short time later. Just before Clea was born we took over a house in North Vancouver, belonging to some friends who had gone to England. The quarrel between us subsided in the excitement of moving; it was never really resolved. We did not move much from the positions we had taken on the phone. I said you don't realize, you never realize, and he said, what do you want me to say? Why do you make such a fuss over this, he asked reasonably. Anybody might wonder. Long after I was away from him, I wondered too. I could have turned on the pump, as I have said, taking responsibility for both of us, as a patient realistic woman, a really married woman, would have done, as I am sure Mary Frances would have done, did many times, during the ten years she lasted. Or I could have told Dotty the truth, though she was not a very good choice to receive such information. I could have told somebody, if I thought it was that important, pushed Hugo out into the unpleasant world and let him taste trouble. But I didn't, I was not able fully to protect or expose him, only to flog him with blame, desperate sometimes, feeling I would claw his head open to pour my vision into it, my notion of what had to be understood. What presumptuousness, what cowardice, what bad faith. Unavoidable. 'You have a problem of incompatibility,' the marriage counsellor said to us a while later. We laughed till we cried in the dreary municipal hall of the building in North Vancouver where the marriage counselling was dispensed. This is our problem, we said to each other, what a relief to know it, incompatibility.

I did not read Hugo's story that night. I left it with Clea and she as it turned out did not read it either. I read it the next afternoon. I got home about two o'clock from the girls' private school where I have a part-time job teaching history. I made tea as I usually do and sat down in the kitchen to enjoy the hour before the boys, Gabriel's sons, get home from school. I saw the book still lying on top of the refrigerator and I took it down and read Hugo's story.

The story is about Dotty. Of course, she has been changed in some unimportant ways and the main incident concerning her has been invented, or grafted on from some other reality. But the lamp is there, and the pink chenille dressing gown. And something about Dotty that I had forgotten: when you were talking she would listen with her mouth slightly open, nodding, then she would chime in on the last word of your sentence with you. A touching and irritating habit. She was in such a hurry to agree, she hoped to understand. Hugo has remembered this, and when did Hugo ever talk to Dotty?

That doesn't matter. What matters is that this story of Hugo's is a very good story, as far as I can tell, and I think I can tell. How honest this is and how lovely, I had to say as I read. I had to admit. I was moved by Hugo's story; I was, I am, glad of it, and I am not moved by tricks. Or if I am, they have to be good tricks. Lovely tricks, honest tricks. There is Dotty lifted out of life and held in light, suspended in the marvellous clear jelly that Hugo has spent all his life learning how to make. It is an act of magic, there is no getting around it; it is an act, you might say, of a special, unsparing, unsentimental love. A fine and lucky benevolence. Dotty was a lucky person, people who understood and value this act might say (not everybody, of course, does understand and value this act); she was lucky to live in that basement for a few months and eventually to have this done to her, though she doesn't know what has been done and wouldn't care for it, probably, if she did know. She has passed into Art. It doesn't happen to everybody.

Don't be offended. Ironical objections are a habit with me. I am half-ashamed of them. I respect what has been done. I respect the intention and the effort and the result. Accept my thanks.

I did think that I would write a letter to Hugo. All the time I was preparing dinner, and eating it, and talking to Gabriel and the children, I was thinking of a letter. I was thinking I would tell him how strange it was for me to realize that we shared, still shared, the same bank of memory, and that what was all scraps and oddments, useless baggage, for me, was ripe and usable, a paying investment, for him. Also I wanted to apologize, in some not-outright way, for not having believed he would be a writer. Acknowledgement, not apology; that was what I owed him. A few graceful, a few grateful, phrases.

At the same time, at dinner, looking at my husband Gabriel, I decided that he and Hugo are not really so unalike. Both of them have managed something. Both of them have decided what to do about everything they run across in this world, what attitude to take, how to ignore or use things. In their limited and precarious ways they both have authority. They are not *at the mercy*. Or think they are not. I can't blame them, for making whatever arrangements they can make.

After the boys had gone to bed and Gabriel and Clea had settled to watch television, I found a pen and got the paper in front of me, to write my letter, and my hand jumped. I began to write short jabbing sentences that I had never planned:

This is not enough, Hugo. You think it is, but it isn't. You are mistaken, Hugo.

That is not an argument to send through the mail.

I do blame them. I envy and despise.

Gabriel came into the kitchen before he went to bed, and saw me sitting with a pile of test papers and my marking pencils. He might have meant to talk to me, to ask me to have coffee, or a drink, with him, but he respected my unhappiness as he always does; he respected the pretence that I was not unhappy but preoccupied, burdened with these test papers; he left me alone to get over it.

HOW I MET MY HUSBAND

We heard the plane come over at noon, roaring through the radio news, and we were sure it was going to hit the house, so we all ran out into the yard. We saw it come in over the tree tops, all red and silver, the first close-up plane I ever saw. Mrs Peebles screamed.

'Crash landing,' their little boy said. Joey was his name.

'It's okay,' said Dr Peebles. 'He knows what he's doing.' Dr Peebles was only an animal doctor, but had a calming way of talking, like any doctor.

This was my first job – working for Dr and Mrs Peebles, who had bought an old house out on the Fifth Line, about five miles out of town. It was just when the trend was starting of town people buying up old farms, not to work them but to live on them.

We watched the plane land across the road, where the

fairgrounds used to be. It did make a good landing field, nice and level for the old race track, and the barns and display sheds torn down now for scrap lumber so there was nothing in the way. Even the old grandstand boys had burned.

'All right,' said Mrs Peebles, snappy as she always was when she got over her nerves. 'Let's go back in the house. Let's not stand here gawking like a set of farmers.'

She didn't say that to hurt my feelings. It never occurred to her.

I was just setting the dessert down when Loretta Bird arrived, out of breath, at the screen door.

'I thought it was going to crash into the house and kill youse all!'

She lived on the next place and the Peebles thought she was a countrywoman, they didn't know the difference. She and her husband didn't farm, he worked on the roads and had a bad name for drinking. They had seven children and couldn't get credit at the Hi-Way Grocery. The Peebles made her welcome, not knowing any better, as I say, and offered her dessert.

Dessert was never anything to write home about, at their place. A dish of Jello or sliced bananas or fruit out of a tin. 'Have a house without a pie, be ashamed until you die,' my mother used to say, but Mrs Peebles operated differently.

Loretta Bird saw me getting the can of peaches.

'Oh, never mind,' she said. 'I haven't got the right kind of a stomach to trust what comes out of those tins, I can only eat home canning.'

I could have slapped her. I bet she never put down fruit in her life.

'I know what he's landed here for,' she said. 'He's got permission to use the fairgrounds and take people up for rides. It costs a dollar. It's the same fellow who was over at Palmerston last week and was up the lakeshore before that. I wouldn't go up, if you paid me.'

'I'd jump at the chance,' Dr Peebles said. 'I'd like to see this neighbourhood from the air.'

Mrs Peebles said she would just as soon see it from the ground. Joey said he wanted to go and Heather did, too. Joey was nine and Heather was seven.

'Would you, Edie?' Heather said.

I said I didn't know. I was scared, but I never admitted that, especially in front of children I was taking care of.

'People are going to be coming out here in their cars raising dust and trampling your property, if I was you I would complain,' Loretta said. She hooked her legs around the chair rung and I knew we were in for a lengthy visit. After Dr Peebles went back to his office or out on his next call and Mrs Peebles went for her nap, she would hang around me while I was trying to do the dishes. She would pass remarks about the Peebles in their own house.

'She wouldn't find time to lay down in the middle of the day, if she had seven kids like I got.'

She asked me did they fight and did they keep things in the dresser drawer not to have babies with. She said it was a sin if they did. I pretended I didn't know what she was talking about.

I was fifteen and away from home for the first time. My parents had made the effort and sent me to high school for a year, but I didn't like it. I was shy of strangers and the work was hard, they didn't make it nice for you or explain the way they do now. At the end of the year the averages were published in the paper, and mine came out at the very bottom, 37 per cent. My father said that's enough and I didn't blame him. The last thing I wanted, anyway, was to go on and end up teaching school. It happened the very day the paper came out with my disgrace in it, Dr Peebles was staying at our place for dinner, having just helped one of our cows to have twins, and he said I looked smart to him and his wife was looking for a girl to help. He said she felt tied down, with the two children, out in the country. I guess she would, my mother said, being polite, though I could tell from her face she was wondering what on earth it would be like to have only two children and no barn work, and then to be complaining.

When I went home I would describe to them the work I had to do, and it made everybody laugh. Mrs Peebles had an automatic washer and dryer, the first I ever saw. I have had those in my own home for such a long time now it's hard to remember how much of a miracle it was to me, not having to struggle with the wringer and hang up and haul down. Let alone not having to heat water. Then there was practically no baking. Mrs Peebles said she couldn't make pie crust, the most amazing thing I ever heard a woman admit. I could, of course, and I could make light biscuits and white cake and a dark cake, but they didn't want it, she said they watched their figures. The only thing I didn't like about working there, in fact, was feeling half hungry a lot of the time. I used to bring back a box of doughnuts made out at home, and hide them under my bed. The children found out, and I didn't mind sharing, but I thought I better bind them to secrecy.

The day after the plane landed Mrs Peebles put both children in the car and drove over to Chesley, to get their hair cut. There was a good woman then at Chesley for doing hair. She got hers done at the same place, Mrs Peebles did, and that meant they would be gone a good while. She had to pick a day Dr Peebles wasn't going out into the country, she didn't have her own car. Cars were still in short supply then, after the war.

I loved being left in the house alone, to do my work at leisure. The kitchen was all white and bright yellow, with florescent lights. That was before they ever thought of making the appliances all different colours and doing the cupboards like dark old wood and hiding the lighting. I loved light. I loved the double sink. So would anybody new-come from washing dishes in a dishpan with a rag-plugged hole on an oilcloth-covered table by light of a coal-oil lamp. I kept everything shining.

The bathroom too. I had a bath in there once a week. They wouldn't have minded if I took one oftener, but to me it seemed like asking too much, or maybe risking making it less wonderful. The basin and the tub and the toilet were all pink, and there were glass doors with flamingoes painted on them, to shut off the tub. The light had a rosy cast and the mat sank under your feet like snow, except that it was warm. The mirror was three-way. With the mirror all steamed up and the air like a perfume cloud, from things I was allowed to use, I stood up on the side of the tub and admired myself naked, from three directions. Sometimes I thought about the way we lived out at home and the way we lived here and how one way was so hard to imagine when you were living the other way. But I thought it was still a lot easier, living the way we lived at home, to picture something like this, the painted flamingoes and the warmth and the soft mat, than it was for anybody knowing only things like this to picture how it was the other way. And why was that?

I was through my jobs in no time, and had the vegetables peeled for supper and sitting in cold water besides. Then I went into Mrs Peebles' bedroom. I had been in there plenty of times, cleaning, and I always took a good look in her closet, at the clothes she had hanging there. I wouldn't have looked in her drawers, but a closet is open to anybody. That's a lie. I would have looked in drawers, but I would have felt worse doing it and been more scared she could tell.

Some clothes in her closet she wore all the time, I was quite familiar with them. Others she never put on, they were pushed to the back. I was disappointed to see no wedding dress. But there was one long dress I could just see the skirt of, and I was hungering to see the rest. Now I took note of where it hung and lifted it out. It was satin, a lovely weight on my arm, light bluish-green in colour, almost silvery. It had a fitted, pointed waist and a full skirt and an off-the-shoulder fold hiding the little sleeves.

Next thing was easy. I got out of my own things and slipped it on. I was slimmer at fifteen than anybody would believe who knows me now and the fit was beautiful. I didn't of course, have a strapless bra on, which was what it needed, I just had to slide my straps down my arms under the material. Then I tried pinning up my hair, to get the effect. One thing led to another. I put on rouge and lipstick and eyebrow pencil from her dresser. The heat of the day and the weight of the satin and all the excitement made me thirsty, and I went out to the kitchen, got-up as I was, to get a glass of ginger ale with ice cubes from the refrigerator. The Peebles drank ginger ale, or fruit drinks, all day, like water, and I was getting so I did too. Also there was no limit on ice cubes, which I was so fond of I would even put them in a glass of milk.

I turned from putting the ice tray back and saw a man watching me through the screen. It was the luckiest thing in the world I didn't spill the ginger ale down the front of me then and there.

'I never meant to scare you. I knocked but you were getting the ice out, you didn't hear me.'

I couldn't see what he looked like, he was dark the way somebody is pressed up against a screen door with the bright daylight behind them. I only knew he wasn't from around here.

'I'm from the plane over there. My name is Chris Watters and what I was wondering was if I could use that pump.'

There was a pump in the yard. That was the way people used to get their water. Now I noticed he was carrying a pail.

'You're welcome,' I said. 'I can get it from the tap and save you pumping.' I guess I wanted him to know we had piped water, didn't pump ourselves.

'I don't mind the exercise.' He didn't move, though, and finally he said, 'Were you going to a dance?'

Seeing a stranger there had made me entirely forget how I was dressed.

'Or is that the way ladies around here generally get dressed up in the afternoon?'

I didn't know how to joke back then. I was too embarrassed.

'You live here? Are you the lady of the house?'

'I'm the hired girl.'

Some people change when they find that out, their whole way of looking at you and speaking to you change but his didn't.

'Well, I just wanted to tell you you look very nice. I was so surprised when I looked in the door and saw you. Just because you looked so nice and beautiful.'

I wasn't even old enough then to realize how out of the common it is, for a man to say something like that to a woman, or somebody he is treating like a woman. For a man to say a word like *beautiful*. I wasn't old enough to realize or to say anything back, or in fact to do anything but wish he would go away. Not that I didn't like him, but just that it upset me so, having him look at me, and me trying to think of something to say.

He must have understood. He said good-bye, and thanked me, and went and started filling his pail from the pump. I stood behind the Venetian blinds in the dining room, watching him. When he had gone, I went into the bathroom and took the dress off and put it back in the same place. I dressed in my own clothes and took my hair down and washed my face, wiping it on Kleenex, which I threw in the wastebasket.

The Peebles asked me what kind of man he was. Young, middle-aged, short, tall? I couldn't say.

'Good-looking?' Dr Peebles teased me.

I couldn't think a thing but that he would be coming

to get his water again, he would be talking to Dr and Mrs Peebles, making friends with them, and he would mention seeing me that first afternoon, dressed up. Why not mention it? He would think it was funny. And no idea of the trouble it would get me into.

After supper the Peebles drove into town to go to a movie. She wanted to go somewhere with her hair fresh done. I sat in my bright kitchen wondering what to do, knowing I would never sleep. Mrs Peebles might not fire me, when she found out, but it would give her a different feeling about me altogether. This was the first place I ever worked but I already had picked up things about the way people feel when you are working for them. They like to think you aren't curious. Not just that you aren't dishonest, that isn't enough. They like to feel you don't notice things, that you don't think or wonder about anything but what they liked to eat and how they like things ironed, and so on. I don't mean they weren't kind to me, because they were. They had me eat my meals with them (to tell the truth I expected to, I didn't know there were families who don't) and sometimes they took me along in the car. But all the same.

I went up and checked on the children being asleep and then I went out. I had to do it. I crossed the road and went to the old fairgrounds gate. The plane looked unnatural sitting there, and shining with the moon. Off at the far side of the fairgrounds, where the bush was taking over, I saw his tent.

He was sitting outside it smoking a cigarette. He saw me coming.

'Hello, were you looking for a plane ride. I don't start taking people up till tomorrow.' Then he looked again and said, 'Oh, it's you. I didn't know you without your long dress on.'

My heart was knocking away, my tongue was dried up. I had to say something. But I couldn't. My throat was closed and I was like a deaf-and-dumb.

'Did you want a ride? Sit down. Have a cigarette.'

I couldn't even shake my head to say no, so he gave me one.

'Put it in your mouth or I can't light it. It's a good thing I'm used to shy ladies.'

I did. It wasn't the first time I had smoked a cigarette, actually. My girl friend out home, Muriel Lowe, used to steal them from her brother.

'Look at your hand shaking. Did you just want to have a chat, or what?'

In one burst I said, 'I wish you wouldn't say anything about the dress.'

'What dress? Oh, the long dress.'

'It's Mrs Peebles'.'

'Whose? Oh, the lady you work for? Is that it? She wasn't home so you got dressed up in her dress, eh? You got dressed up and played queen. I don't blame you. You're not smoking that cigarette right. Don't just puff. Draw it in. Did nobody ever show you how to inhale? Are you scared I'll tell on you? Is that it?'

I was so ashamed at having to ask him to connive this way I couldn't nod. I just looked at him and he saw *yes*.

'Well I won't. I won't in the slightest way mention it or embarrass you. I give you my word of honour.'

Then he changed the subject, to help me out, seeing I couldn't even thank him.

'What do you think of this sign?'

It was a board sign lying practically at my feet.

SEE THE WORLD FROM THE SKY. ADULTS $1.00, CHILDREN 50C. QUALIFIED PILOT.

'My old sign was getting pretty beat up, I thought I'd make a new one. That's what I've been doing with my time today.'

The lettering wasn't all that handsome, I thought. I could have done a better one in half an hour.

'I'm not an expert at sign making.'

'It's very good,' I said.

'I don't need it for publicity, word of mouth is usually enough. I turned away two carloads tonight. I felt like taking it easy. I didn't tell them ladies were dropping in to visit me.'

Now I remembered the children and I was scared again, in case one of them had waked up and called me and I wasn't there.

'Do you have to go so soon?'

I remembered some manners. 'Thank you for the cigarette.'

'Don't forget. You have my word of honour.'

I tore off across the fairgrounds, scared I'd see the car heading home from town. My sense of time was mixed up, I didn't know how long I'd been out of the house. But it was all right, it wasn't late, the children were asleep. I got in bed myself and lay thinking what a lucky end to the day, after all, and among things to be grateful for I could be grateful Loretta Bird hadn't been the one who caught me.

The yard and borders didn't get trampled, it wasn't as bad as that. All the same it seemed very public, around the house. The sign was on the fairgrounds gate. People came mostly after supper but a good many in the afternoon, too. The Bird children all came without fifty cents between them and hung on the gate. We got used to the excitement of the plane coming in and taking off, it wasn't excitement any more. I never went over, after that one time, but would see him when he came to get his water. I would be out on the steps doing sitting-down work, like preparing vegetables, if I could.

'Why don't you come over? I'll take you up in my plane.'

'I'm saving my money,' I said, because I couldn't think of anything else.

'For what? For getting married?'

I shook my head.

'I'll take you up for free if you come sometime when it's slack. I thought you would come, and have another cigarette.'

I made a face to hush him, because you never could tell when the children would be sneaking around the porch, or Mrs Peebles herself listening in the house. Sometimes she came out and had a conversation with him. He told her things he hadn't bothered to tell me. But then I hadn't thought to ask. He told her he had been in the War, that was where he learned to fly a plane, and now he couldn't settle down to ordinary life, this was what he liked. She said she couldn't imagine anybody liking such a thing. Though sometimes, she said, she was almost bored enough to try anything herself, she wasn't brought up to living in the country. It's all my husband's idea, she said. This was news to me.

'Maybe you ought to give flying lessons,' she said.

'Would you take them?'
She just laughed.

Sunday was a busy flying day in spite of it being preached against from two pulpits. We were all sitting out watching. Joey and Heather were over on the fence with the Bird kids. Their father had said they could go, after their mother saying all week they couldn't.

A car came down the road past the parked cars and pulled up right in the drive. It was Loretta Bird who got out, all importance, and on the driver's side another woman got out, more sedately. She was wearing sunglasses.

'This is a lady looking for the man that flies the plane,' Loretta Bird said. 'I heard her inquire in the hotel coffee shop where I was having a Coke and I brought her out.'

'I'm sorry to bother you,' the lady said. 'I'm Alice Kelling, Mr Watters' fiancée.'

This Alice Kelling had on a pair of brown and white checked slacks and a yellow top. Her bust looked to me rather low and bumpy. She had a worried face. Her hair had had a permanent, but had grown out, and she wore a yellow band to keep it off her face. Nothing in the least pretty or even young-looking about her. But you could tell from how she talked she was from the city, or educated, or both.

Dr Peebles stood up and introduced himself and his wife and me and asked her to be seated.

'He's up in the air right now, but you're welcome to sit and wait. He gets his water here and he hasn't been yet. He'll probably take his break about five.'

'That is him, then?' said Alice Kelling, wrinkling and straining at the sky.

'He's not in the habit of running out on you, taking a different name?' Dr Peebles laughed. He was the one, not his wife, to offer iced tea. Then she sent me into the kitchen to fix it. She smiled. She was wearing sunglasses too.

'He never mentioned his fiancée,' she said.

I loved fixing iced tea with lots of ice and slices of lemon in tall glasses. I ought to have mentioned before, Dr Peebles was an abstainer, at least around the house, or I wouldn't have been allowed to take the place. I had to fix a glass for Loretta Bird too, though it galled me, and when I went out she had settled in my lawn chair, leaving me the steps.

'I knew you was a nurse when I first heard you in that coffee shop.'

'How would you know a thing like that?'

'I get my hunches about people. Was that how you met him, nursing?'

'Chris? Well yes. Yes, it was.'

'Oh, were you overseas?' said Mrs Peebles.

'No, it was before he went overseas. I nursed him when he was stationed at Centralia and had ruptured appendix. We got engaged and then he went overseas. My, this is refreshing, after a long drive.'

'He'll be glad to see you,' Dr Peebles said. 'It's a rackety kind of life, isn't it, not staying one place long enough to really make friends.'

'Youse've had a long engagement,' Loretta Bird said.

Alice Kelling passed that over. 'I was going to get a room at the hotel, but when I was offered directions I came on out. Do you think I could phone them?'

'No need,' Dr Peebles said. 'You're five miles away from

him if you stay at the hotel. Here, you're right across the road. Stay with us. We've got rooms on rooms, look at this big house.'

Asking people to stay, just like that, is certainly a country thing, and maybe seemed natural to him now, but not to Mrs Peebles, from the way she said, oh yes, we have plenty of room. Or to Alice Kelling, who kept protesting, but let herself be worn down. I got the feeling it was a temptation to her, to be that close. I was trying for a look at her ring. Her nails were painted red, her fingers were freckled and wrinkled. It was a tiny stone. Muriel Lowe's cousin had one twice as big.

Chris came to get his water, late in the afternoon just as Dr Peebles had predicted. He must have recognized the car from a way off. He came smiling.

'Here I am chasing after you to see what you're up to,' called Alice Kelling. She got up and went to meet him and they kissed, just touched, in front of us.

'You're going to spend a lot on gas that way,' Chris said.

Dr Peebles invited Chris to stay for supper, since he had already put up the sign that said: NO MORE RIDES TILL 7 P.M. Mrs Peebles wanted it served in the yard, in spite of bugs. One thing strange to anybody from the country is this eating outside. I had made a potato salad earlier and she had made a jellied salad, that was one thing she could do, so it was just a matter of getting those out, and some sliced meat and cucumbers and fresh leaf lettuce. Loretta Bird hung around for some time saying, 'Oh, well, I guess I better get home to those yappers,' and, 'It's so nice just sitting here, I sure hate to get up,' but nobody invited her, I was relieved to see, and finally she had to go.

That night after rides were finished Alice Kelling and Chris went off somewhere in her car. I lay awake till they got back. When I saw the car lights sweep my ceiling I got up to look down on them through the slats of my blind. I don't know what I thought I was going to see. Muriel Lowe and I used to sleep on her front veranda and watch her sister and her sister's boy friend saying good night. Afterwards we couldn't get to sleep, for longing for somebody to kiss us and rub up against us and we would talk about suppose you were out in a boat with a boy and he wouldn't bring you in to shore unless you did it, or what if somebody got you trapped in a barn, you would have to, wouldn't you, it wouldn't be your fault. Muriel said her two girl cousins used to try with a toilet paper roll that one of them was the boy. We wouldn't do anything like that; just lay and wondered.

All that happened was that Chris got out of the car on one side and she got out on the other and they walked off separately – him towards the fairgrounds and her towards the house. I got back in bed and imagined about me coming home with him, not like that.

Next morning Alice Kelling got up late and I fixed a grapefruit for her the way I had learned and Mrs Peebles sat down with her to visit and have another cup of coffee. Mrs Peebles seemed pleased enough now, having company. Alice Kelling said she guessed she better get used to putting in a day just watching Chris take off and come down, and Mrs Peebles said she didn't know if she should suggest it because Alice Kelling was the one with the car, but the lake was only twenty-five miles away and what a good day for a picnic.

Alice Kelling took her up on the idea and by eleven o'clock they were in the car, with Joey and Heather and a sandwich lunch I had made. The only thing was that Chris hadn't come down, and she wanted to tell him where they were going.

'Edie'll go over and tell him,' Mrs Peebles said. 'There's no problem.'

Alice Kelling wrinkled her face and agreed.

'Be sure and tell him we'll be back by five!'

I didn't see that he would be concerned about knowing this right away, and I thought of him eating whatever he ate over there, alone cooking on his camp stove, so I got to work and mixed up a crumb cake and baked it, in between the other work I had to do; then, when it was a bit cooled, wrapped it in a tea towel. I didn't do anything to myself but take off my apron and comb my hair. I would like to have put some make-up on, but I was too afraid it would remind him of the way he first saw me, and that would humiliate me all over again.

He had come and put another sign on the gate: NO RIDES THIS P.M. APOLOGIES. I worried that he wasn't feeling well. No sign of him outside and the tent flap was down. I knocked on the pole.

'Come in,' he said, in a voice that would just as soon have said *Stay out*.

I lifted the flap.

'Oh, it's you. I'm sorry. I didn't know it was you.'

He had been just sitting on the side of the bed, smoking. Why not at least sit and smoke in the fresh air?

'I brought a cake and hope you're not sick,' I said.

'Why would I be sick, Oh – that sign. That's all right.

I'm just tired of talking to people. I don't mean you. Have a seat.' He pinned back the tent flap. 'Get some fresh air in here.'

I sat on the edge of the bed, there was no place else. It was one of those fold-up cots, really: I remembered and gave him his fiancée's message.

He ate some of the cake. 'Good.'

'Put the rest away for when you're hungry later.'

'I'll tell you a secret. I won't be around here much longer.'

'Are you getting married?'

'Ha ha. What time did you say they'd be back?'

'Five o'clock.'

'Well, by that time this place will have seen the last of me. A plane can get further than a car.' He unwrapped the cake and ate another piece of it, absent-mindedly.

'Now you'll be thirsty.'

'There's some water in the pail.'

'It won't be very cold. I could bring some fresh. I could bring some ice from the refrigerator.'

'No,' he said. 'I don't want you to go. I want a nice long time of saying good-bye to you.'

He put the cake away carefully and sat beside me and started those little kisses, so soft, I can't ever let myself think about them, such kindness in his face and lovely kisses, all over my eyelids and neck and eyes, all over, then me kissing back as well as I could (I had only kissed a boy on a dare before, and kissed my own arms for practice) and we lay back on the cot and pressed together, just gently, and he did some other things, not bad things or not in a bad way. It was lovely in the tent, that smell of grass and hot tent cloth with the sun beating down on it, and he said, 'I wouldn't do you any harm for the world.' Once, when he had rolled on top of me and we were sort of rocking together on the cot, he said softly, 'Oh, no,' and freed himself and jumped up and got the water pail. He splashed some of it on his neck and face, and the little bit left, on me lying there.

'That's to cool us off, Miss.'

When we said good-bye I wasn't at all sad, because he held my face and said 'I'm going to write you a letter. I'll tell you where I am and maybe you can come and see me. Would you like that? Okay then. You wait.' I was really glad I think to get away from him, it was like he was piling presents on me I couldn't get the pleasure of till I considered them alone.

No consternation at first about the plane being gone. They thought he had taken somebody up, and I didn't enlighten them. Dr Peebles had phoned he had to go to the country, so there was just us having supper, and then Loretta Bird thrusting her head in the door and saying, 'I see he's took off.'

'What?' said Alice Kelling, and pushed back her chair.

'The kids come and told me this afternoon he was taking down his tent. Did he think he'd run through all the business there was around here? He didn't take off without letting you know, did he?'

'He'll send me word,' Alice Kelling said. 'He'll probably phone tonight. He's terribly restless, since the War.'

'Edie, he didn't mention to you, did he?' Mrs Peebles said. 'When you took over the message?'

'Yes,' I said. So far so true.

'Well why didn't you say?' All of them were looking at me. 'Did he say where he was going?'

'He said he might try Bayfield,' I said. What made me tell such a lie? I didn't intend it.

'Bayfield, how far is that?' said Alice Kelling.

Mrs Peebles said, 'Thirty, thirty-five miles.'

'That's not far. Oh, well, that's really not far at all. It's on the lake, isn't it?'

You'd think I'd be ashamed of myself, setting her on the wrong track. I did it to give him more time, whatever time he needed. I lied for him, and also, I have to admit, for me. Women should stick together and not do things like that. I see that now, but didn't then. I never thought of myself as being in any way like her, or coming to the same troubles, ever.

She hadn't taken her eyes off me. I thought she suspected my lie.

'When did he mention this to you?'

'Earlier.'

'When you were over at the plane?'

'Yes.'

'You must've stayed and had a chat.' She smiled at me, not a nice smile. 'You must've stayed and had a little visit with him.'

'I took a cake,' I said, thinking that telling some truth would spare me telling the rest.

'We didn't have a cake,' said Mrs Peebles rather sharply.

'I baked one.'

Alice Kelling said, 'That was very friendly of you.'

'Did you get permission,' said Loretta Bird. 'You never

know what these girls'll do next,' she said. 'It's not they mean harm so much as they're ignorant.'

'The cake is neither here nor there,' Mrs Peebles broke in. 'Edie, I wasn't aware you knew Chris that well.'

I didn't know what to say.

'I'm not surprised,' Alice Kelling said in a high voice. 'I knew by the look of her as soon as I saw her. We get them at the hospital all the time.' She looked hard at me with her stretched smile. 'Having their babies. We have to put them in a special ward because of their diseases. Little country tramps. Fourteen and fifteen years old. You should see the babies they have, too.'

'There was a bad woman here in town had a baby that pus was running out of its eyes,' Loretta Bird put in.

'Wait a minute,' said Mrs Peebles. 'What is this talk? Edie. What about you and Mr Watters? Were you intimate with him?'

'Yes,' I said. I was thinking of us lying on the cot and kissing, wasn't that intimate? And I would never deny it.

They were all one minute quiet, even Loretta Bird.

'Well,' said Mrs Peebles. 'I am surprised. I think I need a cigarette. This is the first of any such tendencies I've seen in her,' she said, speaking to Alice Kelling, but Alice Kelling was looking at me.

'Loose little bitch.' Tears ran down her face. 'Loose little bitch, aren't you? I knew as soon as I saw you. Men despise girls like you. He just made use of you and went off, you know that, don't you? Girls like you are just nothing, they're just public conveniences, just filthy little rags!'

'Oh, now,' said Mrs Peebles.

'Filthy,' Alice Kelling sobbed. 'Filthy little rag!'

'Don't get yourself upset,' Loretta Bird said. She was swollen up with pleasure being in on this scene. 'Men are all the same.'

'Edie, I'm very surprised,' Mrs Peebles said. 'I thought your parents were so strict. You don't want to have a baby, do you?'

I'm still ashamed of what happened next. I lost control, just like a six-year-old, I started howling. 'You don't get a baby from just doing that!'

'You see. Some of them are that ignorant,' Loretta Bird said.

But Mrs Peebles jumped up and caught my arms and shook me.

'Calm down. Don't get hysterical. Calm down. Stop crying. Listen to me. Listen. I'm wondering, if you know what being intimate means. Now tell me. What did you think it meant?'

'Kissing,' I howled.

She let go. 'Oh, Edie. Stop it. Don't be silly. It's all right. It's all a misunderstanding. Being intimate means a lot more than that. Oh, I *wondered*.'

'She's trying to cover up, now,' said Alice Kelling. 'Yes. She's not so stupid. She sees she got herself in trouble.'

'I believe her,' Mrs Peebles said. 'That is an awful scene.'

'Well there is one way to find out,' said Alice Kelling, getting up. 'After all, I am a nurse.'

Mrs Peebles drew a breath and said, 'No. No. Go to your room, Edie. And stop that noise. That is too disgusting.'

I heard the car start in a little while. I tried to stop crying, pulling back each wave as it started over me. Finally I succeeded, and lay heaving on the bed.

Mrs Peebles came and stood in the doorway.

'She's gone,' she said. 'That Bird woman too. Of course, you know you should never have gone near that man and that is the cause of all this trouble. I have a headache. As soon as you can, go and wash your face in cold water and get at the dishes and we will not say any more about this.'

Nor we didn't. I didn't figure out till years later the extent of what I had been saved from. Mrs Peebles was not very friendly to me afterwards, but she was fair. Not very friendly is the wrong way of describing what she was. She never had been very friendly. It was just that now she had to see me all the time and it got on her nerves, a little.

As for me, I put it all out of my mind like a bad dream and concentrated on waiting for my letter. The mail came every day except Sunday, between one-thirty and two in the afternoon, a good time for me because Mrs Peebles was always having her nap. I would get the kitchen all cleaned and then go up to the mailbox and sit in the grass, waiting. I was perfectly happy, waiting, I forgot all about Alice Kelling and her misery and awful talk and Mrs Peebles and her chilliness and the embarrassment of whether she had told Dr Peebles and the face of Loretta Bird, getting her fill of other people's troubles. I was always smiling when the mailman got there, and continued smiling even after he gave me the mail and I saw today wasn't the day. The mailman was a Carmichael. I knew by his face because there are a lot of Carmichaels living out by us and so many of them have a sort of sticking-out top lip. So I asked his name (he was a young man, shy, but good humoured, anybody could ask him anything) and then I said, 'I knew by your face!' He was pleased by that and always glad to see me and got a little less shy. 'You've got the smile I've been waiting on all day!' he used to holler out the car window.

It never crossed my mind for a long time a letter might not come. I believed in it coming just like I believed the sun would rise in the morning. I just put off my hope from day to day, and there was the goldenrod out around the mailbox and the children gone back to school, and the leaves turning, and I was wearing a sweater when I went to wait. One day walking back with the hydro bill stuck in my hand, that was all, looking across at the fairgrounds with the full-blown milkweed and dark teasels, so much like fall, it just struck me: *No letter was ever going to come.* It was an impossible idea to get used to. No, not impossible. If I thought about Chris's face when he said he was going to write to me, it was impossible, but if I forgot that and thought about the actual tin mailbox, empty, it was plain and true. I kept on going to meet the mail, but my heart was heavy now like a lump of lead. I only smiled because I thought of the mailman counting on it, and he didn't have an easy life, with the winter driving ahead.

Till it came to me one day there were women doing this with their lives, all over. There were women just waiting and waiting by mailboxes for one letter or another. I imagined me making this journey day after day and year after year, and my hair starting to go grey, and I thought, I was never made to go on like that. So I stopped meeting the mail. If there were women all through life waiting, and women busy and not waiting, I knew which I had to be. Even though there might be things the second kind of women have to pass up and never know about, it still is better.

I was surprised when the mailman phoned the Peebles' place in the evening and asked for me. He said he missed me. He asked if I would like to go to Goderich where some well-known movie was on, I forget now what. So I said yes, and I went out with him for two years and he asked me to marry him, and we were engaged a year more while I got my things together, and then we did marry. He always tells the children the story of how I went after him by sitting by the mailbox every day, and naturally I laugh and let him, because I like for people to think what pleases them and makes them happy.

WALKING ON WATER

This was a part of town where a lot of old people still lived, though many had moved to high-rises across the park. Mr Lougheed had a number of friends, or perhaps it would be better to say acquaintances, whom he met every day or so on the way downtown, at the bus stop, or on the walks overlooking the sea. Occasionally he played cards with them in their rooms or apartments. He belonged to a lawn-bowling club and to a club which brought in travel films and showed them, in a downtown hall, during the winter. He had joined these clubs not out of a real desire to be sociable but as a precaution against his natural tendencies, which might lead him, he thought, into becoming a sort of hermit. During his years in the drugstore business he had learned how to get through all kinds of conversations with all sorts of people, to skate along affably and go on thinking his own thoughts. He practised the same thing with his wife. His aim was to give people what they thought they wanted, and continue, himself, solitary and unmolested. Except for his wife, few people had ever suspected what he was up to. But now that he was no longer obliged to give anybody anything, in the ordinary daily way, he put himself in a position where now and again he would have to, as he believed in some way it must be good for him. If he left it all to his own choice who would he talk to? Eugene, that was all. He would get to be a nuisance to Eugene.

It was on the sea walk Mr Lougheed heard the first time what Eugene had been proposing.

'Says he can walk on water.'

Mr Lougheed was sure Eugene had said no such thing.

'It's all in the way of thinking your weight out of your body, according to him. There's nothing you can't control if you set out to. So he says.'

This was Mr Clifford and Mr Morey, sitting on the lookout bench catching their breath.

'Mind over matter.'

They invited Mr Lougheed to sit but he remained standing. He was tall and thin and if he kept a sensible pace did not run out of breath.

'Eugene talks a lot of that kind of thing but it's just speculation,' he told them. He did not care for their tone on Eugene although he knew it was partly justified. 'He's very intelligent. He's not cracked.'

'We'll have to wait for the demonstration to make up our minds on that.'

'He's either cracked or I am. Or else he's Jesus Christ.'

'What demonstration is that?' said Mr Lougheed cautiously, and with foreboding.

'He's going to demonstrate walking off the Ross Point pier.'

Mr Lougheed said he was sure Eugene had been joking. Mr Clifford and Mr Morey assured him that it was no joke, a serious undertaking. (Mr Clifford and Mr Morey, saying it was serious, were laughing a bit and shaking their heads cheerfully, while Mr Lougheed, saying it was a joke, was frowning and staying aloof.) The time set was Sunday morning. Today was Friday. Ten o'clock had been the exact time picked so that some people could get to church after the walking or the not-walking was over. But, just as Mr Lougheed suspected, neither Mr Clifford nor Mr Morey had actually heard these arrangements being made, they had heard about them from somebody else. Mr Morey had heard while playing cards with friends and Mr Clifford had heard in the British Israel Reading Room.

'It's getting talked up all over.'

'Well it might as well get talked down, then, because Eugene is not a fool, or anyway not so much of a fool as that,' said Mr Lougheed shortly, and continued on his walk. He cut off home by a shorter route than he usually took.

He knocked on Eugene's door, which was across the hall from his own. Eugene said, in a serene but warning voice, 'Come in.'

Mr Lougheed opened the door and was struck by a brisk cool wind blowing right off the ocean and in at Eugene's window, which was raised as high as it would go.

Eugene was on the bare floor in front of the window, sitting with his legs bent and twisted that unnatural-looking way, which he declared was not entirely natural to him. He wore a pair of jeans, that was all. Mr Lougheed contemplated the slenderness, the delicacy, of this young man's upper body. What work could he do, how many pounds could he lift? Yet he could do all these contortions, twist and stretch his body into the most distressing-looking positions, which he claimed were delightful, of course. He took his pride in that.

'Sit down,' said Eugene. 'I'm coming out.'

He meant that he was coming out of meditating, which was how he finished up his exercises. Sometimes he sat and meditated without bothering to shut his door. Mr Lougheed, walking past, always quickly averted his eyes. He did not look to see the expression on Eugene's face. Rapt, was it supposed to be? He was as alarmed, as appalled, in the furthest corner of himself, as if he had seen somebody making love.

That had happened, too.

Living downstairs in the house were three young people. Their names were Calla, Rex and Rover. Rover was apparently a name given for a joke, to a skinny, sickly boy with a twelve-year-old's body and some days a fifty-year-old face. Mr Lougheed had seen him sleeping on the hall carpet, like a dog. But Rex and Calla were also strange names, more properly belonging to an animal and a flower; were those the names their parents called them? They struck Mr Lougheed as having got here without parents, without any experience of highchairs or tricycles or wagons; they seemed to have sprung up, armed as they were, from the earth. No doubt that was how they thought of themselves.

He had come into the house one day and the downstairs apartment door had been open. Somebody might have just run out. In the back of the hall – in full view though, not under the stairs – were two figures tangled up with each other. Rex and Calla. The girl was in a long skirt as usual and she seemed to be down on all fours, squawking and struggling as if she had been pushed. The skirt was thrown up over her head, she was half trapped and muffled in its cloth. Mr Lougheed saw no more than a crescent of spongy flesh, her hindquarters, and that quickly covered by the boy, mounting. Awareness of Mr Lougheed's presence was presumably what caused him to let out a yap – of glee as well as amazement – and to fall forward so that both he and the girl collapsed, their essential connection probably broken for the time being; their voices joined, however, in laughter that seemed to Mr Lougheed not only unashamed but full of derision. He was apparently the one to be laughed at, for having witnessed, for being shocked at, their copulation.

He was not shocked, he wished to tell them. When a boy going to school, to what was called the Stone School on Fifth Line of Killop Township, he had been part of the paying audience of a show put on by one of the Brewer boys and his younger sister. It took place in the entry way to the boys' toilet, a foul place. It was not simulated. Nobody needed to think they had invented this business.

But if not shocked, what was he? His heart pounded, he felt a gloomy congestion in his head. In his own room, he had to sit down. Their laughter would be heard by him for some time. He imagined their hairy parts driving together, with independent swollen ferocity and squashing noises, ending in that laughter. Like animals. No, he took that back. Animals went about their business without calling attention to it, and with gravity. What he objected to, he had said to Eugene, what he objected to in this generation, if that was what it was, was that they could not do a thing without showing off. Why all this yawping about everything, he asked. They could not grow a carrot without congratulating themselves on it.

For example. There was a little store on the way downtown that he had got into the habit of visiting because he liked the sight of the bins along the sidewalk, filled with lumpy vegetables with a bit of the dirt still clinging to them. These reminded him of the vegetables in the stores when he was a child, and in the cellar of his own house. But the young people in the store, with their long wild hair and Indian headbands and their costumes of striped overalls and underwear with holes (what was that but a costume? No farmer in his right mind, no matter how poor, would appear in town in such a get-up), and their lilting, pious discussions of gardening and food, had disturbed him so much that he had stopped going in. They took too much praise on themselves. Bread had been baked before, turnips had been harvested before. This was artificial, in some way it was more artificial than the supermarkets.

'I think they're more boring than artificial,' Eugene said reasonably. 'Like early Christians. They would have been boring.'

'They won't last. Their farming will fail.'

'Possibly. But some people build their practical lives on a philosophy and are very successful. Hutterites. Mennonites.'

'They have a different mentality,' said Mr Lougheed. He was not unaware of how he sounded – stubborn, querulous, old.

Now, when Eugene came all the way out of his meditating he stood up and stretched himself and asked if Mr Lougheed would like some tea. Mr Lougheed said yes. Eugene plugged in the electric kettle and moved about the room tidying things up. His room was neatly kept. He slept on a mattress on the floor, but he put sheets on it and the sheets were clean, he took them to the laundromat. His books were on plank-and-brick shelves or stacked on the floor and window-sills. He had hundreds of books, nearly all paperbacks, they were the chief thing in the room. Mr Lougheed often gazed at their titles, with a sense of awe and futility. *From Heidegger to Kant*. He knew who Kant was of course though he had never read anything by him, only about him in *The Story of Philosophy*. He might once have known who Heidegger was but he didn't know now. He had not gone to college. In his day you did not have to go to college to become a druggist, you just had to serve an apprenticeship, as he had done with his uncle. But later on he had gone through a period of serious reading. Nothing like this, though. He knew enough to recognize the names, that was all. Meister Eckhart. Simon Weil. Teilhard de Chardin. Loren Eiseley. Respected names. Luminous names. And the thing was that Eugene had not just collected these books, planning to read through them all someday. No. He had read them. Eugene had read virtually everything there was to read on these most important, these most demanding subjects. Philosophy. Religion. Mysticism. Psychology. Science. Eugene was twenty-eight years old and it was safe to say that he had spent the last twenty years of his life reading. He had degrees. He had won scholarships and prizes. All of which he scorned, or at least dismissed, with a kind of apology. He had done little spates of teaching, but no other steady work, it seemed. At some point there had been a breakdown, a lengthy crisis from which he still, perhaps, believed himself to be recovering. Yes, he had the air of someone who gauges and guards his convalescence. He was deliberate, even in his supple movements, his light-heartedness. He wore his hair like a medieval page boy's. His hair and his eyes shone, soft and foxy, reddish brown. He had a little moustache, which did not help him look his age.

'I heard this business about the walking on water,' Mr Lougheed said, attempting to take a jocular tone.

'Honey?' said Eugene, and slid a large dollop of it into Mr Lougheed's tea.

Mr Lougheed, who liked his tea without sweetening, absently accepted a spoon.

'I didn't credit it.'

'Oh, yes,' said Eugene.

'I said you wouldn't be that big a fool.'

'You were wrong.'

Both were smiling. Mr Lougheed's smile was thin but hopeful, tactical. Eugene's was frank and kind. And yet – what was that frankness? It was not natural, it was achieved. Eugene, who knew about military history and mysticism and astronomy and biology, who could discuss Indian art (either Indians) or the art of poisoning, who could have made a fortune in the days of quiz shows as Mr Lougheed had once said to him (Eugene laughing and saying thank God for the good of his soul such days were past) – Eugene in all the ordinary movements and exchanges of life was an achievement, in the face of something he did not mention. His breakdown? His bursting knowledge? His understanding?

'Well I don't know if I took this up wrong,' Mr Lougheed said. 'I understood the proposition was walking on water.'

'That's it.'

'And what is the purpose of this?'

'The purpose is walking on water. If that is possible. Do you think it is?'

For that Mr Lougheed could not find an answer.

'It's some kind of joke?'

'It could be,' said Eugene, and still so brightly. 'A serious kind of joke.'

Mr Lougheed's eyes had strayed to a shelf of another kind of books Eugene read, which did not seem to him to tie in too readily with the first kind. These books were by and about people who made prophecies, they were about astral bodies and psychic experiences and supernatural powers and every kind of hoax or magic, if that was what you wanted to call it. Mr Lougheed had even borrowed some of these books, as he did others, from Eugene, but he was not able to read them. Incredulity clogged his brain. Using a word out of his own youth, he told Eugene that all this had him stumped. He could not believe Eugene took it seriously, even when he heard Eugene say so.

A little while after the incident in the downstairs hall

Mr Lougheed had come home one day and found a sign painted on his door. It was something like a flower, with thin red petals, inexpertly painted, and black petals in between, tapering the wrong way. A red circle in the middle and a black circle, black hole, inside that. He touched the paint and found that it was wet, but not very wet, they had paints nowadays that dried in no time. He called Eugene out to take a look at it.

'That's nothing,' Eugene said. 'At least it's nothing to worry about. I don't recognize it. It's just something they made up.'

Mr Lougheed was a minute or two picking up the meaning of this.

'It's not a sign,' Eugene said.

'Sign,' said Mr Lougheed.

'Like a spell. There's a difference between this and a real sign, just as there would be a difference between a piece of gibberish and a real spell, though they might sound equally like gibberish to the uninitiated.'

'I wasn't worried about it being a – sign,' said Mr Lougheed, collecting himself. 'Is that what you mean, some kind of magic sign? I was worried about them defacing my door. They have no business being up here and no business painting on my door.'

'Well I guess they thought it was a joke. Or they might have done it on a dare. They're very childish – Rex and Calla are incredibly childish. Rover only looks childish, he is something of a mystery. He may have an old soul.'

Mr Lougheed was not interested in the age of Rover's soul. He was interested in, dumbounded by, the possibility that such a thing, a sign on a door, could have real meaning for someone who was not a total fool. 'Do you,' he said in a voice of irrepressible intense curiosity, 'would you, be alarmed by a sign on your door? Would you believe that such a thing could have a real effect?'

'Absolutely.'

'That is almost impossible for me to believe,' said Mr Lougheed. He thought, sighed, and said more firmly. 'That is impossible for me to believe.'

'Impasse,' said Eugene agreeably.

Mr Lougheed thought that he should have realized then, he should have realized the extent of this kind of thinking, and he would not be taken aback now.

'The world that we accept – you know, external reality,' Eugene was saying comfortably, 'is nothing like so fixed as we have been led to believe. It responds to more methods of control that we are conditioned to accept.' When expounding something to Mr Lougheed he was apt to talk in these eager and modulated sentences. When he talked to the trio downstairs he used a language sufficiently broken, tranced, and vague to communicate with them, apparently, on something close to their own level. 'Its so-called laws are not final. The law you are thinking of says that a body like this' – he tapped Mr Lougheed's shoulder – 'cannot move on top of water because it cannot attain weightlessness.'

Still it could be a joke.

'You believe that certain people have walked on hot coals and not received any burns on their skin?'

'I've read about it.'

'It's commonplace. You've seen pictures? You believe it?'

'It looks like it.'

'But their feet are made of flesh and covered with skin which according to all we know should burn? Now doesn't it seem that we have to admit that the mind can work in some ways to control matter to the extent that some laws no longer apply?'

'I'd like to see it control the law of gravity.'

'It has. It has. People have been able to rise by their own will several inches off the ground.'

'Until I see with my own eyes that wastepaper basket rise and float over my head,' said Mr Lougheed with absolute conviction – though trying to stay good-humoured – 'I will believe nothing of the kind.'

'Road to Emmaus,' said Eugene.

He even knew the Bible. He was the only person under forty that Mr Lougheed had come across who did. Not counting Jehovah's Witnesses.

'A wastepaper basket cannot control its own being, it cannot utilize energy. However if a person capable of utilizing a certain kind of energy were sitting where you are now –'

He went on to talk about a woman in Russia who could pull heavy furniture across the room without bothering to touch it. The power was in her solar plexus, she said.

'But what makes you think,' said Mr Lougheed, 'that you have these powers? That you can utilize energy or stop the flow of gravity or whatever?'

'If I could stop anything it would be for the minutest space of time. Seconds only. I am nothing but a neophyte. But it would be enough to make people think. Also I am interested in leaving the body. I have never been able to leave this body.'

'You have to make sure you can get back in.'

'People can. People have. Someday it may be something we learn, just like skating. Now suppose I step out on the water and my apparent body – *this* body – sinks down like a stone, there is a possibility that my *other* body will rise, and I will be able to look down into the water and watch myself.'

'Watch yourself drown,' said Mr Lougheed. Eugene laughed, but not quite reassuringly.

The thing Mr Lougheed wanted to know was, what was behind this? Something was behind it, some game or mockery he did not grasp. If Calla or Rex had talked like this – assuming they could talk, at such length – he would have suspected nothing. With Eugene simple-mindedness had to be a trick, and if it had really taken hold it was somehow even more of a trick.

'So the purpose of this is to give people a jolt, so to speak? To make them doubt their senses?'

'It might do that.'

'How did you get yourself into it?'

'It did start almost as a joke. I was talking to those two ladies – you know, the sisters – the blind one and the other one, I don't know their names –'

'I know which ones.'

Eugene would chat with old people, he was a favourite with them; they saw him as a gentle ambassador from the terrible land of youth.

'We were discussing things like this and I said it was a possibility. It has been done, in fact, walking on water. Recently, I mean. They said would I be willing to try it myself and I said yes.'

'Maybe that was a bit conceited of you,' said Mr Lougheed thoughtfully, craftily.

'Yes I know. That night when I was meditating I let the question go down in my mind, am I doing this for my own ego? It came to me that it didn't matter. What I am doing it for doesn't matter. Whatever put the idea into my head to do it, I have to trust that. It may be an act that has a purpose beyond me. I know how that sounds. But I am just lending myself, I am being used. The whole thing really grew. I was going to do it for just those two old ladies but I couldn't do it right away because I wanted time to prepare, and so we arranged for Sunday and now I'm hearing about it from people on the street, people I don't know at all. I'm amazed.'

'Aren't you bothered by the thought that you might make a fool of yourself in front of that many people?'

'That isn't an expression that means anything to me, really. *Make a fool of yourself.* How can anybody do that? How can you make a fool? Show the fool, yes, expose the fool, but isn't the fool just yourself, isn't it there all the time? Show yourself. What else can you do?'

You can hang on to your sanity, if possible, Mr Lougheed could have said, but did not think of it till later. Even if he had thought of it then, the time for saying it had passed.

Outside his door on Sunday morning, Mr Lougheed found a dead bird. He was prepared to believe a cat had brought it. Cats did come into the house, were fed by Calla or Rover, left the smell of their urine in the downstairs hall. He picked up the bird and carried it downstairs and out into the back yard A bluejay. He admired the cold bright colour. Though they were not admirable birds, jays. He had grown up on a farm and could not help passing such judgements on all forms of plant and animal life. He remembered some visitor to the farm, a lady, not young, crying out over the beauty of a field full of wild mustard. She wore a kind of dusty pink or beige hat, chiffon, if that was the stuff, and the conspicuous folly of the hat blended with the folly of her pleasure, in his mind, and had remained to this day. Of course it was the looks, later the words, of the grown-ups, that informed him where folly lay.

He meant to bury the bird, but he could not find anything to dig a hole with. The door had been broken off the basement. There used to be some tools in there, but he supposed they had been carried away. The ground in the back yard was like cement anyway. Stones everywhere, broken glass. He put the dead bird in the garbage pail.

He had lived in this house for twelve years, ever since he sold his drugstore business and came out here to live near his married daughter. His daughter and her family had moved away but he had stayed on. The house and yard had been in a run-down condition even twelve years ago, though he had not foreseen, nobody had, that they would get to be in the state they were in today. The place had belonged to a Miss Musgrave, whose family had had money. She was still living, then, in the downstairs rooms where Rex and Calla and Rover lived today. Soon after moving in Mr Lougheed got the scythe and started cutting down the long grass in the corners of the yard. He meant to trim it up and make a decent lawn, a favour to all concerned. But he had not been doing this very long when a window was wrenched up and a loud, unlady-like, in fact alcoholic, voice called out to him.

'This is Musgrave property!'

That was Miss Musgrave, who was crazy, but in a familiar way. In his drugstore days he had known ladies like her, coming in with their lipstick crooked and their hats too, diddling with their prescriptions, wheedling, lying, taking offence. Miss Musgrave was long dead now and he almost missed such familiar craziness. He was left with the present crew, and it was beyond him, always beyond him, to judge whether they were crazy or not. Even Eugene. Most of all Eugene.

People had argued with him that he ought to move out of here. Why did he not? He did not like apartment buildings, he said, he did not like heights, did not want the bother of moving. There was more to it than that. Whatever he learned here, he was not sorry to have learned. He listened to his contemporaries talking and he thought that their brains would crack like eggs, if they knew one-tenth of what there was to know. He could not finally regret having seen the performance of Rex and Calla, or having read the newspaper that Rover sold, and had thrust at him one day for a joke. He read every word of it though the blurred type hurt his eyes. The bad type, the spelling, some blotched, possibly obscene drawings, as well as the needs admitted to in the want ads and an editorial which disagreed with the city council – referred to throughout as shit-artists and ass-holes – worried him along the same sore and exasperated nerve; but he kept on, with an odd apprehension of a message that could flash out almost too quick for the eye to catch it, like some commercials he had heard about on television.

But this performance of Eugene's was one thing he did

not mean to watch. It offended him too much, it made him too uneasy. He made his breakfast, which was as usual two slices of brown toast, a boiled egg and tea. He did not hear Eugene, and supposed he had gone out earlier. While he ate he remembered a feeling he had had in the back yard, while he was holding the bird and thinking of the chiffon-hatted lady and the field of mustard and his parents. He had been remembering something else, from that, and now he could tell that he had been remembering his dream. He knew that he must have dreamed it again last night, and he seemed to have no choice but to sit and try to see which part of it he could call to mind.

This dream, which he had dreamed on and off since middle age, had its start in a real incident that had happened when he was a child, and living on a farm, with his older brother Walter and his sister Mary who was to die of diphtheria when she was eighteen. In the middle of the night he had heard the phone ringing, three long rings. Each family along the road had its own number of rings – their own, which Mr Lougheed still remembered, was two longs and two shorts – but three long rings was a general alert, a signal for everyone on the line to pick up their phone. Mr Lougheed's father, in the kitchen directly below the boys' bedroom, shouted into the phone. He never did accept the principle of the telephone, and seemed to rely on the strength of his voice to carry over whatever distance was necessary. With the shouting they were all roused and came down to see their father putting on his boots and jacket – the time of year was May, springtime, but the nights were still cool – and, though Mr Lougheed could not remember what was said, he knew that his father had told them something about where he was going and that his brother Walter asked and received permission to go along, just as he himself asked and was refused, on the grounds that he was too young and could not keep up.

They were going to chase a mad boy, a young man, really, nineteen or twenty years old, who had lived on the next line of the township. Mr Lougheed could not recall what information his father gave out about this boy beyond his name, which was Frank McArter. Frank McArter was the youngest of a large, poor, decent family of Catholics. He had been taken away from home for a while after a series of fits but had returned cured, and was living there quietly taking care of his old parents, now that his brothers and sisters were gone. Mr Lougheed did not think his father mentioned at the time that the reason all the men were called out to track down Frank McArter was that earlier that evening, probably before dark (and before milking, certainly, because it was the bawling of the unrelieved cows that brought in a neighbour passing on the road), he had killed his father in the barn, using a pitchfork and the flat of a shovel, then his mother in the kitchen, using the same shovel which he must have carried from the barn for the purpose.

These were the facts. The dream, as far as he could tell, contained but did not reveal them. Awake he had all this information about the murder, double murder, in his memory, though he could not think when or how it was given to him. In the dream he never understood clearly what all the urgency and commotion were about, he knew only that he had to find his boots and hurry out with his father and brother (if he hurried, in the dream, he would not be left behind). He did not know where he was going and it would not dawn on him until he had gone along for a while that there was something they were going to find. Their progress might be easy and cheerful at the start, but often it would be slowed by confusing and deflecting invisible forces, so that Mr Lougheed would find himself separated, doing things such as mixing a prescription in his drugstore or eating supper with his wife. Then with such too-late desperate regret, through reproachful, unhelpful neighbourhoods, and always some kind of grey weather, not disclosing too much, he would be trying to get back to where he ought to have been. He never dreamed the dream through to the end. Or he never remembered. That was it, more likely. When the dream first came to him his parents and sister were dead but his brother was still alive, in Winnipeg, and he had thought of writing to him, asking him about Frank McArter, and if they had actually found him that night or not. There was a hole in his memory at that point. But he never did write – or when he did write, he did not ask this question, because he forgot, and if he had remembered he might have felt foolish anyway – and then his brother died.

This dream always left some weight on his mind. He supposed it was because he was still carrying around, for part of the day, the presences of dead people, father and mother, brother and sister, whose faces he could not clearly remember when he was awake. How to convey the solidity, complexity, reality, of those presences – even if he had anybody to convey this to? It almost seemed to him there must be a place where they moved with independence, undiminished authority, outside his own mind; it was hard to believe he had authored them himself. A commonplace experience. He remembered his own mother, sitting down at the breakfast table, saying in a voice of astonishment that was almost complaint, 'I've been having a dream about your grandma! Oh, it was *her!*'

Another thing he was made to think about was the difference between that time and now. It was too much. Nobody could get from one such time to another, and how had he done it? How could one man know Mr Lougheed's father and mother, and now know Rex and Calla? It occurred to him, and had occurred to him before, that there was after all something to be said for dealing with things the way most people of his age seemed to do. It was sensible perhaps to stop noticing, to believe that this was still the same world they were living in, with some dreadful but curable aberrations, never to understand how the whole arrangement had altered.

The dream had brought him in touch with a world of which the world he lived in now seemed the most casual imitation – in texture, you might say, in sharpness, in authority. It was true, of course, that his senses had dimmed. Nevertheless. The weight of life, the importance of it, had some way disappeared. Events took place now in a diminished landscape, and were of equal, or no, importance. Mr Lougheed riding on a bus through city streets or even through the countryside would not have been much amazed to see anything you could name – a mosque, for instance, or a white bear. Whatever it looked to be, it would turn out to be something else. Girls at the supermarket wore grass skirts to sell pineapples and he had seen a gas station attendant, wiping windshields, wearing on his head a fool's hat with bells. Less and less was surprising.

Sometimes in the records they played downstairs he would hear an absolutely clear, and familiar, unmolested line of music. And he knew what would happen, how this would be mocked and twisted around, blown up, blasted out of all recognition. There were similar jokes everywhere, and it must be considered that people found them satisfying.

The Ross Point pier was a long-unused, broken-down pier which disappeared almost entirely at high tide and at low tide slipped into the ocean at its far end. Mr Lougheed coming around the bend in the sea walk – he had had to come after all, he had been too restless to stay away – half expected to see no one there, to discover that he had imagined the whole thing, or, more likely, that it had been an elaborate hoax concocted by others. But this was not so; people had gathered. There were no steps here – there were steps a quarter of a mile back and a little way ahead, past Ross Point – but Mr Lougheed got himself down the bank, hanging onto broom bushes, and not thinking of the risk of broken bones until later. He hurried along the beach.

The first people he recognized were running along the pier and jumping from one of its broken concrete chunks to another. Rex and Calla and Rover and a number of their indistinguishable friends. Calla was wrapped in what looked like – what was – an old chenille bedspread, half the pink and brown tufts worn away. They cavorted, they splashed barefoot in the water. One boy on the shore was playing a

flute, or the thing like a flute, the same thing Eugene had –
a recorder. He played well, though monotonously. The two
old sisters were there, the blind one with her white cane
lifted while she talked, pointed at the water. She reminded
you of Moses at the Red Sea. The other one talked to her,
explaining. Mr Clifford and Mr Morey and a few other old
men, judicious, chatting, had stationed themselves not too
close by. Altogether there were maybe three dozen people,
all over sixty or under thirty. Eugene was sitting rather far
out on the pier, by himself. Mr Lougheed had thought he
might put on some special outfit for the occasion, some
rough robe, or loincloth, if he could locate such a thing,
but he was wearing his usual jeans and white T-shirt.

One of the old men took a watch out of his pocket and
called straight ahead, as if addressing nobody in particular,
'I see here it's ten o'clock.'

'Ten o'clock, Eugene!' called Rex who had jumped into
the water and was naked from the waist up, wet to the
thighs.

Eugene's back was to them all, his knees were bent, his
head was on his knees.

'Holy, holy, holy,' intoned Rex, throwing back his bushy
head, spreading his arms wide.

'We should sing,' a girl said.

At the same time two ladies wearing hats, in front of Mr
Lougheed, spoke to each other.

'I didn't expect so many of them would be here.'

'I didn't come to listen to sacreligion.'

The girl began to sing by herself, in competition with
the recorder player. She whirled unsteadily around on the
shore, singing without words, a scarf of many soft colours

flying out from her throat. After a bit of this the two ladies in front of Mr Lougheed looked at each other, cleared their throats, nodded, and started up in shaky sweet voices, modestly determined.

> *We gather together to ask the Lord's blessing,*
> *He chastens, and hastens, His will to make known . . .*

'Let's get the show on the road!' called out Mr Morey rambunctiously.

'What's happening?' said the blind sister. 'Is he on it yet?'

Eugene got up and walked farther out on the pier. He walked without hesitation into the water which lapped around his ankles, then his knees, then his thighs.

'He's in it more than he's on it,' said Mr Morey. 'Say a prayer, boy!'

Rover squatted down on the stones and began to say loudly, 'Om, om, om, om –'

'What, what?' said the blind sister, and the girl who was singing paused long enough in her song to call, 'Oh, Eugene! Eugene!' in a voice of loving hopelessness, renunciation.

> *So from the beginning, the fight we were*
> *winning . . .*

Eugene walked to his waist, to his chest, and Mr Lougheed roared in a voice he thought he had lost, 'Eugene, come out of that water!'

'Weightlessness!' Mr Morey shouted at the same time. 'Turn your weightlessness on!'

Eugene bowed his head and went under.

The singing girl gave a joyful scream.

Mr Lougheed had gone down to the pier and a little way out on it. He said to Calla, wrapped in her bedspread like a Biblical woman, 'Do you know if he can swim?'

'Swim, swim!' cried Rex, that buffoon, and fell upon the water, while the not-blind sister was spinning around calling, 'Somebody, somebody! Don't let him drown!'

Eugene appeared hanging onto the pier where it came out of the water. He got to his feet, dripping, and stood braced there clearing the hair out of his eyes, while a girl called, 'Sea monster, sea monster!' The men, led by Mr Morey, broke into ironical clapping.

The recorder player had not paused for any of this.

'That's what it amounts to, walking on water,' Mr Morey said.

'Don't let anybody torment him,' said the blind sister. 'He did his best.'

Eugene walked slowly towards them, smiling. 'I don't even know how to swim,' he said, gladly drawing in air. He sounded nearly triumphant. 'I crawled along the pier. I could have stood up sooner but I liked – being under water.'

'Go home and change your clothes if you don't want to get pneumonia,' said Mr Lougheed.

'Was it just a joke then?' said one of the hymn-singing ladies, and though she was not speaking to him Mr Lougheed turned and said to her harshly, 'What did you think it was?' The two ladies looked at each other, pressing in their lips at his rudeness.

'I'm sorry if this has not been what you all hoped for,' said Eugene in a gently raised voice, looking around. 'The fault is all in me. I haven't reached the point I hoped I might have reached, in my control. However if this has been disappointing for you it has been very interesting and wonderful for me and I have learned something important. I want to thank you.'

The ladies clapped now kindly, and some of the young people joined them, clapping more exaggeratedly. Two groups with more in common than they knew, Mr Lougheed was thinking. Neither would have admitted that. But didn't their expectations run along the same lines? And what was it in them that prompted such expectations? It was despair, it was being at the end of the track. Nevertheless pride should forbid one.

Without speaking any more to anyone he went off by himself. He went along the beach and up the steps wondering how he had ever managed to get down the bank without breaking a leg, which at his age would have finished him, and all for this nonsense. He walked a mile or so along the sea to a café he knew stayed open Sundays. He sat for a long time over a cup of coffee and then walked back. There was music coming from the open downstairs windows of the house, from Miss Musgrave's windows; the kind of music they always played. He walked upstairs and knocked on Eugene's door, calling out, 'I just wanted to see if you got those wet clothes off!'

No answer. After a moment he opened the door. Eugene never locked it.

'Eugene?'

Eugene was not there and neither were his wet clothes. Mr Lougheed had seen the room without Eugene in it before, when he had brought back a book. The sight of it had not bothered him then as it did now. The window was all the way up now, for one thing. Eugene usually put it down before he went out, for fear of rain getting at his books or a wind coming up. There was some wind now. Papers had blown off the top of the bookcase and were scattered on the floor. Otherwise the place was tidy. The blanket and sheets were folded at the end of the mattress, as if he did not intend to sleep there any more.

Mr Lougheed knocked on the downstairs door. Calla came.

'Eugene's not home. Do you know where he is?'

Calla turned and called into the room, which was darkened by red and purple curtains, dyed bedsheets, always shut.

'Did anybody see Eugene?'

'He went out towards the golf course. He was headed east.'

'What do you want him for?' said Rex amiably, leaning on Calla's shoulder.

Somebody in the background shouted, 'Ask him how he liked his door.'

'Ask him how he liked his bird.'

Not the cat, then. Calla smiled at him. She had a large, sweet white face, white as chalk, dotted by many little inflamed pimples.

'Thank you,' said Mr Lougheed. He ignored Rex.

'What does he want Yew-gene for?' said another voice in the background, probably Rover's, his tinny whine. This voice offered a conjecture Mr Lougheed immediately and ever afterwards pretended he had not heard.

'Have a fig?' said Calla.

★

He took their word for it, there was nothing else he could do. He went east, walking along the sea, retracing his route of that morning. Past the pier, deserted now, past the café where he had drunk his coffee, on to the golf course. It was a pleasant afternoon, there were many people walking. Sometimes he thought he saw Eugene. Half the young men in the world seemed to be wearing jeans and white T-shirts, to be short and slight and have hair of about that length. He found himself looking into people's faces and wanting to ask them, 'Have you seen a young man?' He thought he might meet somebody who had been at the pier this morning. He looked for Mr Clifford or Mr Morey. But it was too far, it was out of their territory.

On the other side of the golf course was an area of wild brush, bushes about as high as a man's head. There were rocks slipping into the water. No beach here. The water looked fairly deep. A man was standing out on the rocks holding onto a kite string. There were small boats out on the water, with red and blue sails. Could a man fall here, and not be noticed? Could a man slide in quietly causing no stir, and be gone?

Earlier in the day, in fact while he was sitting drinking his coffee in that café, something had come to him, a scene which he took to be the ending of his dream. It was a clear and detailed scene effortlessly retrieved from somewhere – either from the dream or from his memory, and he did not see how it could have come from his memory.

He was walking behind his father in some long grey grass. It was grey because the night was ending and everything could be seen clearly but the sun was not yet up. They seemed to have become separated from the other men searching. They were near a river, and in a little while climbed a bank onto a dirt road. The road led to a bridge, crossing the river, and Mr Lougheed, a child of course in this scene, hurried out onto the bridge. He was about a third of the way across it before it occurred to him what an unlikely, and positively unsafe, structure this was. Boards were missing from its floor, and the girders seemed crumpled up in some way, as if the bridge were a toy someone had stepped on. He looked back for his father, but his father was not there; this was as expected. Then he had to look down through the floor of the bridge where a plank was missing and in the shallow water of the river which flowed among white stones he saw a boy's body spread out, face down. Which in the dream, if that was what it was, seemed just as natural a sight as the stones, and as clean and white.

But in his wakened mind of course this sight could not be received so casually and he asked himself if that was Frank McArter, if that young man after killing both his parents had actually thrown himself into the river. There was no way now of finding out.

Once he had suffered what the doctor told him later was a tiny stroke, in which a jagged line, blinding white, danced in a corner of his vision for forty-eight hours or so, then disappeared. There was no damage, such things were not uncommon, the doctor told him. Now the dream, or the ending of the dream, kept doing the same thing in his mind. He expected it would go away after a while. And another thing which he hoped would go away, when he got back to himself, were these fears or strange thoughts about Eugene going into the water – committing suicide would not be his words for it, not Eugene's; you might be sure he would have some far-fetched and tricky way of describing it – for which that morning's show might have been only a rehearsal, an imitation.

He was very tired. Finally he came to an empty bench and sat there a long time, wondering if he would ever gather the strength to walk home.

'Eugene's door is unlocked and his window is wide open,' he said to Calla. The room behind her was silent now. She smiled at him as before. He thought to look at her eyes but as far as he could see they were normal. He was so tired, so shaken he had to hang onto the newel post.

'He always leaves his door open,' Calla said.

'I have reason to worry about him,' said Mr Lougheed, trembling. 'I think we ought to get in touch with some authority.'

'The *police*?' said Calla in a soft horrified voice. 'Oh, you can't do that. You can't ever do that.'

'I think something might have happened to him.'

'He might have gone away.'

'If he did, he left all his belongings behind.'

'He might have done that. He might have just – you know, he might have suddenly thought he wanted to go away, and so he went.'

'I think his mind was disturbed. I think he might have tried to – he might have gone into the water again.'

'You think so?' said Calla. He had expected her to be surprised, to exclaim against this, even to smile at him for such an idea, but instead she seemed to be letting the possibility blossom slowly, seductively, in her head. 'You think he might have?'

'I don't know. I think he was disturbed. I think so. I find it hard to tell when one of you is disturbed or not.'

'He wasn't one of us,' said Calla. 'He was fairly old.'

'He might have wanted to do that, though,' she said in a minute. 'It's just another thing he might have wanted to do. If that's what he was going to do, then nobody ought to stop him, should they? Or feel sad about him. I never feel sad about anybody.'

Mr Lougheed turned away. 'Good night now,' said Calla persuasively. 'I'm sorry if you don't like your door.'

Mr Lougheed thought for the first time ever that he might not be able to get to the top of the stairs. He doubted his powers even for that. It was possible that he would have to go into an apartment building, like the rest of them, if he wanted to continue.

FORGIVENESS IN FAMILIES

I've often thought, suppose I had to go to a psychiatrist, and
he would want to know about my family background,
naturally, so I would have to start telling him about my
brother, and he wouldn't even wait till I was finished,
would he, the psychiatrist, he'd commit me.

I said that to Mother; she laughed. 'You're hard on that
boy, Val.'

'Boy,' I said. '*Man*.'

She laughed, she admitted it. 'But remember,' she said,
'the Lord loves a lunatic.'

'How do you know,' I said, 'seeing you're an atheist?'

Some things he couldn't help. Being born, for instance.
He was born the week I started school, and how's that for
timing? I was scared, it wasn't like now when the kids have
been going to playschool and kindergarten for years. I was

going to school for the first time and all the other kids had their mothers with them and where was mine? In the hospital having a baby. The embarrassment to me. There was a lot of shame about those things then.

It wasn't his fault getting born and it wasn't his fault throwing up at my wedding. Think of it. The floor, the table, he even managed to hit the cake. He was not drunk, as some people thought, he really did have some violent kind of flu, which Haro and I came down with, in fact, on our honeymoon. I never heard of anybody else with any kind of flu throwing up over a table with a lace cloth and silver candlesticks and a wedding cake on it, but you could say it was bad luck; maybe everybody else when the need came on them was closer to a toilet. And everybody else might try a little harder to hold back, they just might, because nobody else is quite so special, quite so centre-of-the-universe, as my baby brother. Just call him a child of nature. That was what he called himself, later on.

I will skip over what he did between getting born and throwing up at my wedding except to say that he had asthma and got to stay home from school weeks on end, listening to soap operas. Sometimes there was a truce between us, and I would get him to tell me what happened every day on 'Big Sister' and 'Road of Life' and the one with Gee-Gee and Papa David. He was very good at remembering all the characters and getting all the complications straight, I'll say that, and he did read a lot in *Gateways to Bookland*, that lovely set Mother bought for us and that he later sneaked out of the house and sold, for ten dollars, to a secondhand book dealer. Mother said he could have been brilliant at school if he wanted to be. That's a deep one, your brother, she used to say, he's got some surprises in store for us. She was right, he had.

He started staying home permanently in Grade Ten after a little problem of being caught in a cheating-ring that was getting maths tests from some teacher's desk. One of the janitors was letting him back in the classroom after school because he said he was working on a special project. So he was, in his own way. Mother said he did it to make himself popular, because he had asthma and couldn't take part in sports.

Now. Jobs. The question comes up, what is such a person as my brother – and I ought to give him a name at least, his name is Cam, for Cameron, Mother thought that would be a suitable name for a university president or honest tycoon (which is the sort of thing she planned for him to be) – what is he going to do, how is he going to make a living? Until recently the country did not pay you to sit on your uppers and announce that you had adopted a creative life-style. He got a job first as a movie usher. Mother got it for him, she knew the manager, it was the old International Theater over on Blake Street. He had to quit, though, because he got this darkness-phobia. All the people sitting in the dark he said gave him a crawly feeling, very peculiar. It only interfered with him working as an usher, it didn't interfere with him going to the movies on his own. He got very fond of movies. In fact, he spent whole days sitting in movie houses, sitting through every show twice then going to another theatre and sitting through what was there. He had to do something with his time, because Mother and all of us believed he was working then in the office of the Greyhound Bus Depot. He went off to work at the right time every morning and came home at the right time every night, and he told all about the cranky old man in charge of the office and the woman with curvature of the spine who had been there since 1919 and how mad she got at the young girls chewing gum, oh, a lively story, it would have worked up to something as good as the soap operas if Mother hadn't phoned up to complain about the way they were withholding his pay cheque – due to a technical error in the spelling of his name, he said – and found out he'd quit in the middle of his second day.

Well. Sitting in movies was better than sitting in beer parlours, Mother said. At least he wasn't on the street getting in with criminal gangs. She asked him what his favourite movie was and he said *Seven Brides for Seven Brothers*. See, she said, he is interested in an outdoor life, he is not suited to office work. So she sent him to work for some cousins of hers who have a farm in the Fraser Valley. I should explain that my father, Cam's and mine, was dead by this time, he died a way back when Cam was having asthma and listening to soap operas. It didn't make much difference, his dying because he worked as a conductor on the P.G.E. when it started at Squamish, and he lived part of the time in Lillooet. Nothing changed, Mother went on working at Eaton's as she always had, going across on the ferry and then on the bus; I got supper, she came trudging up the hill in the winter dark.

Cam took off from the farm, he complained that the cousins were religious and always after his soul. Mother could see his problem, she had after all brought him up to be a freethinker. He hitchhiked east. From time to time a letter came. A request for funds. He had been offered a job in northern Quebec if he could get the money together to get up there. Mother sent it. He sent word the job had folded, but he didn't send back the money. He and two friends were going to start a turkey farm. They sent us plans, estimates. They were supposed to be working on contract for the Purina Company, nothing could go wrong. The turkeys were drowned in a flood, after Mother had sent him money and we had too against our better judgement. Everywhere that boy hits turns into a disaster area, Mother said. If you read it in a book you wouldn't believe it, she said. It's so terrible it's funny.

She knew. I used to go over to see her on Wednesday afternoon – her day off – pushing the stroller with Karen in it, and later Tommy in it and Karen walking beside, up Lonsdale and down King's Road, and what would we always end up talking about? That boy and I, we are getting a divorce, she said. I am definitely going to write him off. What good will he ever be until he stops relying on me, she asked. I kept my mouth shut, more or less. She knew my opinion. But she ended up every time saying, 'He was a nice fellow to have around the house, though. Good company. That boy could always make me laugh.'

Or, 'He had a lot to contend with, his asthma and no dad. He never did intentionally hurt a soul.'

'One good thing he did,' she said, 'you could really call it a good turn. That girl.'

Referring to the girl who came and told us she had been engaged to him, in Hamilton, Ontario, until he told her he could never get married because he had just found out there was hereditary fatal kidney disease in his family. He wrote her a letter. And she came looking for him to tell him it didn't matter. Not at all a bad-looking girl. She worked for the Bell Telephone. Mother said it was a lie told out of kindness, to spare her feelings when he didn't want to marry her. I said it was a kindness, anyway, because she would have been supporting him for the rest of her life.

Though it might have eased things up a bit on the rest of us.

But that was then and now is now and as we all know times have changed. Cam is finding it easier. He lives at home, off and on, has for a year and a half. His hair is thin in front, not surprising in a man thirty-four years of age, but shoulder-length behind, straggly, greying. He wears a sort of rough brown robe that looks as if it might be made out of a sack (is that what sackcloth is supposed to be, I said to Haro, I wouldn't mind supplying the ashes), and hanging down on his chest he has all sorts of chains, medallions, crosses, elk's teeth or whatnot. Rope sandals on his feet. Some friend of his makes them. He collects welfare. Nobody asks him to work. Who could be so crude? If he has to write down his occupation he writes priest.

It's true. There is a whole school of them, calling themselves priests, and they have a house over in Kitsilano, Cam stays there too sometimes. They're in competition with the Hare Krishna bunch, only these ones don't chant, they just walk around smiling. He has developed this voice I can't stand, a very thin, sweet voice, all on one level. It makes me want to stand in front of him and say, 'There's an earthquake in Chile, two hundred thousand people just died, they've burned up another village in Vietnam, famine as usual in India.' Just to see if he'd keep saying,

'Ve-ery ni-ice, ve-ery ni-ice,' that sweet way. He won't eat meat, of course, he eats whole-grain cereals and leafy vegetables. He came into the kitchen where I was slicing beets – beets being forbidden, a root vegetable – and, 'I hope you understand that you're committing murder,' he said.

'No,' I said, 'but I'll give you sixty seconds to get out of here or I may be.'

So as I say he's home part of the time now and he was there on the Monday night when Mother got sick. She was vomiting. A couple of days before this he had started her on a vegetarian diet – she was always promising him she'd try it – and he told her she was vomiting up all the old poisons stored up in her body from eating meat and sugar and so on. He said it was a good sign, and when she had it all vomited out she'd feel better. She kept vomiting, and she didn't feel better, but he had to go out. Monday nights is when they have the weekly meeting at the priests' house, where they chant and burn incense or celebrate the black mass, for all I know. He stayed out most of the night, and when he got home he found Mother unconscious on the bathroom floor. He got on the phone and phoned *me*.

'I think you better come over here and see if you can help Mom, Val.'

'What's the matter with her?'

'She's not feeling very well.'

'What's the matter with her? Put her on the phone.'

'I can't.'

'Why can't you?'

I swear he tittered. 'Well I'm afraid she's passed out.'

I called the ambulance and sent them for her, that was

how she got to the hospital, five o'clock in the morning. I called her family doctor, he got over there, and he got Dr Ellis Bell, one of the best-known heart men in the city, because that was what they had decided it was, her heart. I got dressed and woke Haro and told him and then I drove myself over to the Lions Gate Hospital. They wouldn't let me in till ten o'clock. They had her in Intensive Care. I sat outside Intensive Care in their slick little awful waiting room. They had red slippery chairs, cheap covering, and a stand full of pebbles with green plastic leaves growing up. I sat there hour after hour and read *The Reader's Digest*. The jokes. Thinking this is how it is, this is it, really, she's dying. Now, this moment, behind those doors, dying. Nothing stops or holds off for it the way you somehow and against all your sense believe it will. I thought about Mother's life, the part of it I knew. Going to work every day, first on the ferry then on the bus. Shopping at the old Red-and-White then at the new Safeway – new, fifteen years old! Going down to the Library one night a week, taking me with her, and we would come home on the bus with our load of books and a bag of grapes we bought at the Chinese place, for a treat. Wednesday afternoon too when my kids were small and I went over there to drink coffee and she rolled us cigarettes on that contraption she had. And I thought, all these things don't seem that much like life, when you're doing them, they're just what you do, how you fill up your days, and you think all the time something is going to crack open, and you'll find yourself, *then* you'll find yourself, in life. It's not even that you particularly want this to happen, this cracking open, you're comfortable enough the way things are, but you do expect it. Then you're dying, Mother is dying, and it's just the same plastic chairs and plastic plants and ordinary day outside with people getting groceries and what you've had is all there is, and going to the Library, just a thing like that, coming back up the hill on the bus with books and a bag of grapes seems now worth wanting, O God doesn't it, you'd break your heart wanting back there.

When they let me in to see her she was bluish-grey in the face and her eyes were not all-the-way closed, but they had rolled up, the slit that was open showed the whites. She always looked terrible with her teeth out, anyway, wouldn't let us see her. Cam teased her vanity. They were out now. So all the time, I thought, all the time even when she was young it was in her that she was going to look like this.

They didn't hold out hope. Haro came and took a look at her and put his arm around my shoulders and said, 'Val, you'll have to be prepared.' He meant well but I couldn't talk to him. It wasn't his mother and he couldn't remember anything. That wasn't his fault but I didn't want to talk to him, I didn't want to listen to him telling me I better be prepared. We went and ate something in the hospital cafeteria.

'You better phone Cam,' Haro said.

'Why?'

'He'll want to know.'

'Why do you think he'll want to know? He left her alone last night and he didn't know enough to get an ambulance when he came in and found her this morning.'

'Just the same. He has a right. Maybe you ought to tell him to get over here.'

'He is probably busy this moment preparing to give her a hippie funeral.'

But Haro persuaded me as he always can and I went and phoned. No answer. I felt better because I had phoned, and justified in what I had said because of Cam not being in. I went back and waited, by myself.

About seven o'clock that night Cam turned up. He was not alone. He had brought along a tribe of co-priests, I suppose they were, from that house. They all wore the same kind of outfit he did, the brown sacking nightgown and the chains and crosses and holy hardware, they all had long hair, they were all a good many years younger than Cam, except for one old man, really old, with a curly grey beard and bare feet – in March, bare feet – and no teeth. I swear this old man didn't have a clue what was going on. I think they picked him up down by the Salvation Army and put that outfit on him because they needed an old man for a kind of mascot, or extra holiness, or something.

Cam said, 'This is my sister Valerie. This is Brother Michael. This is Brother John, this is Brother Louis.' Etc., etc.

'They haven't said anything to give me hope, Cam. She is dying.'

'We hope not,' said Cam with his secret smile. 'We spent the day working for her.'

'Do you mean praying?' I said.

'Work is a better word to describe it than praying, if you don't understand what it is.'

Well of course, I never understand.

'Real praying is work, believe me,' says Cam and they all smile at me, his way. They can't keep still, like children who have to go to the bathroom they're weaving and jiggling and doing little steps.

'Now where's her room?' says Cam in a practical tone of voice.

I thought of Mother dying and through that slit between her lids – who knows, maybe she can see from time to time – seeing this crowd of dervishes celebrating around her bed. Mother who lost her religion when she was thirteen and went to the Unitarian Church and quit when they had the split about crossing God out of the hymns (she was for it), Mother having to spend her last conscious minutes wondering what had happened, if she was transported back in history to where loonies cavorted around in their crazy ceremonies, trying to sort her last reasonable thoughts out in the middle of their business.

Thank God the nurse said no. The intern was brought and he said no. Cam didn't insist, he smiled and nodded at them as if they were granting permission and then he brought the troupe back into the waiting room and there, right before my eyes, they started. They put the old man in the centre, sitting down with his head bowed and his eyes shut – they had to tap him and remind him how to do that – and they squatted in a rough sort of circle round him, facing in and out, in and out, alternately. Then, eyes closed, they started swaying back and forth moaning some words very softly, only not the same words, it sounded as if each one of them had got different words, and not in English of course but Swahili or Sanskrit or something. It got louder, gradually it got louder, a pounding singsong, and as it did they rose to their feet, all except the old man who stayed where he was and looked as if he might have gone to sleep, sitting, and they began a shuffling kind of dance where they stood, clapping, not very well in time. They did this for a long while, and the noise they were making, though it was not terribly loud, attracted the nurses from their station and nurses' aids and orderlies and a few people like me who were waiting, and nobody seemed to know what to do, because it was unbelievable, so crazy in that ordinary little waiting room. Everybody just stared as if they were asleep and dreaming and expecting to wake up. Then a nurse came out of Intensive Care and said, 'We can't have this disturbance. What do you think you're doing here?'

She took hold of one of the young ones and shook him by the shoulder, else she couldn't have got anybody to stop and pay attention.

'We're working to help a woman who's very sick,' he told her.

'I don't know what you call working, but you're not helping anybody. Now I'm asking you to clear out of here. Excuse me. I'm not asking. I'm telling.'

'You're very mistaken if you think the tones of our voices are hurting or disturbing any sick person. This whole ceremony is pitched at a level which will reach and comfort the unconscious mind and draw the demonic influences out of the body. It's a ceremony that goes back five thousand years.'

'Good Lord,' said the nurse, looking stupefied as well she might. 'Who are these people?'

I had to go and enlighten her, telling her that it was my brother and what you might call his friends, and I was not in on their ceremony. I asked about Mother, was there any change.

'No change,' she said. 'What do we have to do to get them out of here?'

'Turn the hose on them,' one of the orderlies said, and all this time, the dance, or ceremony, never stopped, and the one who had stopped and done the explaining went back to dancing too, and I said to the nurse, 'I'll phone in to see how she is, I'm going home for a little while.' I walked out of the hospital and found to my surprise that it was dark. The whole day in there, dark to dark. In the parking lot I started to cry. Cam has turned this into a circus for his own benefit, I said to myself, and said it out loud when I got home.

Haro made me a drink.

'It'll probably get into the papers,' I said. 'Cam's chance for fame.'

Haro phoned the hospital to see if there was any news and they said there wasn't. 'Did they have – was there any difficulty with some young people in the waiting room this evening? Did they leave quietly?' Haro is ten years older than I am, a cautious man, too patient with everybody. I used to think he was sometimes giving Cam money I didn't know about.

'They left quietly,' he said. 'Don't worry about the papers. Get some sleep.'

I didn't mean to but I fell asleep on the couch, after the drink and the long day. I woke up with the phone ringing and day lightening the room. I stumbled into the kitchen dragging the blanket Haro had put over me and saw by the clock on the wall it was a quarter to six. She's gone, I thought.

It was her own doctor.

He said he had encouraging news. He said she was much better this morning.

I dragged over a chair and collapsed in it, both arms and my head too down on the kitchen counter. I came back on the phone to hear him saying she was still in a critical phase and the next forty-eight hours would tell the story, but without raising my hopes too high he wanted me to know she was responding to treatment. He said that was especially surprising in view of the fact that she had been late getting to hospital and the things they did to her at first did not seem to have much effect, though of course the fact that she survived the first few hours at all was a good sign. Nobody had made much of this good sign to me yesterday, I thought.

I sat there for an hour at least after I had hung up the phone. I made a cup of instant coffee and my hands were shaking so I could hardly get the water into the cup, then couldn't get the cup to my mouth. I let it go cold. Haro came out in his pyjamas at last. He gave me one look and said, 'Easy, Val. Has she gone?'

'She's some better. She's responding to treatment.'

'The look of you I thought the other.'

'I'm so amazed.'

'I wouldn't've given five cents for her chances yesterday noon.'

'I know. I can't believe it.'

'It's the tension,' Haro said. 'I know. You build yourself up ready for something bad to happen and then when it doesn't, it's a queer feeling, you can't feel good right away, it's almost like a disappointment.'

Disappointment. That was the word that stayed with

me. I was so glad, really, grateful, but underneath I was thinking, so Cam didn't kill her after all, with his carelessness and craziness and going out and neglecting her he didn't kill her, and I was, yes, I was, sorry in some part of me to find out that was true. And I knew Haro knew this but wouldn't speak of it to me, ever. That was the real shock to me, why I kept shaking. Not whether Mother lived or died. It was what was so plain about myself.

Mother got well, she pulled through beautifully. After she rallied she never sank back. She was in the hospital three weeks and then she came home, and rested another three weeks, and after that went back to work, cutting down a bit and working ten to four instead of full days, what they call the housewives' shift. She told everybody about Cam and his friends coming to the hospital. She began to say things like, 'Well, that boy of mine may not be much of a success at anything else but you have to admit he has the knack of saving lives.' Or, 'Maybe Cam should go into the miracle business, he certainly pulled it off with me.' By this time Cam was saying, he is saying now, that he's not sure about that religion, he's getting tired of the other priests and all that not eating meat or root vegetables. It's a stage, he says now, he's glad he went through it, self-discovery. One day I went over there and found he was trying on an old suit and tie. He says he might take advantage of some of the adult education courses, he is thinking of becoming an accountant.

I was thinking myself about changing into a different sort of person from the one I am. I do think about that. I read a book called *The Art of Loving*. A lot of things seemed clear while I was reading it but afterwards I went back to being more or less the same. What has Cam ever done that actually hurt me, anyway, as Haro once said. And how am I better than he is after the way I felt the night Mother lived instead of died? I made a promise to myself I would try. I went over there one day taking them a bakery cake – which Cam eats now as happily as anybody else – and I heard their voices out in the yard – now it's summer, they love to sit in the sun. Mother saying to some visitor, 'Oh yes I was, I was all set to take off into the wild blue yonder, and Cam here, this *idiot*, came and danced outside my door with a bunch of his hippie friends –'

'My God, woman,' roared Cam, but you could tell he didn't care now, 'members of an ancient holy discipline.'

I had a strange feeling, like I was walking on coals and trying a spell so I wouldn't get burnt.

Forgiveness in families is a mystery to me, how it comes or how it lasts.

TELL ME YES OR NO

I persistently imagine you dead.
    You told me that you loved me years ago. Years ago.
And I said that I too, I was in love with you in those days.
An exaggeration.

In those days I was a young girl, but didn't know it because
times were different then. At the age when young girls
nowadays are growing their hair to their waists, travelling through Afghanistan, moving – it seems to me – as
smoothly as eels among their varied and innocent and
transitory loves, I was sleepily rinsing diapers, clad in a red
corduroy dressing gown, wet across the stomach; I was
pushing a baby carriage or a stroller along the side of the
road to the store (so habitually that without this prop my
arms felt a disturbing lightness, my body weight had to be

redistributed, tilted back), I was reading and falling asleep on the evening couch. We are pitied for this bygone drudgery, women of my age are, we pity ourselves, but to tell the truth it was not always bad, it was sometimes comfortable – the ritual labours, small rewards of coffee and cigarettes, the desperate, humorous, formalized exchanges with other women, the luxurious dreams of sleep.

We lived then in a community called The Huts, on the edge of the campus. They were in fact old army huts, used as married students' quarters. I was reading *The Magic Mountain*, all one winter, I would fall asleep with it across my stomach. Sometimes I would read aloud to Douglas, when he was too tired to work any more. When I finished *The Magic Mountain* I meant to get us through *Remembrance of Things Past*. We stumbled to bed with our arms around each other, united in our longing for sleep. But occasionally I would have to get out of bed, later, and go into the bathroom to put in my diaphragm. If I looked out the top half of the bathroom window, through the gap in the plastic curtains, I could see lights on in some of the other bathroom windows in the colony, and I would imagine other wives risen in the night on a similar errand. Creatures of daily use, inseparable from infants, stoves, and tubs, turned now to our nightly use, with its connotations – rapidly fading – of sin and splendour. I remembered from far back – from four or five years back, actually, that seemed a long time to me – how sex had seemed apocalyptic (we read Lawrence, many of us were virgins at twenty). Now it had shrunk to this brisk, unvarying, satisfactory, localized exchange, contained appropriately enough in these domestic quarters. I felt nothing so definite as dissatisfaction. I simply registered the change, as I would still register the diminished glamour of Christmas. I believed such changes had taken place because I had grown up and become at home in the world. I was young enough to think that, we all were. A word we often used was 'mature'. We would meet somebody we had known a few years ago and we would report that this person had greatly matured. You know, everybody knows, the catalogue of delusions we subscribed to in the fifties; it is too easy to mock them, to announce that maturity was indicated by possession of automatic washers and a muting of political discontent, by addiction to childbearing and station wagons. Too easy and not the whole truth, because it leaves out something that was appealing, I think, in our heaviness and docility, our love of limits.

There was no infidelity in The Huts, or none that I knew of. We lived so close together, we were poor and too busy. Few flashes of lust at parties; perhaps we could not afford to drink enough. You say you were in love with me and I reply that I was in love with you, but the truth was surely different. More likely we got a glimpse of something, through each other, that we had not been thinking about – had put aside, in your case, or not yet discovered, in mine.

I remembered the same day you remembered, when we met two years ago totally unexpectedly in a city where neither of us lived. We spoke of it after we had drunk a lot of wine at our spur-of-the-moment lunch.

'One day we went for a walk. I had to lift that thing –'
'Stroller. I had Jocelyn in it then.'
'Over rocks and mud. I remember.'
A sunny day, a beautiful hot day, in spring, April or maybe

even March. I had gone to the drugstore in the campus shopping centre wearing my winter car coat, because I did not believe it could really be as warm a day as it looked. As soon as I saw you I wished I could go home and start over again, comb my hair more carefully and put on a brushed-wool, dark grey sweater I had. I could not take off my coat because I was wearing the T-shirt Jocelyn had spilled orange juice on.

I did not know you well, you lived at the other end of The Huts. You were older than most of us, you had come back to university as a graduate student, from the real world of work and war (a mistake, you didn't stay, you left and got a job with a magazine soon after that day we took the walk). Your wife drove off every morning to teach at a dancing school. She was little, dark, gypsyish, emphatically confident, in comparison to the blurred and sleepy, stay-at-home wives.

We talked in front of the drugstore and you said it was too nice a day to go on working, we ought to go for a walk. We did not head for the campus, with its wide easy paths, but for that wild, partly wooded patch of land above the river, where students – the unmarried ones, of course – went to make halfway love in the daytime, all-the-way love at night. Nobody was there that day. It was too early in the year, the munificence of the weather had taken everybody by surprise. It was an awkward place to walk with the stroller. As you said, you had to lift it over rocks and muddy stretches of the path. Our conversation had to be hauled over similar difficulties. We said nothing of importance. We never touched each other. We became more and more uncomfortable as it became apparent that our walk was not going to accomplish what we pretended we wanted it to do – give us an hour's easy company in the pleasure of the day – or what we really wanted it to do. This kind of tension was new to me then. I could not gauge and manipulate, as later with other men. I could not even be sure it extended beyond myself. I said good-bye to you feeling as if I had behaved awkwardly, uninterestingly, on a date. Next day, or the day after, when I was reading as usual on the couch, I felt myself drop a lovely distance, thinking of you, and that was the beginning, I suppose, the realization of what more there could still be. So I said to you, 'I was in love.'

Would you like to know how I was informed of your death? I go into the faculty kitchen, to make myself a cup of coffee before my ten o'clock class. Dodie Charles who is always baking something has brought a cherry pound cake. (The thing we old pros know about, in these fantasies, is the importance of detail, solidity; yes, a cherry pound cake.) It is wrapped in waxed paper and then in a newspaper. *The Globe and Mail*, not the local paper, that I would have seen. Looking idly at this week-old paper as I wait for my water to boil I see the small item, the modest headline VETERAN JOURNALIST DIES. I think about the word *veteran*, does it mean a veteran, someone who fought in the war, or is it a simple adjective, though in this case, I think, it could be either, since it says the man was a war correspondent – Only then do I realize. Your name. The city where you lived and died. A heart attack, that will do.

I am in the habit of carrying around your last letter in my purse. When the next letter comes, I replace it, I put it with all the earlier letters in a box in my closet. While it is fresh in my purse I like to take the letter out and read it at odd moments, for instance if I am sitting having coffee in some little café, or waiting at the dentist's. Later on I never take the letter out at all, I grow to dislike the sight of it, folded and dog-eared, reminding me what weeks, what months, I have been waiting for the new letter. But I leave it there, I don't put it in the box, I don't dare.

Now, however, after I have taught my class, lunched with my colleagues, met my students, done whatever else is required of me, I go home and remove this letter, this last letter, from my purse, put it with the others and shove the box out of sight. Deliberately, almost painlessly I do this, having thought the act out beforehand. I make myself a drink. I continue with my life.

Every day when I come back from teaching I see the mailbox and to tell the truth I experience something pleasant, a lack of expectation. For two years that tin box has been the central object in my life, and now to see it go neutral again, to see it promise and withhold nothing very much, that is like feeling a pain gone. Nobody knows I have lost anything, nobody knew that part of my life, except in a general, rumoured way; when you came here we did not see people. So I am able to continue, as if it never happened, you never happened. But after a while I do tell somebody, a man I work with, Gus Marks. He has recently separated from his wife. He takes me out to dinner and we drink and tell each other our stories, then mostly on my initiative go to bed. He is hairy and sad, I am frenzied. I surprise myself. A few days later he asks me for coffee and says, 'I've been worried about you, I've been wondering if maybe you should – see somebody.'

'A psychiatrist, you mean?'

'Well. To talk.'

'I'll consider it.'

But I laugh at him to myself, for I am absorbed by another plan. As soon as the term ends, in late April, I mean to go to visit you, to visit the city where you have died. I have never been there. It was never suggested. Looking forward to this trip, I become remarkably cheerful. I buy some fashionable sunglasses, some new, light clothes.

Love is not in the least unavoidable, there is a choice made. It is just that it is hard to know when the choice was made, or when, in spite of seeming frivolous, it became irreversible. There is no clear warning about that. I remember sitting at lunch with you, and when you said, 'I loved you. I love you now,' I looked past you at myself in the restaurant mirror, and I felt embarrassed for you. I thought, God knows why, that you were being gallant; I did not take the words seriously, and I thought that in a moment you would look at me and see that you had said this to the wrong person, to a woman who had abandoned the whole posture, the vocabulary, for dealing with such tributes. I had some time before this given up on intrigues, on anxious subplots. I had stopped using a dark rinse on my hair and I no longer put white of egg, or oatmeal-and-honey, or hormone creams, or blush stick, or anything much at all, on my face.

Then I understood that you meant what you said and it seemed to me more than ever that you must be mistaken.

'You're sure you're not remembering somebody else?'

'My mind has not deteriorated so much as that.'

Before this we had talked easily. I asked about your wife.

'She doesn't dance any more. She had an operation on her knee.'

'It must be hard on her not to be active.'

'She's busy. She has a store. A bookstore.'

You asked about Douglas and I told you that we were divorced. I told you the children were away, both away this year for the first time. You told me you had not had any children. I was a little drunk and I even told you how in the last couple of years Douglas talked all the time to himself. I would hide behind the curtains and watch him talking to himself, and chuckling, making faces of recognition or distaste, while he cut the grass. And what a furiously interested private flow of conversation he would keep up while he was shaving, supposing his voice to be masked by the sound of the electric razor. I told you that I realized, that I did not want to find out what he was saying.

My plane left at four-thirty. You drove me out of town towards the airport. I was not unhappy at the thought of leaving you and never seeing you again, though I was very happy to be with you in the car. It was November, the day was dark soon after three o'clock, car lights were on.

'You could take a later plane, you know.'

'I don't know.'

'You could come to a hotel with me and phone up and cancel, and get yourself booked onto a later flight.'

'I don't know. No, I don't think I can. I'm too tired.'

'I am not so strenuous.'

'No.' We were holding hands all the way, in the car. I freed my hand and made a gesture meaning I was tired of something else – experience? – and easily put it back. I was not sure what I meant myself but expected, rightly, that you would understand.

We made a turn on to a freeway north of the city. As we came off the access road we faced west. The streaks of sky between the clouds were a fiery pink. The lights of the cars seemed to stream together, mile after mile. It was all like the kind of vision of the world – a fluid, peaceful vision, utterly reassuring – that I used to get when I was drunk. It said to me, why not? It urged me to have faith, to float upon the present, which might stretch out forever. And I was not drunk. I had been drunk at lunch but I was not any more.

'Why not?'

'Why not what?'

'Why not go to a hotel and phone up and get a later flight?'

'I hoped it might be that,' you said.

Was that when the choice was made, do you think, when I saw the sky and the car lights? It seemed lighthearted, nothing much. The hotel/motel was built of white blocks. The walls were the same on the inside as the outside, so that the rich-looking curtains and carpets, the heavy imitation-Spanish furniture, seemed to have been set up incongruously, in some temporary, barren sort of shelter. The picture we could see from the bed was of orange boats, dark and orange buildings, reflected in blue-black water. You told me a story of a man you knew who painted exclusively for motels. He painted boats, flamingoes, and brown nudes, nothing else; you said he made a lot of money at it.

Planes screamed overhead. Sometimes I could not hear

what you said, with your face pressed against me. I could not ask you to repeat, I would have felt ridiculous, and anyway such things are usually not repeatable. But what if you asked me a question, and hearing no answer were unable to ask it again? This possibility tormented me at a later time, when I wanted to give you every hoped-for answer.

We both trembled. We barely managed it, being overcome – both of us, both of us – with gratitude, and amazement. The flood of luck, of happiness undeserved, unqualified, nearly unbelieved-in. Tears stood in our eyes. Undeniably. Yes.

If you had been a man I had met that day, or at that time in my life, could I have loved you? Not so much. I don't think so. Not so much. I loved you for linking me with my past, with my young self pushing the stroller along the campus paths, innocent through no fault of my own. If I could kindle love then and take it now there was less waste than I had thought. Much less than I had thought. My life did not altogether fall away in separate pieces, lost.

I decide to leave, then, on the first of May. I have almost two months free before any child comes home to me, before summer school starts. I fly to the city where I have all this time been sending my letters. My joyful letters, my chattering and confiding letters, my apprehensive and finally begging letters. Where I would still be sending them, if I had not been clever enough to take note of your death.

The city where you lived, which you described to me wryly, but on the whole contentedly, in your letters. Full of old crocks and bewildered tourists, you said. No. Full of old crocks, *like me*, you said, making yourself out as usual to be older than you were. You loved to do that, to pretend to be tired and lazy, to stress your indifference. I thought it a pose, to tell you the truth. What I could not credit, did not have the imagination to credit, was that it might be real. You told me once that you did not care at all whether you died soon or went on living for another twenty-five years. Blasphemy from a lover. You told me that you did not think about happiness, the word did not occur to you. What pomposity, I thought, taking such things as if a young man had said them, unwilling to strain myself to understand a man for whom these statements were flat truth, in whom some energy I expected to find was worn down or entirely forgotten. Though I had stopped dyeing my hair and learned to live, as I thought, with a decent level of expectation, I did send hope in your direction, gigantic hope. I refused, I refuse, to see you as you seemed to see yourself.

I do think of you I suppose as a warm and sentient flood, you wrote one time to me, *and I have the normal human concerns with being overwhelmed, which is what floods do.*

I wrote back that I was nothing but the tamest little creek you could go wading in. You knew better.

How I tried to charm and mislead you, by that time, both in my letters and when we were together! Half my concern in love became how to disguise love, to make it harmless and merry. What humiliating charades those were. And you, you would smile in a certain way, a gentle way; I think you were a good deal ashamed for me.

I find an apartment building close to the sea, a building

dating I should think from the twenties, creamy yellow stucco with flaking window-sills, black medallion and indecipherable scroll above the door. Many old people, as you told me, walking past in the dazzling sea-light. I go out into the streets and walk everywhere. I don't bother to go to the cemetery. I don't know which cemetery it would be, in any case. I walk on sidewalks you may have walked on and look at things you almost certainly looked at. Windows which hosted your reflection give me back mine. It is a game. This city I find quite different from the cities I am used to. The steep streets, the pale stucco houses, so many of them flat-roofed and built in that strange filling-station style called 'modern' before the Second World War. Oblong ornamental windows of thick glass bricks. Sometimes a Spanish roof, or misplaced portholes and decks. The famous gardens. Rhododendrons, azaleas, hydrangeas, in red and orange and purple colours that hurt the eyes. Tulips big as goblets, endless showing-off. And the shops so strange to anyone from an industrial/university town, someone used, in spite of shopping-centre dress-ups, to some commercial modesty and functionalism. Turn-of-the-century ice-cream parlours. WILD WEST SPORTING GOODS. HAWAIIAN CASUALS, with palms in tubs. Tudor teashops with flimsy gables. Rope-soled sandals in a sort of cave, from which issue recorded jungle noises. Candy stores with false fronts like miniature castles. These masquerades are too various, too tiring. One day I go into a supermarket to buy some bread and oranges and the girl at the cash register is dressed in a burlap sack, her face is smeared with mud and red paint, she has a plastic bone stuck through her hair. They are promoting raisins, and beef from Australia.

But she smiles at me humanly, wearily, through the mud and paint, she reassures me; there is somebody in most of these places who can do that.

I see myself searching these streets for some memory of you as I once looked for clues in the articles you wrote for newspapers and magazines, in the books you wrote so efficiently to serve others' purposes, never your own. Amusing and informative you are, so skilled you verge on elegance, but you hold back, even from that. Is that all there is, I hear myself asking, and you laughing, indulgently; what more could there be? But I am not convinced, I keep after you, I desire revelations.

If I had to describe you, as I secretly see you, I would say that you are uncompromising. And you would say impatiently that you have compromised all your life. But that is not what I mean. I will say it: you are uncompromising, angular in some thorough-going way (body and spirit together), chaste, kind but not compassionate. I would emphasize that there is something chivalric about you. I do expect you, like a knight, to be capable of acts of outmoded self-sacrifice and also of marvellous brutality, both performed with the kind of style that indicates obedience to secret orders.

You, on the other hand, would describe yourself as genial, corrupt, ordinarily selfish and pleasure-loving. You would look over your glasses at me like some mild inflexible school-master, put out by my extremity. We would have to consider my being in love, the way I am in love, as if it were a curable extravagance, a highhanded assumption in an essay.

From the beginning, of course, I knew that this was a

dangerous way to live. At any moment the ties may be cut, have been cut, there is no knowing where the failure originated, whether it was by your wish or beyond your control; there is nobody I can complain to. Always before, at the last moment, rescue arrived. My brief wild letter, final desperation, and then your letter of humorous, somewhat tender, apology, which tells me there was never any danger. I was on solid ground all the time, you never left me. As if this hole I fall into, which is the permanent absence of you, is nothing but a dream I scare myself with, or at worst a place from which I have only to cry out hard enough, convincingly enough, for help, and help will come.

I find myself reading articles in women's magazines. Case histories. When my faith is restored, and riding high, I skip over these lessons superstitiously; when it is low, and very low, and gone, I read them for comfort, because it is a comfort to discover that one's own case holds no particular agony, only some shopworn recognizable pain. Other women have recovered and offered encouragement. Martha T., mistress for five years to a man who deceived, mocked, and fascinated her. I fell in love with him because he seemed so gentle, she says. Emily R., whose lover was not married as he claimed. And how often talking to both men and women I hear myself in witty and rueful pursuit of this theme – how women build their castles on foundations hardly strong enough to support a night's shelter; how women deceive themselves and uselessly suffer, being exploitable because of the emptiness of their lives and some deep – but indefinable, and not final! – flaw in themselves. And further and further along this line which everybody is learning these days like an easy song. Meanwhile my heart is cracked, also like the heart in a song, it is dry and cracked like a bare bit of landscape marked with gullies. I cry with Martha T. and Emily R. and wonder what possible way they managed to cure themselves. By learning macramé? By deep breathing? Once a friend of mine – a woman, of course – said to me that since pain was only possible if you looked backward to the past or forward to the future she had eliminated the whole problem by living every moment by itself; every moment, she said, was filled with absolute silence. I have tried this, I will try anything, but I don't understand how it works.

I have bought a map. I have found your street, the block where your house is. It is not very far from my apartment. Ten blocks or so to walk. I don't go there yet. I walk within a block or two of it and turn aside. That is a house you never meant me to see. (The places where I live are just the opposite; I deck them out and wait for them to come to life, when you visit me.) Now I can see it if I want to. I can walk past on the other side of the street, my heart pounding, able only to glance at it once or twice, then growing bolder I can walk slowly. Dusk is the time I would choose, to loiter not far from the open windows, to listen for music or voices. Imagine this real, a real house, where people wash dishes and oversleep. At night if she doesn't draw the curtains I can look into your rooms. Are the pictures your choice, or hers? Neither. Both. These discoveries cause me ordinary pain.

Once I read a story, a true story, in a magazine – it may have been one of the magazines you worked for – about a woman who had lost both her young daughters in a car accident, and every day when the other children were coming home from school she would go out and walk along the streets as if she expected to meet her daughters. But she never went as far as the school, she never looked into their empty classrooms, she could not risk that.

I go to your wife's store, that is what I can do. I don't know the name. I look up bookstores in the yellow pages of the phone book. BARBARA'S BOOK MART, that must be it. From the name I expected something self-conscious and quaint; I am surprised to find it so large, bright, busy and commonplace. No medieval or Tudor trappings; no trappings of any kind. This is a solid, year-round business, not tricked out for tourists.

I know her at once, though she has changed. Her hair is grey, greyer than mine, pulled into a bun. Features less sharp than they were, no make-up, a sallow skin, and still those flashes of vivid attractiveness; her quivering, witty, irritable style. She wears a faded purple smock with bands of Indian embroidery. She moves stiffly, having had to learn to walk again, after the cartilage in one knee was removed. And she is heavier, as you said; she is a stocky middle-aged woman.

She has come from the back of the store carrying a couple of large art books. She goes behind the desk, puts them on a shelf, speaks to the salesgirl as if continuing a conversation started earlier.

'Well, I don't know how – invoice – phone them up and tell them that isn't the way we do things around here – whole damn lot's got to be returned.'

I remember her voice, the same voice I heard all that

time ago at one or two parties – a clear challenging voice that seems to come into its own on a certain level of exasperation, a voice that excels in saying *My God what are those idiots thinking of*! Suppose she recognizes my voice, or my face? I don't think she will. She is not a person to remember people at the fringes, she is always at the centre, and she has no information about me, has she? She cannot expect me here.

Nevertheless I feel conspicuous, guilty, strange. Yet I stay for a long time, I wander all over the store. It's frightening, there are so many books. I always seem to stop in front of books telling people various ways to be happy, or at any rate peaceful. You have no idea – well, maybe you do have an idea – how many books of this sort there are. I am not scornful. I think I ought to read them. Or at least some of them. But all I can do is stare at them in stupefaction. Other books deal with magic, there are really hundreds of books about witches, spells, clairvoyance, rituals, all kinds of tricks and wonders. These books seem to me all the same – the happiness-and-peace ones and the magic wonders – they don't seem like separate books at all, that is why I cannot touch them. They are all flowing together around the store like some varicoloured marvellous stream, or wide river, and I can really no more understand what is inside them than I can breathe underwater.

I come day after day. I do buy a few paperbacks. I browse, as they must think, for hours. Once she looks at me, and smiles, but it is only the quick blind smile she has for a customer, I listen to her talking to the salesgirls, laughing, carrying on a joking, also serious, feud with somebody on the phone, demanding her tea with honey, mock-righteously refusing cakes. I hear her successfully, sometimes charmingly, bully the customers. I can imagine becoming her friend, listening to her confidences. I am ashamed of such a fantasy. I feel envy in her presence, and a precarious triumph, and this frivolous desperate curiosity; I am ashamed of all this when I remember.

I come at night – the store is open till nine – but she is usually not there. One night I come and she is there by herself. No one else is in the store. She goes to the back room and comes back carrying something, comes directly to me.

'I think I know who you are.'

She looks straight into my face. She has to lift her chin, she is much shorter than I am.

'We've all noticed you hanging around here. At first I thought you were a shoplifter. I told everybody to keep an eye on you. But you're not a shoplifter, are you?'

'No.'

She gives me what she has in her hand, a brown paper bag full of papers.

'He's dead.' She smiles at me as a teacher would who finds you fatally compromised at school. 'That's why you haven't been hearing from him. He died in March. He had a heart attack, at his desk at home. I found him when I came in at supper time.'

I cannot, and should not, speak to her.

'Should I say I'm sorry to tell you? I'm not sorry. How you feel is not important to me. Not at all. I don't want to see you here. Good-bye.'

I leave the store without saying another word to her.

In my apartment I open the bag and take out the letters.

They are letters, not in their envelopes. That is what I knew I would find, I knew I would find my letters. I don't want to read them, I dread reading them, I think that I will put them away. But then I notice that the writing is not mine. I start to read. These letters are not mine, they were not written by me. I skip through every one of them in a panic and read the signature. *Patricia. Pat. P.* I go back and read them carefully one by one.

My dear love,

You leave me so happy. I went to the park with Samantha and it was lovely. I pushed her on the swings and watched her on the slide and thought I will have to love this park forever and ever, because I went there when I was so happy and after I had been with you.

Darling,

Remember the crazy old man next door? He came and ate the things off that pink tree in the garden. I mean the ornamental plum tree, they must be the ornamental plums, they are hard as rocks and nobody ever was meant to eat them I'm sure but I saw him grabbing them and swallowing them down by the handful. I was sitting on the floor in the sun room on the purple cushions, where you and I were —

My darling,

I had a dream about you last night. It was a beautiful strange dream. You were holding my hair in your hands and saying, this is all too heavy for you, you'll have to cut it off, it will sap your strength. And the way you said it was so lovely, so sympathetic, as if you meant something else not just my hair. How can I tell, love, what you're saying in my dreams if you never write to me? So please write and tell me, tell me what you're saying to me in my dreams –

Love,

I try and try to keep from writing because I believe I must give you the choice, I don't want to chase after and torment you but it is so hard when you just drop off the earth like this, I feel so terrible alone. If you could tell me you didn't want to see me or hear from me any more I could accept that, I really think I could, it's just the awfulness of not knowing. I could deal with my feelings if I had to and recover from loving you but I must know whether you love me and want me any more so please, please, tell me yes or no.

And the last letter, really no letter at all, a large scribble on the page, without salutation or signature:

Please write to me or phone me, I am going crazy. I hate to be like this but it is more than I can stand so I beg you.

'I didn't write these letters.'
  'Aren't you her?'
  'No. I don't know who she is. I don't know.'
  'Why did you take them?'
  'I didn't understand. I didn't know what you were talking about. I've had a grief lately and sometimes I'm not – paying attention.'
  'You must have thought I was crazy.'
  'No. I didn't know what to think.'
  'You see what happened is – my husband died. He

died in March. Well, I told you. And these letters keep coming. There's no return address. There's no surname. The postmark is Vancouver but what help is that? I've been expecting her to turn up. She is getting to sound so desperate.'

'Yes.'

'Did you read them all?'

'Yes.'

'Did it take you that long to figure out there'd been a mistake?'

'No. I was curious.'

'You look familiar to me. So many people do, because of the store. I see so many people.'

I tell her my name, my real name, why not? It means nothing to her.

'I see so many people.' She holds the bag of letters over the wastebasket, lets it drop. 'I can't keep them around any more.'

'No.'

'I will just have to let her suffer.'

'Eventually she will figure it out.'

'What if she doesn't? It's not my concern.'

'No.'

I no longer want to talk to her, I no longer want to hear her stories. The air around her seems harsh, as if she gave off a shrivelling light.

She looks at me. 'I don't know why I got the idea it might be you. You don't look much younger than I am. I always understood they were younger.'

Then she says, 'You know more about my life than the girls who work for me or my friends or anybody, except I suppose her. I'm sorry. I really would like not to see you any more.'

'I don't live here. I'm going away. In fact I might go away tomorrow.'

'It's just life, you know. It's just the usual thing. It isn't that we didn't have a good life together. We didn't have children, but we did what we wanted. He was a very kind man, easy to be with. And successful, if he had pushed himself. But even so. If I told you his name you might recognize it.'

'You don't need to.'

'No. Oh, no. I wouldn't.'

She makes a little bitter face, a swallowing face, ending with a humorous line of the mouth, that would dispose of you. I turn away almost in time not to see it.

I go out onto the street and it is still light in the long evening. I walk and walk. In this city of my imagination I walk past stone walls up and down steep hills, and see in my mind that girl Patricia. Girl, woman, the sort of woman who would call her daughter Samantha – very slim, dark, fashionably dressed, slightly nervous, slightly artificial. Her long black hair. Her long black hair uncombed and her face blotched. She sits in the dark. She walks around the rooms. She tries smiling at herself in the glass. She tries putting on make-up. She confides in a woman, goes to bed with a man. She takes her daughter to the park but not to the same park. She avoids certain streets, never opens certain magazines. She suffers according to rules we all know, which are meaningless and absolute. When I think of her I see all this sort of love as you must have seen, or see it, as something going on at a distance; a strange, not even pitiable, expenditure; unintelligible ceremony in an unknown faith. Am I right, am I getting close to you, is that true?

But you were the one, I keep forgetting, *you were the one who said it first.*

How are we to understand you?

Never mind. I invented her. I invented you, as far as my purposes go. I invented loving you and I invented your death. I have my tricks and my trap doors, too. I don't understand their workings at the present moment, but I have to be careful, I won't speak against them.

THE FOUND BOAT

At the end of Bell Street, McKay Street, Mayo Street, there was the Flood. It was the Wawanash River, which every spring overflowed its banks. Some springs, say one in every five, it covered the roads on that side of town and washed over the fields, creating a shallow choppy lake. Light reflected off the water made everything bright and cold, as it is in a lakeside town, and woke or revived in people certain vague hopes of disaster. Mostly during the late afternoon and early evening, there were people straggling out to look at it, and discuss whether it was still rising, and whether this time it might invade the town. In general, those under fifteen and over sixty-five were most certain that it would.

Eva and Carol rode out on their bicycles. They left the road – it was the end of Mayo Street, past any houses – and rode right into a field, over a wire fence entirely flattened by the weight of the winter's snow. They coasted a little way before the long grass stopped them, then left their bicycles lying down and went to the water.

'We have to find a log and ride on it,' Eva said.

'Jesus, we'll freeze our legs off.'

'Jesus, we'll freeze our legs off!' said one of the boys who were there too at the water's edge. He spoke in a sour whine, the way boys imitated girls although it was nothing like the way girls talked. These boys – there were three of them – were all in the same class as Eva and Carol at school and were known to them by name (their names being Frank, Bud and Clayton), but Eva and Carol, who had seen and recognized them from the road, had not spoken to them or looked at them or, even yet, given any sign of knowing they were there. The boys seemed to be trying to make a raft, from lumber they had salvaged from the water.

Eva and Carol took off their shoes and socks and waded in. The water was so cold it sent pain up their legs, like blue electric sparks shooting through their veins, but they went on, pulling their skirts high, tight behind and bunched so they could hold them in front.

'Look at the fat-assed ducks in wading.'

'Fat-assed fucks.'

Eva and Carol, of course, gave no sign of hearing this. They laid hold of a log and climbed on, taking a couple of boards floating in the water for paddles. There were always things floating around in the Flood – branches, fence-rails, logs, road signs, old lumber; sometimes boilers, wash-tubs, pots and pans, or even a car seat or stuffed chair, as if somewhere the Flood had got into a dump.

They paddled away from shore, heading out into the cold lake. The water was perfectly clear, they could see the brown grass swimming along the bottom. Suppose it was the sea, thought Eva. She thought of drowned cities and countries. Atlantis. Suppose they were riding in a Viking boat – Viking boats on the Atlantic were more frail and narrow than this log on the Flood – and they had miles of clear sea beneath them, then a spired city, intact as a jewel irretrievable on the ocean floor.

'This is a Viking boat,' she said. 'I am the carving on the front.' She stuck her chest out and stretched her neck, trying to make a curve, and she made a face, putting out her tongue. Then she turned and for the first time took notice of the boys.

'Hey, you sucks!' she yelled at them. 'You'd be scared to come out here, this water is ten feet deep!'

'Liar,' they answered without interest, and she was.

They steered the log around a row of trees, avoiding floating barbed wire, and got into a little bay created by a natural hollow of the land. Where the bay was now, there would be a pond full of frogs later in the spring, and by the middle of summer there would be no water visible at all, just a low tangle of reeds and bushes, green, to show that mud was still wet around their roots. Larger bushes, willows, grew around the steep bank of this pond and were still partly out of the water. Eva and Carol let the log ride in. They saw a place where something was caught.

It was a boat, or part of one. An old rowboat with most of one side ripped out, the board that had been the seat just dangling. It was pushed up among the branches, lying on what would have been its side, if it had a side, the prow caught high.

Their idea came to them without consultation, at the same time:

'You guys! Hey, you guys!'

'We found you a boat!'

'Stop building your stupid raft and come and look at the boat!'

What surprised them in the first place was that the boys really did come, scrambling overland, half running, half sliding down the bank, wanting to see.

'Hey, where?'

'Where is it, I don't see no boat.'

What surprised them in the second place was that when the boys did actually see what boat was meant, this old flood-smashed wreck held up in the branches, they did not understand that they had been fooled, that a joke had been played on them. They did not show a moment's disappointment, but seemed as pleased at the discovery as if the boat had been whole and new. They were already barefoot, because they had been wading in the water to get lumber, and they waded in here without a stop, surrounding the boat and appraising it and paying no attention even of an insulting kind to Eva and Carol who bobbed up and down on their log. Eva and Carol had to call to them.

'How do you think you're going to get it off?'

'It won't float anyway.'

'What makes you think it will float?'

'It'll sink. Glub-blub-blub, you'll all be drownded.'

The boys did not answer, because they were too busy

walking around the boat, pulling at it in a testing way to see how it could be got off with the least possible damage. Frank, who was the most literate, talkative and inept of the three, began referring to the boat as *she*, an affectation which Eva and Carol acknowledged with fish-mouths of contempt.

'She's caught two places. You got to be careful not to tear a hole in her bottom. She's heavier than you'd think.'

It was Clayton who climbed up and freed the boat, and Bud, a tall fat boy, who got the weight of it on his back to turn it into the water so that they could half float, half carry it to shore. All this took some time, Eva and Carol abandoned their log and waded out of the water. They walked overland to get their shoes and socks and bicycles. They did not need to come back this way but they came. They stood at the top of the hill, leaning on their bicycles. They did not go on home, but they did not sit down and frankly watch, either. They stood more or less facing each other, but glancing down at the water and at the boys struggling with the boat, as if they had just halted for a moment out of curiosity, and staying longer than they intended, to see what came of this unpromising project.

About nine o'clock, or when it was nearly dark – dark to people inside the houses, but not quite dark outside – they all returned to town, going along Mayo Street in a sort of procession. Frank and Bud and Clayton came carrying the boat, upside-down, and Eva and Carol walked behind, wheeling their bicycles. The boys' heads were almost hidden in the darkness of the overturned boat, with its smell of soaked wood, cold swampy water. The girls could look ahead and see the street lights in their tin reflectors, a necklace of lights climbing Mayo Street, reaching all the way up to the standpipe. They turned onto Burns Street heading for Clayton's house, the nearest house belonging to any of them. This was not the way home for Eva or for Carol either, but they followed along. The boys were perhaps too busy carrying the boat to tell them to go away. Some younger children were still out playing, playing hopscotch on the pavement though they could hardly see. At this time of year the bare pavement was still such a novelty and delight. These children cleared out of the way and watched the boat go by with unwilling respect; they shouted questions after it, wanting to know where it came from and what was going to be done with it. No one answered them. Eva and Carol as well as the boys refused to answer or even look at them.

The five of them entered Clayton's yard. The boys shifted weight, as if they were going to put the boat down.

'You better take it round to the back where nobody can see it,' Carol said. That was the first thing any of them had said since they came into town.

The boys said nothing but went on, following a mud path between Clayton's house and a leaning board fence. They let the boat down in the back yard.

'It's a stolen boat, you know,' said Eva, mainly for the effect. 'It must've belonged to somebody. You stole it.'

'You was the ones who stole it then,' Bud said, short of breath. 'It was you seen it first.'

'It was you took it.'

'It was all of us then. If one of us gets in trouble then all of us does.'

'Are you going to tell anybody on them?' said Carol as

she and Eva rode home, along the streets which were dark
between the lights now and potholed from winter.

'It's up to you. I won't if you won't.'

'I won't if you won't.'

They rode in silence, relinquishing something, but not
discontented.

The board fence in Clayton's back yard had every so often
a post which supported it, or tried to, and it was on these
posts that Eva and Carol spent several evenings sitting,
jauntily but not very comfortably. Or else they had just
leaned against the fence while the boys worked on the
boat. During the first couple of evenings neighbourhood
children attracted by the sound of hammering tried to get
into the yard to see what was going on, but Eva and Carol
blocked their way.

'Who said you could come in here?'

'Just us can come in this yard.'

These evenings were getting longer, the air milder.
Skipping was starting on the pavements. Further along
the street there was a row of hard maples that had been
tapped. Children drank the sap as fast as it could drip into
the buckets. The old man and woman who owned the
trees, and who hoped to make syrup, came running out
of the house making noises as if they were trying to scare
away crows. Finally, every spring, the old man would come
out on his porch and fire his shotgun into the air, and then
the thieving would stop.

None of those working on the boat bothered about
stealing sap, though all had done so last year.

The lumber to repair the boat was picked up here and

there, along back lanes. At this time of year things were lying around – old boards and branches, sodden mitts, spoons flung out with the dishwater, lids of pudding pots that had been set in the snow to cool, all the debris that can sift through and survive winter. The tools came from Clayton's cellar – left over, presumably, from the time when his father was alive – and though they had nobody to advise them the boys seemed to figure out more or less the manner in which boats are built, or rebuilt. Frank was the one who showed up with diagrams from books and *Popular Mechanics* magazines. Clayton looked at these diagrams and listened to Frank read the instructions and then went ahead and decided in his own way what was to be done. Bud was best at sawing. Eva and Carol watched everything from the fence and offered criticism and thought up names. The names of the boat that they thought of were: *Water Lily*, *Sea Horse*, *Flood Queen*, and *Caro-Eve*, after them because they had found it. The boys did not say which, if any, of these names they found satisfactory.

The boat had to be tarred. Clayton heated up a pot of tar on the kitchen stove and brought it out and painted slowly, his thorough way, sitting astride the overturned boat. The other boys were sawing a board to make a new seat. As Clayton worked, the tar cooled and thickened so that finally he could not move the brush any more. He turned to Eva and held out the pot and said, 'You can go in and heat this on the stove.'

Eva took the pot and went up the back steps. The kitchen seemed black after outside, but it must be light enough to see in, because there was Clayton's mother standing at the ironing board, ironing. She did that for a living, took in wash and ironing.

'Please may I put the tar pot on the stove?' said Eva, who had been brought up to talk politely to parents, even wash-and-iron ladies, and who for some reason especially wanted to make a good impression on Clayton's mother.

'You'll have to poke up the fire then,' said Clayton's mother, as if she doubted whether Eva would know how to do that. But Eva could see now, and she picked up the lid with the stove-lifter, and took the poker and poked up a flame. She stirred the tar as it softened. She felt privileged. Then and later. Before she went to sleep a picture of Clayton came to her mind; she saw him sitting astride the boat, tar-painting, with such concentration, delicacy, absorption. She thought of him speaking to her, out of his isolation, in such an ordinary peaceful taking-for-granted voice.

On the twenty-fourth of May, a school holiday in the middle of the week, the boat was carried out of town, a long way now, off the road over fields and fences that had been repaired, to where the river flowed between its normal banks. Eva and Carol, as well as the boys, took turns carrying it. It was launched in the water from a cow-trampled spot between willow bushes that were fresh out in leaf. The boys were first. They yelled with triumph when the boat did float, when it rode amazingly down the river current. The boat was painted black, and green inside, with yellow seats, and a strip of yellow all the way around the outside. There was no name on it, after all. The boys could not imagine that it needed any name to keep it separate from the other boats in the world.

Eva and Carol ran along the bank, carrying bags full of peanut butter-and-jam sandwiches, pickles, bananas, chocolate cake, potato chips, graham crackers stuck together with corn syrup and five bottles of pop to be cooled in the river water. The bottles bumped against their legs. They yelled for a turn.

'If they don't let us they're bastards,' Carol said, and they yelled together. 'We found it. We found it!'

The boys did not answer, but after a while they brought the boat in, and Carol and Eva came crashing, panting down the bank.

'Does it leak?'

'It don't leak yet.'

'We forgot a bailing can,' wailed Carol, but nevertheless she got in, with Eva, and Frank pushed them off, crying, 'Here's to a Watery Grave!'

And the thing about being in a boat was that it was not solidly bobbing, like a log, but was cupped in the water, so that riding in it was not like being on something in the water, but like being in the water itself. Soon they were all going out in the boat in mixed-up turns, two boys and a girl, two girls, and a boy a girl and a boy, until things were so confused it was impossible to tell whose turn came next, and nobody cared anyway. They went down the river – those who weren't riding, running along the bank to keep up. They passed under two bridges, one iron, one cement. Once they saw a big carp just resting, it seemed to smile at them, in the bridge-shaded water. They did not know how far they had gone to the river, but things had changed – the water had got shallower, and the land flatter. Across an open field they saw a building that looked like a house, abandoned. They dragged the boat up on the bank and tied it and set out across the field.

'That's the old station,' Frank said. 'That's Pedder Station.' The others had heard this name but he was the one who knew, because his father was the station agent in town. He said that this was a station on a branch line that had been torn up, and that there had been a sawmill here, but a long time ago.

Inside the station it was dark, cool. All the windows were broken. Glass lay in shards and in fairly big pieces on the floor. They walked around finding the larger pieces of glass and tramping on them, smashing them, it was like cracking ice on puddles. Some partitions were still in place, you could see where the ticket window had been. There was a bench lying on its side. People had been here, it looked as if people came here all the time, though it was so far from anywhere. Beer bottles and pop bottles were lying around, also cigarette packages, gum and candy wrappers, the paper from a loaf of bread. The walls were covered with dim and fresh pencil and chalk writings and carved with knives.

I LOVE RONNIE COLES

I WANT TO FUCK

KILROY WAS HERE

RONNIE COLES IS AN ASS-HOLE

WHAT ARE YOU DOING HERE?

WAITING FOR A TRAIN

DAWNA MARY-LOU BARBARA JOANNE

It was exciting to be inside this large, dark, empty place, with the loud noise of breaking glass and their voices ringing back from the underside of the roof. They tipped the old beer bottles against their mouths. That reminded them that they were hungry and thirsty and they cleared a place in the middle of the floor and sat down and ate the lunch. They drank the pop just as it was, lukewarm. They ate everything there was and licked the smears of peanut butter and jam off the bread-paper in which the sandwiches had been wrapped.

They played Truth or Dare.

'I dare you to write on the wall, I am a Stupid Ass, and sign your name.'

'Tell the truth – what is the worst lie you ever told?'

'Did you ever wet the bed?'

'Did you ever dream you were walking down the street without any clothes on?'

'I dare you go outside and pee on the railway sign.'

It was Frank who had to do that. They could not see him, even his back, but they knew he did it, they heard the hissing sound of his pee. They all sat still, amazed, unable to think of what the next dare would be.

'I dare everybody,' said Frank from the doorway, 'I dare – Everybody.'

'What?'

'Take off all our clothes.'

Eva and Carol screamed.

'Anybody who won't do it has to walk – has to *crawl* – around this floor on their hands and knees.'

They were all quiet, till Eva said, almost complacently, 'What first?'

'Shoes and socks.'

'Then we have to go outside, there's too much glass here.'

They pulled off their shoes and socks in the doorway, in

the sudden blinding sun. The field before them was bright as water. They ran across where the tracks used to go.

'That's enough, that's enough,' said Carol. 'Watch out for thistles!'

'Tops! Everybody take off their tops!'

'I won't! We won't, will we, Eva?'

But Eva was whirling round and round in the sun where the track used to be. 'I don't care, I don't care! Truth or Dare! Truth or Dare!'

She unbuttoned her blouse as she whirled, as if she didn't know what her hand was doing, she flung it off.

Carol took off hers. 'I wouldn't have done it, if you hadn't!'

'Bottoms!'

Nobody said a word this time, they all bent and stripped themselves. Eva, naked first, starting running across the field, and then all the others ran, all five of them running bare through the knee-high hot grass, running towards the river. Not caring now about being caught but in fact leaping and yelling to call attention to themselves, if there was anybody to hear or see. They felt as if they were going to jump off a cliff and fly. They felt that something was happening to them different from anything that had happened before, and it had to do with the boat, the water, the sunlight, the dark ruined station, and each other. They thought of each other now hardly as names or people, but as echoing shrieks, reflections, all bold and white and loud and scandalous, and as fast as arrows. They went running without a break into the cold water and when it came almost to the tops of their legs they fell on it and swam. It stopped their noise. Silence, amazement, came over them in a rush. They dripped and floated and separated, sleek as mink.

Eva stood up in the water her hair dripping, water running down her face. She was waist deep. She stood on smooth stones, her feet fairly wide apart, water flowing between her legs. About a yard away from her Clayton also stood up, and they were blinking the water out of their eyes, looking at each other. Eva did not turn or try to hide; she was quivering from the cold of the water, but also with pride, shame, boldness, and exhilaration.

Clayton shook his head violently, as if he wanted to bang something out of it, then bent over and took a mouthful of river water. He stood up with his cheeks full and made a tight hole in his mouth and shot the water at her as if it was coming out of a hose, hitting her exactly, first one breast and then the other. Water from his mouth ran down her body. He hooted to see it, a loud self-conscious sound that nobody would have expected, from him. The others looked up from wherever they were in the water and closed in to see.

Eva crouched down and slid into the water, letting her head go right under. She swam, and when she let her head out, downstream, Carol was coming after her and the boys were already on the bank, already running into the grass, showing their skinny backs, their white, flat buttocks. They were laughing and saying things to each other but she couldn't hear, for the water in her ears.

'What did he do?' said Carol.

'Nothing.'

They crept in to shore. 'Let's stay in the bushes till they go,' said Eva. 'I hate them anyway. I really do. Don't you hate them?'

'Sure,' said Carol, and they waited, not very long, until
they heard the boys still noisy and excited coming down to
the place a bit upriver where they had left the boat. They
heard them jump in and start rowing.

'They've got all the hard part, going back,' said Eva,
hugging herself and shivering violently. 'Who cares?
Anyway. It never was our boat.'

'What if they tell?' said Carol.

'We'll say it's all a lie.'

Eva hadn't thought of this solution until she said it, but
as soon as she did she felt almost light-hearted again. The
ease and scornfulness of it did make them both giggle, and
slapping themselves and splashing out of the water they
set about developing one of those fits of laughter in which,
as soon as one showed signs of exhaustion, the other would
snort and start up again, and they would make helpless
– soon genuinely helpless – faces at each other and bend
over and grab themselves as if they had the worst pain.

EXECUTIONERS

Helena the skunk,
Her father must be drunk.

What was that to cry about? I don't know if I cried, I don't remember. I became familiar with sidewalks, and the ground under trees, neutral things that I could look down at, meaning no offence. I did marvel at the way some people managed, not being pulled down by anything – not by having crossed eyes, or a little brother who was an idiot, or living in a dirty house beside the tracks. I was the opposite, thin-skinned as Robina said. I expected blame.

Good-bye Helena
Good-bye Helena
Good-bye Helena
Good-bye Helena

They used to bunch behind me walking down the school hill. Sweet voices they had, just on the edge of sincerity, deadly innocence. If I had known what to do, if I had known how to turn around. That can't be taught. It's a gift, like being able to carry a tune.

My clothes were strange, that was one thing. A navy blue tunic, resembling the uniforms worn at private schools. (Where my mother would have sent me, certainly, if she had had the money.) Long white stockings, winter and summer, never mind the mud on our road. In the winter they showed the lumpy folds of the long underwear I was compelled to wear underneath. On top of my head a large bow, sticking up in ironed points. My hair in ringlets, put in with a comb dipped in water, not a style favoured by anybody else. But what could I have worn that would have been right? Once I got a new winter coat, which I thought lovely. It had a squirrel collar. *Rat fur, rat fur, skinned a rat and wore the fur!* they called after me. After that I didn't like the fur, didn't like the touch of it; something too soft about it, private humiliating.

I used to look for places to hide. In buildings, in big public buildings I looked for little high windows, dark places. The old Bank of Commerce building had a tower I was fond of. I imagined myself hiding there, or in any small high-up room, safe in the middle of town, disregarded, forgotten. Except that somebody could come at night and bring me food.

It was true about my father. But he was usually away, taking a cure, resting in a sanatorium, travelling. Before I was born he had been a Member of Parliament. He suffered a great defeat in 1911, the year Laurier went out. Much later, when I learned about Reciprocity, I discovered that this defeat had been only a corner of a national calamity (if indeed you were inclined to see it as a calamity), but when I was a child I always believed that my father had been personally, tauntingly, shamefully rejected. My mother likened the event to the Crucifixion. He had come out on the balcony of the Queen's Hotel, to speak, to concede his defeat, and was prevented, jeered down, by Tories carrying brooms on fire. I had no idea, hearing this, that such were the scenes politicians sometimes have to face. My mother dated his downfall from this time. Though she did not specify what form the downfall took. Alcoholic was not a word spoken in our home; I don't believe it was spoken much anywhere, at that time. Drunk was the word used, but that was in the town.

My mother would no longer shop in this town, except for groceries, which she had Robina order by phone. She would not speak to various ladies, wives of taunters and Tories.

I will never darken this door.

That was what she would say about a church, a store, somebody's house.

'He was too *fine* for them.'

She had nobody but Robina to say these things to. But Robina was satisfactory, in a way. She was a person with her own list of people not to be spoken to, stores not to be entered.

'They're all ignorant around here. It's them ought to be swept out with a broom.'

And she would start telling about some injustice done to

her brothers Jimmy and Duval, accused of stealing when they were only trying to see how a flashlight worked.

Past the buildings in town I had to walk a mile on a straight country road. Our house was at the end of it, a big brick house with bay windows upstairs and down. They always looked unpleasant to me, swollen out like insects' eyes. I was glad when they tore that house down, years later; they turned our land into the Municipal Airport. Along the road there were only two or three other houses. One of them was Stump Troy's.

Stump Troy was a bootlegger, who had lost his legs in an accident at Ryan's Mill. It was said that the Ryan family supported his bootlegging and kept him out of trouble, so that he would not bring a lawsuit against them. Certainly he flourished as a bootlegger and was never interfered with by anybody. He had a son Howard, who came to school now and then – no knowing by whose whim – and was put in whatever class had room for him, seated at the back with empty seats around him if possible so that no mother could complain. No truant officer, if there was such a thing as a truant officer then, can have bothered with this case. In those days it was expected, even necessary, that people should stay as they were and not be improved or changed. Teachers would make jokes about Howard Troy in his presence and absence, and it was never thought odd or cruel. Beyond that they let him alone.

During one of his sessions at school he was in our class, sitting diagonally behind me, and I did him a favour, which afterwards and even at the time I knew to be a mistake. We were copying from the board. Howard Troy was not copying. He was sitting without a pencil or a paper, doing nothing at all. He came to school without any equipment. Carrying pencils, paper, erasers, crayons, would have been as unlikely for him as growing feathers. He was looking straight ahead, maybe looking at the board trying to read or make sense of what was written there, maybe not looking at anything. What was he thinking? It bothered me to wonder. I didn't like to think of him being still there, underneath, looking out, through all the things, the stupidity and ugliness, that had been put onto him and accepted by him and were so firmly believed in it would not matter now if they were really there at all. I did not think that he would like me, I did not go that far, I was just afraid of him in a way it had not occurred to me to be afraid before.

His eyes were the colour of a cat's. They were round, clear, close together.

I opened my scribbler in the middle, so that I could detach a page without tearing anything, and I passed this back to him along with a sharpened pencil. He did not reach to take them. I laid them on his desk. He did not thank me or take any notice, but I saw later that he was at least using the pencil on the paper – whether to copy from the board or draw pictures or just make wire-rolls of O's, I have no idea.

That was the mistake, the thing that brought me to his attention, as well as the accident – no accident, it seemed to me! – of our living on the same road. I needed to be taught a lesson. He may have thought that. For presumption. For condescension. Or he may have seen the glimmer of a novel, interesting, surprising weakness.

*

The snowbanks were high, the road went like a tunnel between. Under the fresh snow were boulders of old snow, hard and grey. Ribbons of dog urine ran down the shovelled paths. Stump Troy's drive was kept ploughed, and for whose convenience, asked Robina. She asked most things in a voice that already knew the answer. I walked with a knife in my pocket, a paring knife stolen from Robina's kitchen. I took my mitten off to touch it. Hidden by the snowbank, in his father's driveway, once a week, twice a week, I never knew when, Howard Troy was waiting for me. He would step out as if to go in front of me, to block me in the narrow road.

Fuck

You want to fuck

I walked past him with my head down and my breath drawn, just like somebody walking through a wall of flame. It was important not to look at him, not to hurry, and to feel the blade. I never thought that he could come after me. If he did not move at once, he would not move at all. Danger was in the aura of the word.

All that's beyond explaining now. I hear young children saying lazily, 'What the fuck?' as they ride past on their bicycles. I hear a father yelling, 'Get the fucking lawn mower off the drive!' It used to be a word that could be thrown against you, that could bring you to an absolute stop. Humiliation was promised, but was perhaps already there, was contained in the hearing, the being stopped, having to acknowledge. Shame could choke you. I mean that. Not at the moment when the whole point was to keep safe and get past but later, what quantities of greasy shame, what indigestible bad secrets. The vulnerability which is in itself a shame. We are shamefully made.

I would never have told anybody, never asked anybody's help. I would have borne any danger, risked any violence, or final indignity, rather than repeat, or admit what was said to me. I saw this as being out of reach of all help, all authority. I believed of course that this could only be said to me, that Howard Troy would understand how he could threaten me, that it was a sign. And so it had to be concealed and blotted out, stamped out, quick, quick, but I could never get it all, the knowledge, the memory, it was running underground and spurting out at another place in my mind.

Robina used to take me home with her. We walked through the bush, behind where the airport is now, a mile, or maybe a mile and a half, to that little farm with stonepiles in the middle of the fields. We went in the wintertime, too, and Robina showed me what she said were wolf tracks. She knew of a case where a baby had been put in a sleigh, with a dog to pull it, and the dog had heard wolves howling, in the bush, and taken off to join them, with the baby still attached. Then when the dog got to where the wolves were it turned wolf too, and they all together pulled the baby out and ate it.

Walking through the bush Robina increased in authority, or took on authority of another kind than she had in my mother's kitchen, where she went under the inadequate altogether misleading title of maid. Her tall flat body seemed to loosen, to swing like a door on its hinges, controlled, but dangerous if you got in the way. She was maybe twenty years old at this time but she seemed to me as old as my mother, as old as the powerful older teachers, the ladies looking after stores. Her hair was shingled, dark, pulled tight across her forehead and held with a bobby pin. Her smell was of the kitchen, and of dried sweaty cloth. There was something sooty, smokey, about her – about her skin and her hair and her clothes and her smell. None of this seemed objectionable. Who would object to Robina, who would be so foolhardy?

We had to cross a bridge that was nothing but three logs, irregularly spaced. Robina swung her arms out, for balance. The one sleeve that was half-empty flopped like an injured wing over the water.

Her most important story was about how she used to go tagging after her mother, who did housework, years ago, for ladies in town. At one of the houses there was an electric wringer-washer, a new contrivance then. Robina, five years old, stood on a chair to put clothes through the wringer. (Even then, I understood, she would have been unable to let anything alone, would have had to show herself boss of any process.) The wringer caught her hand, her arm. That arm ended now between the elbow and the wrist. She never showed it. She always wore a dress or a blouse with long sleeves. But it seemed to me this was not for shame; it was to increase the mystery, and importance. Sometimes on the road young children would trail after her, calling, 'Robina, Robina, show us your arm!' Their calls were wistful, and full of respect. She would let them go on for a bit before she shooed them away, like chickens. She was chief of those people I have mentioned, who can turn disabilities into something enviable, mockery into tributes. I never thought of that arm except as something she had chosen, a sign of perversity and power.

I longed to see it. I thought that it would be sawed off straight, like a log, revealing bone and muscle and blood vessels in their gristly, fibrous, intimate nakedness. I knew I had as much chance of laying eyes on that as I had of looking at the far side of the moon.

Other stories concerned her family.

'Duval when he was little he was up on the roof all day, he was helping them shingle. He shouldn't've been up there, because he had a light skin, he has the lightest skin of all our family. Our whole family is fair, except for me and Findley, the beginning and the end. Nobody thought about how hot it would be for Duval or put a hat on him. I was the one would've thought, and I wasn't home. But even if you had put a hat on him he'd've took it off, probably, because he thinks he's too smart to wear a hat if the men aren't wearing one. So after supper he laid down on the couch like to have a sleep. Then after a while he opens his eyes and says as loud as anything, *Get them feathers outa my face.* Well, we couldn't see feathers. So we all wondered. Then he sits up, looks right through us, didn't even know us. *Grandma,* he says, *get me a drink of water. Please Grandma,* he says, *get me a drink of water.* Grandma wasn't there at all. She was dead. But to hear him talk you'd think she was sitting there right beside him and none of the rest of us was in the room at all or anywhere he could see.'

'Was he having sunstroke?'

'He was having a sight of Heaven.'

Her voice was flat and scornful.

About all members of her family, from Duval and Jimmy

who came right after her down to Findley the five-year-old, Robina spoke with peculiar respect and severity, to let you know that nothing that happened to them, no preference or ailment or feud or habitual saying or daily adventure of theirs, was to be taken lightly. Her own importance shone through them, or theirs through her. I understood that I did not weigh much in comparison. Nevertheless I was the child of the house where Robina worked; that meant something. I was not jealous.

As we walked through the bush we might hear nuts or pine cones dropping, at a distance, and Robina would say, 'Maybe that's Duval or Jimmy or them out shaking a tree.' Then I was somehow excited to think that we were within range of them, in the territory of their excursions and adventures. I would look forward as much as Robina did to the sight of the unpainted slightly listing house, with no shade tree near it, adrift on the weedy fields – in winter, adrift on the snow – just out of reach of the bush, like an unlucky boat on a pond. Children would come spilling out of it when they saw us, white-haired except for Findley, barefoot until the ground was frozen hard. They would shout and show off and dangle from the pump handle; they would deliberately raise storms of dust and chicken feathers in the yard.

They did not go to the school in town. Their school was a mile or two through the bush, in another direction. According to Robina they were at all times the major part of the school population. I could imagine them making school more or less an extension of home, cupping their hands under the pump to get a drink and sitting on the roof to enjoy the view.

This meant I came to them free, as somebody strange and new. With them I was not who I was. I wore my coat; they asked to touch the fur. I swaggered then. This was magic, it was intoxication. *Listen*, I said to them. I told them riddles. I taught them the rules of games, which I knew from watching. 'Red Rover.' 'Take a Giant Step.' 'Statues.' They who were daring and quarrelsome but still scared of town, ragged but not envious, took me as their leader. I accepted. It seemed natural. 'Hide and Seek.' 'Aunty Aunty over the Shanty.' They had a rope-and-tyre swing. They would climb anywhere, and so would I when I was with them. We put a board across an open well, and walked on it. I was unfailingly happy, or so I think now. The only problem I had was with the food. Robina who in my mother's kitchen produced such complicated puddings, such moist black devil's food, incomparable pastry, velvety mashed potatoes, thought nothing here of giving you a piece of bread with a greasy bit of bacon on it, and that nearly cold, barely cooked. The others would chew it and swallow it down in a hurry and want more; they were always hungry. I would have given somebody mine, but protocol made them turn it down.

Jimmy and Duval were big boys, big as men but still playful, unpredictable. They might chase us and pick us up and swing us by the arms until we flew straight out. They would not say a word, and would look very stern the whole time. Or they would come and stand on either side of me and say, 'Can you remember, is this the one who ain't ticklish?'

'I don't know. I can't remember if that's the one.'

'I think it is. I think it's her.'

They would nod heavily, considering. Then they would just have to move, as if they were about to close in, to make me break into screams of jittery pleasure. I did not scream just at being tickled, or at the threat of being tickled. My joy was at being recognized. This teasing did seem to me a recognition, and a reprieve; I was never afraid of Duval and Jimmy, despite their size. I never minded, when I understood by their solemnity that they were making fun of me. I thought them powerful, benevolent, mystifying, rather like clowns. They actually could do tricks, as clowns do. They sometimes performed silently, amazingly, in the dust of the yard, turning cartwheels, leap-frogging. Robina said they were good enough to go in the circus but they wouldn't leave home, they loved their home. They did not go to school, either. They had not gone back since the day the teacher beat up on Jimmy for throwing the chalk-brush out the window, and Jimmy and Duval together – so Robina said – beat up on the teacher. That had been years ago.

'Whose girl friend is she?' they said, *Mine. Mine.* And they play-fought over me, each of them grabbing me from the other and trapping me in a hard hug. I loved their smell, which was of barns and engines and Buckingham's Fine Cut.

They had enemies who could not be so readily disposed of as that teacher. There was Stump Troy. He was known to me as an enemy of Jimmy's and Duval's – and therefore, of course, of Robina's – long before his son Howard became an enemy of mine. But I had not paid much attention till then.

Robina said that Stump Troy had got the police on Jimmy and Duval for siphoning petrol out of one of the cars that was parked in front of his place on a Saturday night. It was true all right that they were taking petrol – this would be for the old car that was usually laid open on the gangway, not running – but it was from the car of a man who had never paid them for a job they did for him and it was their only way of getting back at him. Even before this time Stump Troy had been spreading lies about them, Robina said, and he was the one who paid a whole gang from Dungannon to wait for Jimmy and Duval and beat them up – even Jimmy and Duval could not beat more than maybe three men apiece – outside the Paramount Dance Hall.

I think now they may have been rivals, or fallen-out accomplices, in the bootlegging business. My mother was opposed to drinking, as was natural in her circumstances, and Robina in my mother's house appeared to share this view. She said their whole family was on the Pledge, their Grandma had demanded it. This may have been an exaggeration. Whatever the truth was, Stump Troy had got Jimmy and Duval into trouble, and had the means of getting them into more trouble, and they hated him.

'Oh, they hate him! If they was out on a dark night and old Stump was out on the road, he'd soon be sorry he ever heard of them!'

'How would he get out on the road?'

'That's it. Lucky for him he can't.'

'Jimmy and Duval are good-natured,' Robina said. 'They are not mean boys. But they don't forget when somebody has played a dirty trick on them. They don't let up on a person then.'

*

Punishments. I thought of myself walking on Howard Troy's eyes. Driving spikes into his eyes. The spikes would be on the soles of my shoes, they would be long and sharp. His eyeballs would bulge out, unprotected, as big as overturned basins, and I would walk on them, puncturing, flattening, bloodying, at a calm pace. It wasn't anything clean and magical I dreamed of, no saying the right word in my head and shrivelling him in an instant. I would have liked his head torn from his body, flesh pulpy and dripping like watermelon, limbs wrenched away; axes, saws, knives and hammers applied to him. If I could surprise him with that knife, making not a slit in him but a round hole such as they make in maple trees for sap, I would jab in deep and then all kinds of pus, venomous substances, would spurt and flow, everything would leak away.

The fire filled the house the way blood fills a boil. It seemed every minute ready to burst, but the skin still held. The skin was the roof, the walls, of Stump Troy's house. Wood could seem as thin as that.

'The roof'll go next!' people were saying, and, 'Lucky there's no wind!'

I did not understand why it was lucky, or what could be lucky, now. The house which I had never quite dared or wanted to look at turned out to be as simple as a house in a drawing – the door in the middle and a narrow window on either side, a dormer window over the door. Both downstairs windows had been smashed, by Howard Troy trying to get inside. Men had pulled him back. Now he was sitting on the ground in front of the burning house. He was reduced, apparently powerless, just as he had been in school.

The town fire truck had come, but by the time they got there there was nothing for the firemen to do but praise the lack of wind. They took the ladders off but did not put them anywhere. They managed after some time to get water from the last hydrant – this was of course beyond the town limits – and they sprayed some falling-down outbuildings, the fence, and the toilet. They played water on the flames too, but that seemed just silliness and vainglory. 'You might as well all stand back and spit on it!' yelled Robina, who was in a great state of excitement. She trembled and crackled, she was like a burning beam herself. She stood by the gate, where a big neglected forsythia bush had sprung into bloom, early bloom, with the snow hardly gone. She kept me beside her. My mother, who had driven us down, sat in the car a little way up the road. She was watching, presumably, but did not care to mingle.

I was the one who had first seen the fire from my upstairs window, seen something beautiful, a flush in a corner of the night landscape, separate from the glow of the town lights, a warm spreading pool. That was the house giving off such light, through its cracks and windows.

The trouble with Robina, I thought, was that she could not do anything about this fire. She could not boss the firemen. She tried, but they went on morosely doing what they were doing, none of them in any hurry. She could correct the information people were exchanging; that was something.

'Lucky there's nobody in there,' some latecomer said.

And Robina said sternly, 'Don't you know this house?'

Apparently there were people who did not.

'Don't you know who lives in this house? It's Stump Troy.'

There was not sufficient comprehension, so she went on.

'It's Stump Troy that hasn't got any legs! He's not going to walk out of there, is he? He's in there yet.'

'Jesus,' a man said reverently. 'Jesus, he'll be fried!'

The sound the fire made was surprising. It was like something scraping, like boards, or a lawn mower being dragged over concrete. I had never thought a fire would sound like that. A harsh, busy noise, the sort people call a racket. Inside this racket was Stump Troy yelling, was he calling out for help? If he was, the fire was too loud for him, nobody could hear.

It was not yet midnight, so most people had not gone to bed, or had been ready to get up again. The road was clogged with cars now. Many people were just sitting in the cars, watching, but there were plenty of them out, too, wandering after the firemen or standing against the fence, their faces lighted up. Even children did not run around, the fire took too much of their attention. I saw Robina's young brothers and sisters, some of them at least. They must have seen the fire from their place – by this time there would be a proclamatory light in the sky – and walked all this way to it, through the bush at night. Robina saw them too and called to them at once.

'Florence! Carter! Findley! You stay back out of this!'

They were staying back anyway, they were not as near as we were.

She did not ask where Jimmy and Duval were, who would surely not have wanted to miss a sight like this. I yelled it for her.

'Florence! Where are Jimmy and Duval?'

Robina with a swing of her one full arm caught me across the face, across the mouth, the hardest blow I had ever felt, or was likely to feel. It was so sudden I thought it had something to do with the fire (for people all along had been saying, 'Watch out, the whole thing's going to give way, boards'll fly!') or that Robina's arm had shot out to keep something else from hitting me. At the same moment, it seemed, the roof at last did give way, and people ran, backing off. Flames tore through at the sky. There was also, and almost at the same time, a shout from another part of the yard, though I did not understand till later what this shout was for. I even thought, in my confusion, that it had to do with Robina hitting me. It was really for Howard Troy, who had made a dash from where he had been sitting right into the flaming, collapsing doorway, far too late to save anybody, if that was his intention, too late to be saved himself.

There were explanations offered for this later. One was that he meant to run the other way, away from the fire, but in his temporary craziness ran instead straight into it. Another was that he heard his father yelling for him and still thought he could get him out. Or thought he heard him yell. Stump Troy would have been in no condition to yell, by then. This explanation would have made Howard Troy heroic, and it was not popular, though a few surprising people hung onto it, among them my mother.

Another explanation was that Howard Troy had set the fire himself, perhaps after an argument with his father, perhaps for no particular reason, but to demonstrate what he could do, had been all this time preparing and waiting to do, while people rightly mistrusted him.

There was backing for this opinion, because of an empty petrol can. Those who believed that the fire had been set argued sometimes that Stump himself might have set it, or ordered it, a trick to get the insurance. He had meant to be outside or had counted on Howard to get him out, and Howard through cowardice or ill-timing had failed him. On account of remorse, then, or fear of facing the authorities, Howard had run into the fire.

At the time, however, there were no explanations. All that people could do was hurry and tell other people, who might not have seen. I was not surprised. The fire itself, and the blow across my face, had cut me off from further surprise. I held my hands to my mouth, but for a wonder my teeth were not loosened; the only blood came from a small cut on the inside of my lip, where the edge of a tooth had caught it.

Robina seemed all at once to be sick of the fire. She pulled me with her out the gateway and along the road. My mother's car was not to be seen.

'She's gone home ahead of us,' Robina said. 'I don't blame her. Those fools can stand there all night if they want to. I know what they're waiting on. They're waiting to see them take out the body. Bodies,' she corrected herself. 'They can wait.'

I did not answer, or look back at the fire once. I walked ahead. Robina pushed me once, to keep me from going into the ditch. When she touched me I jumped.

'You're going like a person walking in its sleep. I only grabbed you to keep you from going headlong into that ditch.'

When we got past the cars, and there was room, Robina

came up to walk beside me. I had the feeling that if she could have moved all around me, been in front and behind and on both sides at once, that was what she would do. She would close me off, she would peer into me until she found whatever she wanted, and got it rearranged. Meanwhile she said, 'If you let one bad thing like this bother you there's going to be a lot of trouble for you in this world.'

I was not trying in any way to punish Robina or worry her. I did mean to answer. Some of the time I believed that I had answered, just as in a light sleep you will keep telling yourself you must do something – shut a window, turn off a light – and so convince yourself, in your sleep, that you have actually done it. And after such a sleep you can never be sure at all what has happened, what has really been said, and what you have dreamed. I never did know afterwards if Robina had really spoken to me from time to time as I thought she had, in an uncharacteristically soft and bothered voice, threatening or promising something, scaring and reassuring.

Or if she had ever said, 'Listen. I'll show you my arm.'

If she did, I never answered that either.

When I was in high school, or home from college for the weekend, I sometimes saw Robina walking along the main street, with her flopping sleeve, her one whole swinging arm, her long steps that always seemed to be taking her downhill. She had not worked for us for a long time. When my father came home for good, with a nurse who wanted her own way in the kitchen, there was no place left for her, and no money either. When I saw her I had to be reminded of my childhood, which seemed so long ago, and full of panic and disgrace. For I had changed, things had changed for me, I believed that with luck and good management I could turn out to seem like anybody else. And this is in fact what I have done.

She looked odd to me, Robina did; absurd, obsessed, not very clean. Nevertheless I would have spoken to her, I was prepared. But she would turn her head away and never speak, showing me that I had become one of those people who had committed an offence against her.

She may be dead now, Robina. Jimmy and Duval may be dead too, though that is hard to imagine. I am still a few years away from retiring. I am a widow, a civil servant, I live on the eighteenth floor of an apartment building. I don't mind being alone. In the evenings I read, I watch television. No, that is not always true. Sometimes I sit in the dark, drinking whiskey and water, thinking uselessly and helplessly, almost comfortably, about things like this that I had forgotten, or could not bear to think about for a long time.

When everybody is dead who could have remembered it, then I suppose the fire will be finished with, it will be just as if nobody had ever run through the door.

MARRAKESH

Dorothy was sitting in a straight-backed chair on the side porch, eating nuts. She had taken to buying nuts from the machine in the drugstore. She ate them from the white paper bag with the picture of a squirrel on it. At the age of seventy she had been forced to give up cigarettes, because of chest pains. The school board had never been able to get her to do that. A one-time petition, signed by parents, had failed. Gordie Lomax – dead now himself – brought her the petition which had been sent first to the school board. She looked over it critically as if it had been a spelling test. 'Tell them it's my only vice,' she said firmly, and Gordie went back and told them.

'She says it's her only vice.'

Viola predicted that Dorothy would get fat, switching to nuts, but nothing could make Dorothy fat and never had. Viola was put out because she could not do the same, could not eat nuts and apples. Viola had a plate.

Dorothy was by herself at present. Viola had gone to the cemetery, taking Jeanette. Early in the morning, before breakfast, she had stripped the flower border of delphiniums, which were at their peak now, blooming in every shade of blue and purple. She wanted a bouquet for her husband's grave, one for Dorothy's husband's grave (she had taken him over, because Dorothy seldom went near the cemetery) and one for their parents'.

'I thought you might like to take a drive out to Last Lookout,' she said to Jeanette at breakfast. That was her husband's name for it, his joke. Naturally Jeanette did not know what she was talking about. Viola had spoken confidentially, coquettishly. She could not help it. To the cashier at the grocery store, the mechanic at the garage, the teenager who mowed the lawn, she bent her silver, smoothly waved head in this mystifying way, she murmured deprecatingly some words that half the time they did not bother to pick up. Dorothy was embarrassed. To offset Viola's silliness she had to be more brusque and to the point than she might have been otherwise.

'She means the cemetery,' Dorothy said.

'Oh, I love the cemetery,' said Jeanette, with her tender, charming smile.

'What is there to love?' said Dorothy, looking down into her cup of black coffee as if it were a well.

'Well I love the view,' said Jeanette gamely. 'And the old tombstones. I love reading the inscriptions on the old tombstones.'

'Dorothy thinks I'm morbid,' said Viola slyly.

'I don't think anything,' said Dorothy, and brightened up, remembering something. 'Glass jars are prohibited in the cemetery.' She looked at the bouquets which Viola had put in preserving jars. 'You'll have to take them out and put them in those plastic ice-cream things.'

'Prohibited?' Viola said. 'Whyever is that?'

'Vandalism,' replied Dorothy with satisfaction. 'I heard it on the radio.'

Jeanette was Dorothy's granddaughter. People here in town, seeing her with the two old ladies – and seeing her with Viola, who still drove her car, more frequently than with Dorothy – were not usually aware of this. They thought her some distant young relative. Though Dorothy had lived in and around this town all her life it was not well remembered that she had been left a widow with a young boy to raise, that his name had been Bobby, that he had gone to high school four years here, before he left to look for work out west in the final years before the War. From the time she was widowed until the time of her retirement Dorothy had taught Grade Seven in the public school, and because of this people were apt to forget that she had had any life that might be called private. She had become a fixed star in many, many, shifting, changing, ongoing lives. Seeing her on the street, truck drivers, storekeepers, mothers pushing baby carriages – now, as a matter of fact, even grandmothers pushing baby carriages – would be reminded of maps, percentages, spelling bees, the serious but not oppressive, well-run, sensible, atmosphere of her class. She herself seldom thought of the classroom where she had spent most of her life, and could not have gone back to visit it if she had wanted to, because they had torn down the building five years ago and put up a new, low, unimpressive, pastel school; but as far as those people were concerned, she carried it around with her, forever, and they never looked at her for anything beyond that. The Mrs in front of her name was as empty as a courtesy title.

Bobby, her son, had died before the War, killed in a car accident in the interior of British Columbia. He had found time to get married first and father a baby girl. That was Jeanette. Jeanette's mother, whom Dorothy had never met to this day, had moved to Vancouver and in a couple of years had married again and started in on what was to be a large family. When Jeanette was fourteen years old she had come east for the first time, on the train, to spend a month of the summer with her grandmother. For a few years after that she came every summer. Dorothy and the stepfather splitting the cost. Dorothy's correspondence was with the stepfather who explained that there was some natural friction between the girl and her mother and her mother's many children; it was a good thing to give them a holiday from each other. He seemed a sensible man. Now he was dead too. Jeanette seemed to see hardly anything nowadays of her mother and her step-family.

But she continued to visit Dorothy and, after Viola had moved in, Dorothy and Viola. She had won scholarships which had taken her to college. She remained to get her M.A. Then her Ph.D. She stayed at college for good, teaching. She travelled. Her visits never lasted longer than a week, and sometimes only three or four days. She had friends to see, she had made arrangements. Dorothy supposed that she was bored.

When she first came to visit, as a young girl, Jeanette's

hair had been short and brown. Later on it was blonde. One year she appeared with it puffed up in what looked like a heap of bubbles on top of her head. In those days she would colour her eyelids blue up to the eyebrows, she wore sheath dresses in patterns of orange and purple, yellow and scarlet. Her stylish, provocative air, after her thoughtful drabness as a young girl, came as a surprise. But the way she looked now was even more surprising. She had let her hair grow long and wore it either in a single braid down her back or loose, pale, and frizzy. She wore jeans and a peasant blouse and a collection of beads and metal jewellery. Most of the time no shoes. She also wore little childish print dresses, short as playsuits which bared her back and revealed that she was wearing no brassiere. Not that there was any need. She was a thirtyish woman with the figure of an eleven-year-old child.

'Is she trying to be a hippie, do you think?' said Viola mildly. 'They must think it funny when she's teaching.' Viola was a great one for the smile to the face and the knife in the back. It was her social life as a banker's wife that had trained her. She was getting at Dorothy, really, because Jeanette was Dorothy's granddaughter. Both Dorothy and Viola were well-enough satisfied with the arrangement of living together. It was economical and provided company, as well as help in case of accident or illness. They drew comfort from each other's presence in the way young quarrelsome children do, or long-married apparently uncongenial couples, the comfort being so inexplicable and largely unrecognized that what showed on the surface – what they thought they felt – was mostly wariness, irritation, concern for strategy.

'That's the way the majority of them dress around the college nowadays,' Dorothy said.

'Teachers too?'

'It makes no difference.'

'I wonder will she ever get married?' remarked Viola, not at random.

Dorothy had seen pictures in magazines of this new type of adult who appeared to have discarded adulthood. Jeanette was the first one she had seen close up and in the flesh. It used to be that young boys and girls would try to look like grown men and women, often with ridiculous results. Now there were grown men and women who would try to look like teen-agers until, presumably, they woke up on the brink of old age. It was a strange thing to see the child already meeting the old woman in Jeanette's face. One moment she looked younger than she had done ten years ago, her face pale without make-up, her mouth wide and secretive. She looked fresh, clean, dreamy and self-absorbed. Then with a change of light or mood or body chemistry this same face showed itself bruised, bluish, sharp, skin more than a little shrivelled under the eyes. A great deal had been simply skipped out.

From where Dorothy sat on the porch the street looked hotter and shabbier than it had looked any other summer. This was because the trees were gone. Last fall the men who worked for the municipality had come along and cut down all the elm trees, those tall, old, deeply shading trees whose branches used to darken and brush against the upstairs windows of many of the houses, and in October bury the lawns in leaves. The trees were all diseased, some already half-dead, and they had to be taken down before the winter storms made them dangerous. During the winter it was not obvious how much this had changed the street, since the trees were not the main thing about the street then; the snowbanks were. But now Dorothy noticed a great difference. The overhanging trees had isolated the houses and made the yards seem bigger; they had kept the patched narrow pavement flowing with light and shade, like a river.

Jeanette had raised a lament at once.

'The trees!' she said, as soon as she stepped out of her little cream-coloured foreign car. 'The beautiful trees! Who cut them down?'

'The municipality,' Dorothy said.

'They would.'

'They had no choice,' said Dorothy, exchanging with her granddaughter a dry kiss, a token embrace. 'It was Dutch elm disease.'

'The same thing that's happening everywhere,' Jeanette cut in on her, hardly listening. 'It's all part of the same destruction. The whole country is turning into a junkyard.'

Dorothy could not agree. She could not speak for the country but this town was hardly turning into a junkyard. In fact the Kinsmen had recently drained and cleared a waste area by the river and turned it into a very nice park, something the town had been lacking in its entire hundred years. She understood that Dutch elm disease had wiped out all the elm trees in Europe during the last century and had been making headway across this continent for fifty years. God knows the scientists had worked hard enough looking for a cure. She felt compelled to point all this out. Jeanette smiled wanly, yes, but you don't know what's happening, it's everywhere, technology and progress are destroying the quality of life.

Well, thought Dorothy; she had forgotten what a black view Jeanette always took and how it always annoyed her and drove her to defending things she supposed she knew nothing about and had no business defending. Quality of life. She did not think in those terms or talk to people who did. Jeanette was a problem to understand.

'She has that lovely car,' Viola had said, 'and she has education and her job and nobody to spend her money on but herself, and she has been all over – wouldn't it have seemed like a dream to you or me – and yet she isn't happy.' Viola of course thought that Jeanette was unhappy and embittered because she had failed to get some man to marry her. Dorothy did not think that, and she was not sure that embittered or even unhappy was the word to describe what Jeanette was. Adolescent was the word that came to her mind, but that did not explain enough.

Dorothy herself as a young girl – she remembered this clearly – had flung herself down in the grass beside the lane of her father's farm, howling and weeping, and why? Because her father and her brothers were replacing a fence, a crooked old mossy rail fence, with barbed wire! Of course no one paid any attention to her protests and in time she got up and washed her face and got used to the barbed wire. How she hated change, then, and clung to old things, old mossy rotten *picturesque things*. Now she had changed, herself. She saw what beauty was, all right; she acknowledged the dappling shadows on the grass, the grey pavement, but she saw that it was, in a way, something to get round. It did not matter greatly to her. Nor did familiarity. Those houses across the street had been across from her for forty years, and long before that, she supposed, they must have been casually familiar to her, for this town had been Town to her when she was a child, and she had often driven along this street with her family, coming in from the country, on the way to put the horse in the Methodist Church shed. But if those houses were all pulled down, their hedges and vines and vegetable plots and apple trees and whatnot obliterated, and a shopping centre put up in their place, she would not turn her back. No, she would sit just as now, looking out, looking not emptily but with strong curiosity at the cars and pavement and flashing signs and flat-roofed stores and the immense, curved, dominating shape of the supermarket. Anything would do for her to look at; beautiful or ugly had ceased to matter, because there was in everything something to be discovered. This was a feeling that had come on her as she got older, and it was not at all a peaceful, letting-go sort of feeling, such as old people were supposed to get; it was the very opposite, pinning her where she was in irritable, baffled concentration.

'You don't look as if you're thinking very pleasant thoughts,' Viola had more than once said to her. 'Pleasant thoughts keep you young.'

'Is that so?' said Dorothy. 'Well. I've been young.'

With the trees gone it was possible to see as far as the corner of Mayo and Harper Streets. Dorothy saw Blair King coming around the corner, walking home from work. He worked at the radio station, which was only a couple of blocks away. Like most of the people who worked at the radio station he was not a native of this town and in a few years would probably move on. He and his wife rented the house next to Dorothy's, but his wife was not there now. For several weeks she had been in the hospital.

Blair King paused to look at the out-of-province licence plates on Jeanette's car.

'That belongs to my granddaughter visiting us!'

Why had she called out that? She and Viola did not know the Kings well; they never visited back and forth. He was friendly enough, in what seemed a half-professional way, but she was cool. They did little work on their yard. She had worked in the town library, until she got sick. Dorothy and Viola were more apt to see her there than around her own house. She wore a college girl's skirt and sweater, a barrette in her shoulder-length hair (she was the college girl of fifteen years ago, she hadn't kept up with the times in quite the way Jeanette had) and she had a lowpitched well-bred voice that many people in town found subtly insulting. Also such confidence and homeliness as Dorothy had seldom seen met together in one face.

'Good-looking men will often pick a girl like that,' Viola said. 'Could it be they are not interested in looks when they have got so much themselves?'

Blair King in a neighbourly way approached the porch, but did not come up. Instead he rested a foot on the step and leaned on his knee. He was good-looking, but his looks were getting set, worn. His smile, like his voice, was accomplished, mechanical. The trouble with his wife was telling on him.

'I've been admiring her car every time I go in and out.'

'She bought it in Europe last year and had it shipped back. How is your wife?'

It did not bother Dorothy to ask that, though she knew

the story: Nancy King was dying of cancer. Death at thirty-six might be tragic, but she no longer, to tell the truth, understood the meaning of the word tragic. She asked to make conversation.

'She's not too uncomfortable at the moment.'

'Is it hot in the hospital?' She kept him talking because an idea was coming to her.

'The new wing is all air conditioned.'

'I asked Blair King next door,' said Dorothy. 'I asked him to come over and spend the evening with us.'

'You inviting people,' said Viola. 'What next? The skies may fall.'

'I don't know what we'll give him,' she said later. 'He'll probably expect a drink. Those radio people don't go out for the evening and drink tea.'

'Radio people?' said Jeanette. 'I thought it sounded like a fancy name. A *media* name.'

'Where is that sherry?' said Dorothy. She did not drink; she had been telling the truth when she reported that smoking was her only vice; but Viola had got to like sherry in her bank-managing-hostessing days, and usually kept a bottle of it in the house.

'How can we offer him sherry?' Viola appealed to Jeanette. 'You know what they always call sherry? *The old ladies' drink.*'

'I'll go to the liquor store,' Jeanette said comfortingly, 'and get a bottle of gin, and I'll pick up some tonic and see if I can get a few limes, and that will be very nice on a hot night. Nobody can complain of a gin and tonic.'

Viola was still not satisfied. 'He'll want something to eat.'

'Cucumber sandwiches,' said Dorothy.

'Lovely. Like Oscar Wilde,' said Jeanette mystifyingly. 'I'll pick up a cucumber too.' She rebraided her hair, humming – happy at the prospect of getting out by herself for half an hour? – and ran out to her car, singing. 'Gin a-and ton-ic, lime a-and cucumber –'

'She is going to the stores in her bare feet,' said Viola.

In the middle of the afternoon Jeanette lay out in the back yard, in the sun. Viola could not see her, that was something to be thankful for. 'Is that what passes for a bikini?' Viola would have said. 'I thought it was a couple of ribbons she had tied around herself.'

But Viola's bedroom was at the front of the house, Dorothy's at the back. They always took afternoon naps, it broke up the day. When she was a teacher, Dorothy had thought of afternoon naps as a summer luxury. Teaching tired her during the last years, and she did not even have the whole summer to herself, since the Department of Education in its infinite wisdom had decided that she should spend three weeks living in a hot rented room in Toronto taking courses that would enable her to introduce new methods and perspectives into her classroom teaching. (Naturally, she did nothing of the sort, but went on successfully teaching just as she always had.) When she came home from Toronto, there was Jeanette. But Jeanette did little to upset her pattern of life, and she would go upstairs every afternoon and stretch out for her nap. Sometimes she pictured Jeanette downstairs in the living room, reading a book, or out on the porch lying in the swing, with one foot now and then tapping the floor boards, to keep the swing rocking, and she wondered whether the child was happy, whether she ought to be doing more things for her – taking her to the new swimming pool, registering her for tennis lessons. Then she remembered that Jeanette was too big to be taken anywhere, and if she wanted tennis lessons surely she would ask about them. Most of the time Jeanette liked to read. This was exactly what Dorothy herself had liked to do when she was young, and still did like to do. It seemed quite natural to them both to sit through meals together, each of them reading a book. Now Jeanette seemed to read very little. Perhaps her education had made her tired of it.

Dorothy was less curious in those days. In the classroom, she never sought to know anything but whether her pupils had grasped those principles of arithmetic and spelling, those facts of history and science and geography which it was her duty to teach them. She saw Jeanette as a shy serious girl, a bit older than her pupils. Studious was the word she would have used for her, an old-fashioned word. She believed then, without having to inquire or think about it, that Jeanette was in some important way a continuation of herself. This was not apparent any longer; the connection had either broken or gone invisible. Dorothy looked down for some time from her bedroom window at her granddaughter's spare brown body, as if it were a hieroglyph on her grass.

'And on the M1 –' said Blair King despairingly, sitting on the side porch drinking gin. It was Jeanette he despaired to. Dorothy followed the conversation with attention, but not with ease.

'Oh, the M1! That was the worst experience of my life,

driving down to London in the fog, and they do sixty in the fog, you can't do less, pure fog and you literally cannot see ten feet. My friend and I had just hired a camper, and I wasn't even that used to driving it, and we got into one of those roundabouts and we couldn't get off. We literally couldn't see where to get off and we were going round and round forever, it was like some very symbolic under-graduate play.'

Did Blair King know what she meant? He seemed to. He watched her face and murmured encouragingly. This was the first Dorothy had heard of the camper, or the friend, or for that matter of the M1. To her grandmother and Viola, Jeanette had not said much more about Europe than that most places were overrun with tourists, the houses in Greece were clammy in the winter, and that frozen fish brought in from Athens cost less than local fish caught by the villagers. She had described some things they ate, until Viola said she felt queasy.

Was the friend a man friend or a girl? Dorothy could tell Viola was wondering.

Blair King and his wife had spent six months in Europe three years ago. He did not let them forget her. Nancy and I. Nancy did the driving in Switzerland. Nancy loved Portugal but didn't care as much for Spain. Nancy preferred the Portuguese style of bullfighting. Viola got in her oar occasionally about the three weeks she and her husband had spent in Great Britain in 1956. Dorothy sat and listened and sipped her drink, which she did not like the taste of, though Jeanette had promised to be parsimonious with the gin. She could not complain, really, even if she had trouble keeping up with what they said. This was what she had been counting on – that Blair King might turn out to be more the sort of person Jeanette was used to, that she could talk to, and that she herself listening to this talk could get a better idea of what Jeanette was like than she had been able to get up to now. So she sat concentrating, with not much more than the sound of their voices to concentrate on, because it was dark on the porch. Shall we turn the lights on, Dorothy had asked, and Jeanette had cried no, no, then it's like sitting in a hot little box here with all the bugs beating at the screen.

'I don't mind sitting in the dark do you?' she said to Blair King, and Dorothy caught something in her tone – was it arch, deferential, disparaging? – that she put away for future consideration.

They talked about food and drink and illness and medicine and a strange doctor in Crete who assumed, Jeanette said, that all foreign women who consulted him had come for an abortion, so that he could only with the greatest difficulty be persuaded to treat a sore throat. Blair King told about a doctor in Spain, consulted for Nancy's stomach trouble, who had given her such a rending purgative that two hours later, in the Alhambra, she was doubled up, desperate.

'That's what Nancy always remembers about Spain. Here we are in this incredibly beautiful place we've seen all the pictures of, and it was one of the places Nancy had most looked forward to seeing, and we can only think of one thing – where is the ladies' john?'

'Ah, one's baser needs,' said Jeanette, mock-solemnly. 'One's baser needs are so inconvenient. They get to be so important. I remember my first stoopers. On the boat to Greece.'

Is that the way men and women talk to each other nowadays?
Dorothy could tell Viola was thinking. And further: *No*
wonder she isn't married.

'And for Nancy, of course. Nancy is dignified. You haven't
met her. She isn't anything you would call a snob, but she
is – well, I used to think of her as the sorority-girl type.'

'Ah,' said Jeanette, combining flattery and a delicate sort
of contempt in a way that Blair King was probably not
even aware of, going on talking about his wife. What was
Jeanette up to? Was this flirtation, some new style of it? In
spite of all her talking and animation there was something
quite still about Jeanette, something not playful, but
acquiescent, almost forlorn.

They had progressed from talking about doctors to
talking about places where people would rob you blind,
and other places where you could leave an unlocked, loaded
car for days parked safely on the street. 'In North Africa
I had everything stolen,' said Jeanette. 'I had everything
stolen even though the camper was locked. I was alone by
that time, my friend and I had separated and I felt badly
about that too –' So *it was a man*, thought Dorothy, but
immediately had to correct herself and think, *unless it was*
a girl, and they were – Sometimes she wished she had not
kept up with the world as she had done, reading.

'It was in Marrakesh,' Jeanette said. 'I had everything,
everything, stolen, lovely things – Moroccan dresses,
cloth I had bought for friends, jewellery – as well as my
camera naturally and all the stuff I had come with. I just
sat there all alone in my camper and I cried. And then
two young Arab boys – well, not boys really, young Arab
men – but they were very slender and at first I took them

for younger than they were – they came by and saw me and stopped and tried to talk to me. One spoke English quite well. At first I wouldn't even talk to them, I hated all Arabs, hated all Moroccans, I blamed them personally for my stuff being stolen. I wouldn't even tell them what had happened but they kept on at me – or the one that talked did – until I finally quite rudely explained, and they said, you must go to the police. Ha, I said, the police were probably watching them do it. But they finally persuaded me to go. They got in and directed. It did cross my mind that they were probably not taking me to the police at all and that I was being totally stupid, but I really didn't care much. And do you know what? I was inclined to trust the one talking to me, because he had *blue eyes*. What abysmal prejudice; *Nazis* had blue eyes. But his eyes made me feel more comfortable somehow and I went along even when we had to leave the camper and walk through all those twisty turny smelly streets in the Arab quarter, and by the time I knew for sure we weren't going to the police I couldn't have found my way back anyhow. You're not taking me to the police, are you, I said, and they said no. Not right away, the blue-eyed one said. I'm going to take you home and introduce you to my mother!'

'Well that was very nice of him. After all,' said Viola encouragingly.

But Blair King laughed.

'I *know*. Introduce me to his mother. And his sister, he said. Eventually we did come to a house or rather a door, that was all I noticed because you know how the walls all run together. And we were in a little bare room with a couch and a bright bulb. Wait a minute, he said, and he went through another door. His friend stayed behind. I didn't like the friend at all. He had a sullen face. He didn't talk. I sat on the couch and after a long time No.1 came back and said he was sorry, his mother and sister had gone to bed. Then he said he was going to get some food. I said could he take me back and he said later. So he left me again with this friend and no sooner was he gone than peculiar things started to happen. The friend came over and sat on the couch and started stroking my hands and arms and trying to talk to me. I tried to keep control and ask him – well, *normalizing*, questions, but I was getting very nervous. He began sort of crawling over me there on the couch so I had to get up, and then he just dropped all pretence and cornered me against the wall and took out a knife –'

'Ahhh,' cried Viola. 'How could you go to such a country?'

'And he held it under my throat and demanded – well, by this time he was getting very graphic about the whole thing, but I just said no, *no*, and refused to look at anything.'

'But the knife was at your throat,' said Blair King, almost as if this was a joke.

'Well I somehow did think he was bluffing. I somehow could tell. It was all like a play. And then the blue-eyed one came back. He really had gone to buy food; he had some cheese and so on, and he got very annoyed or seemed to when he saw what was going on. The other one put the knife away of course. The blue-eyed one apologized with great eloquence and we all sat down and ate. It seems incredible. Then the blue-eyed one said he would show me the way back. And he did. He was very courteous. On the way back he asked me to marry him.'

When she said this Jeanette's voice dipped with embarrassment, as it had not done during any other part of the story.

'He was hoping I would get him out of the country or something. Or maybe it's a kind of extreme Arab courtesy. He came to the hotel every day until I left and repeated his proposal. He said he loved me, naturally.'

What is there here that is not being told? thought Dorothy. She had had a great deal of experience listening to the voices of children who were leaving things out. Maybe she slept with the blue-eyed Arab when she got him back to the hotel. Maybe she slept with both of them in the Arab house. Something more than that. Maybe she loved him. Maybe the whole story is made-up.

'I think,' said Jeanette apologetically, 'I think I was a little in love with him. Very odd things happen to your feelings in those countries. And being alone.'

'Odd things happen,' Blair King agreed.

'Of course the impossible thing is to tell what they feel about you. Impossible.'

She and Blair King had drunk about the entire bottle of gin between them.

Dorothy got ready for bed. She felt restless and not at all tired, though it was far past her usual bedtime. If this is what a drink is going to do to me, she thought, then I had better not get in the habit. She heard Viola go to the bathroom and go back to her room and shut the door. She heard Viola's light click out. She put out her own light. Jeanette was sleeping downstairs. No sound in the house.

Dorothy sat on the bed in her nightgown, with her hair,

which was worn coiled up in the daytime, lying like a stiff grey broom, still fairly thick, around her shoulders. She could after a while make out her old face in the glass. There was a moon. She looked like a character to scare children, like an old Norse witch. The sight was enough to make her decide to go downstairs to get a glass of milk or a cup of tea, to bring herself back to normal.

She went down in her bare feet, with her old maroon dressing gown tied over her nightdress. She did not turn on any lights. She could see by the moon in the back rooms of the house and by the street light in the front. She unlocked the front door and went down the steps.

She stood on the pavement in her dressing gown, her pale nightdress trailing underneath, and thought, *What if anybody should see?* She walked around the house on the grass. The grass was heavily damp. August dew. She walked past the spirea bushes and stood by the flower border from which all the delphiniums had been cut. There was no fence or hedge between this yard and the Kings'. On the other side of the border the Kings' ragged grass began.

The Kings had a glassed-in porch at the back of their house. The light was on in it. The porch had been renovated a few years ago and the windows now came right down to the floor.

Dorothy walked across the flower border, trying not to step on plants. She stood on the Kings' grass. In the lighted porch she could see two figures, and when she walked closer she could see they were Jeanette and Blair King. Jeanette seemed to be kneeling on some sort of low stool or hassock. She was pulling her embroidered blouse over her head. Then she was bare. Blair King, standing apart, was removing his clothes too, taking his time. Of course. Nowadays it was nothing to do that. This was what Dorothy had set in motion but she need not worry. They would have forgotten it themselves by tomorrow. Or by a week from tomorrow. Wouldn't they? You could hardly say they loved each other, and they were drunk as sailors.

Blair King knelt down in front of Jeanette, pressing his face against her. She bent over him and held his head. Her tanned body looked golden in the porch light, his white. Pressed together. Dorothy was finally halted. Her breath drew in at the sight of them. Now that they had put their clothes, and what looks and movements she knew of them – all they could give her to know – aside, they seemed strange and familiar to her, both more and less than themselves. Like figures in a museum. But too live, too awkward – even if she could have kept them still! – for that. Flaunting themselves in the light as if nothing mattered, guzzling and grabbing now, relishing and plundering each other. If she had been able to call out to them, *Stop that, stop that at once!* in her old schoolyard voice, it would have been a warning she called, more than a rebuke. Bold as they were, they looked helpless to her, helpless and endangered as people on a raft pulled out on the current. And nobody could call to them. They tumbled, they caught and bore each other down silently, behind the glass.

She noticed now that her whole body was trembling, her knees weak, her head battered from within. She wondered if this was how a person felt at the onset of a stroke. It would be terrible to have a stroke here, in her nightclothes, and not even on her own property. She made her way back through the flower bed and around to the front of the house. She felt better as she walked, and by the time she reached the steps she felt fairly satisfied that she was not going to have a stroke after all. She sat on the steps for a few moments to get control of herself, closing her eyes.

On the underside of her eyelids there promptly appeared the two welded figures, solid and bright, like those chalked-in drawings she used to put on the blackboard – surprising herself – for festive occasions.

What if Viola had seen any of that? More than she could stand. Strength is necessary, as well as something like gratitude, if you are going to turn into a lady peeping Tom at the end of your life.

THE SPANISH LADY

Dear Hugh and Margaret,

I have been by myself a good deal these past weeks and have been able to think about us all and have reached several interesting though not perhaps original conclusions:

1) Monogamy is not a natural condition for men and women.

2) The reason that we feel jealous is that we feel abandoned. This is absurd, because I am a grown-up person capable of looking after myself. I cannot, literally, be abandoned. Also we feel jealous – I feel jealous – because I reason that if Hugh loves Margaret he is taking something away from me and giving it to her. Not so. Either he is giving her extra love – in addition to the love he feels for me – or he does not feel love for me but does for her. Even if the latter is true it does not mean that I am unlovable. If I can feel strong and happy in myself then Hugh's love is not necessary for my self-esteem. And if Hugh loves Margaret I

*should be glad, shouldn't I, that he has this happiness in his life?
Nor can I make any demands on him –*

Dear Hugh and Margaret,
   *The thing that makes me suffer is not just that you were having
an affair but that you deceived me so skilfully. It is terrible when
you find out that your idea of reality is not the real reality. Surely
having Margaret at the house all the time and having us three
go out together and Margaret pretending to be my friend was
unnecessary treachery? How often you must have been laughing
at me exchanging your careful heartless glances when we were
together. It was all a show put on for your own cruel amusement
and my being such a dupe and a fool of course lent spice to your
lovemaking. I despise you both. I could never do that. I could
never make a fool of someone I had loved and been married to
or even someone who had been good to me and was my friend –*

   I tear those letters off, both of them, crumple them and
put them in the tiny receptacle for waste paper. Everything
in the roomette is well-planned, adequate. In this cubicle
of metal and upholstery a human being could without
real inconvenience or discomfort pass a life. The train
is westbound out of Calgary. I sit watching the brown
oceanic waves of dry country rising into the foothills and
I weep monotonously, seasickly. Life is not like the dim
ironic stories I like to read, it is like a daytime serial on
television. The banality will make you weep as much as
anything else.
   Girlfriend. Mistress. Nobody says mistress any more, that
I know of. Girl friend sounds brash, yet has a spurious
innocence, is curiously evasive. The possibilities of

mystery and suffering that hung around the old-fashioned word have entirely disappeared. Violetta could never have been anybody's girl friend. But Nell Gwyn could, she was more modern.

Elizabeth Taylor: mistress.

Mia Farrow: girl friend.

This is exactly the sort of game Hugh and Margaret and I would have taken up in our old evenings together, or more likely Margaret and I would have taken it up, amusing then irritating Hugh with our absorption in it.

Neither word would hang well on Margaret.

Last spring we went downtown to buy her a new dress. I was amused and touched by her thriftiness, her cautious taste. She is a rich girl, she lives in the Uplands with her old mother, but she drives a six-year-old Renault, dented along one side, she carries sandwiches to school, she wishes not to give offence.

I tried to persuade her to buy a long straight dress, heavy dark green cotton with gold and silver embroidery.

'It makes me feel like a courtesan,' she said. 'Or like somebody trying to look like a courtesan, which is worse.'

We left the shop and went to a department store where she bought a rose-coloured wool with three-quarter sleeves and self-covered buttons and belt, the sort of dress she always wore, in which her tall-chested figure appeared as usual dry, shy, unyielding. Then we went to a secondhand bookshop, and decided to buy each other presents. I bought her *Lala Rookh* and she bought me a copy of *The Princess*, from which we recited to each other as we walked down the street:

Tears, idle tears, I know not what they mean . . .

We were often giddy, like high school girls. Was this normal, when you come to think of it? We made up stories about people we saw on the street. We laughed so hard we had to sit down on a bus-stop bench, and the bus came, and we still laughed, waving it on. The edge of hysteria. We were attracted to each other because of the man, or to the man because of each other. I used to go home worn out from talking, from laughing, and say to Hugh, 'It's ridiculous. I haven't had a friend like this in years.'

Sitting at the dinner table with us, where she so often sat, she told us she wanted to be called Margaret, not Marg any more. Marg is what most people call her, what the other teachers call her. She teaches English and Physical Education at Hugh's school, the school where Hugh is Principal. Marg Honecker, they say, she's a great girl when you get to know her, really Marg is a wonderful *person*, and you know from the way they say it that she isn't pretty.

'*Marg* is so gawky, in fact it's just like me. I think *Margaret* would make me feel more graceful,' she said at the dinner table, surprising me with the modest hope behind the droll tone. I was concerned for her as I would have been for a daughter and I always remembered, afterwards, to say Margaret. But Hugh did not bother, he said Marg.

'Margaret has quite nice legs. She should wear her skirts shorter.'

'Too muscular. Too athletic.'

'She should grow her hair.'

'She has got hair growing. On her face.'

'What a mean thing to say.'

'I didn't pass judgement on it, I stated a fact.'

It is a fact, Margaret has a soft down growing in front of her ears, at the corners of her mouth. She has the face of a fair, freckled, twelve-year-old boy. Alert, intelligent, bony in a delicate way, often embarrassed. There is something very attractive about Margaret, I would often say, and Hugh would say yes, she was just the sort of woman about whom other women would say there was something very attractive. And why did they say that? he asked. Because she was no threat.

No threat.

Why is it a surprise to find that people other than ourselves are able to tell lies?

We entertained the young teachers. Young men in jeans, young girls in jeans too, or tiny leather skirts. Long-haired, soft-spoken, passive but critical. Teachers have changed. Margaret wore her knee-length rose wool, sat on a hassock for which her legs were too long, helped with the coffee, did not say twenty words all evening. I was in one of my long, peacock dresses, I tried for rapport. I was not above congratulating myself on my flexibility, my *au-courant*-ness, yes, my un-middle-aged style. I was flaunting myself in front of somebody. Margaret? Hugh? Hugh's real pleasure came from Margaret, when everybody had gone.

'The trouble is I just don't know if I *relate*. I don't know if I relate to all this interpersonal *relating*. I mean, sometimes I think all I am is head tripping –'

I laughed at her too, I was proud of her in the perverse way a parent will be proud of a demure child who imitates

self-important guests after they have gone home. But it
was between Hugh and Margaret, really, that such bracing
airs of boundless scepticism blew. He loved her for her
wit, her cynicism, her deceptions. Less than lovable these
seem to me now. They are both shy, Hugh and Margaret,
they are socially awkward, easily embarrassed. But cold
underneath, you may be sure, colder than us easy flirts with
our charms and conquests. They do not reveal themselves.
They will never admit to anything, never have to talk
about anything, no, I could claw their skin and it would be
my own fingers that would bleed. I could scream at them
till my throat bursts and never alter their self-possession,
change the look of their sly averted faces. Both blonde,
both easy blushers, both cold mockers.

They have contempt for me.

That is rubbish of course. Nothing for me. All for each
other. *Love.*

I am coming back from visiting relatives in various parts
of the country. These are people to whom I feel bound
by irritable, almost inexpressible, bonds of sympathy, and
whose deaths I dread nearly as much as I do my own. But
I cannot tell them anything and they cannot do anything
for me. They took me fishing and out to dinner and to
see the view from high buildings, what else could they
do? They never want to hear bad news from me. They
value me for my high spirits and my good looks and my
modest but tangible success – I have translated a collection
of short stories and some children's books from French
into English, they can go into libraries and find my name
on the book jackets – and the older and unluckier among
them, particularly, feel that I have an obligation to bring

them these things. My luck and happiness is one of the few indications they have now that life is not entirely a downhill slide.

So much for kin, so much for visiting.

Suppose I come back to the house and they are both there, I come in and find them in bed, just as in the Dear Abby letters in the paper (at which I do not intend to laugh again)? I go to the closet and take out my remaining clothes, I begin to pack, I talk diplomatically to the bed.

'Would you like a cup of coffee, I imagine you're awfully tired?'

To make them laugh. To make them laugh as if they were reaching out their arms to me. Inviting me to sit on the bed.

On the other hand, perhaps I go into the bedroom and without a word pick up everything I can find – a vase, a bottle of lotion, a picture off the wall, shoes, clothes, Hugh's tape recorder – and hurl these things at the bed, the window, the walls; then grab and tear the bedclothes and kick the mattress and scream and slap their faces and beat their bare bodies with the hairbrush. As the wife did in *God's Little Acre*, a book I read aloud to Hugh, with a comic accent, during a long dusty car trip across the prairies.

We may have told her that. Many anecdotes, of our courtship and even our honeymoon, were trotted out for her. Showing off. I was. What Hugh was doing I have no way of knowing.

A howl comes out, out of me, amazing protest.

I put my arm across my open mouth and to stop the pain I bite it, I bite my arm, and then I get up and lower the little sink and wash my face at it, and put on blusher and comb my hair, and smooth my eyebrows and go out.

The cars in the train are named after explorers, or mountains or lakes. I often travelled by train when the children were small, and Hugh and I were poor, because the train allowed children under six to ride free. I remember the names written on the heavy doors, and how I used to have to push the doors and hold them open and urge the scrambling unsteady children through. I was always nervous between cars, as if the children could fall off somehow, though I knew they couldn't. I had to sleep close beside them at night and sit with them climbing around me in the daytime; my body felt bruised by their knees and elbows and feet. I did think then that it would be lovely to be a woman travelling alone, able to sit after a meal drinking coffee and looking out of the window, able to go to the club car and have a drink. Now one of my daughters is hitchhiking in Europe and the other is a counsellor at a camp for handicapped children, and all that time of care and confusion that seemed as if it would never end seems as if it never was.

Somehow without my noticing it we have got into the mountains. I ask for a gin and tonic. The glass catches the sunlight, reflecting a circle of light on the white mat. This makes the drink seem pure and restorative to me, like mountain water. I drink thirstily.

From the club car a little staircase goes up to the dome, where people have been sitting no doubt since Calgary, waiting for the mountains. Latecomers hoping for seats climb part way up the stairs, crane their necks, come down disgruntled.

'Them that's up there's going to stay for a week,' says

a fat woman in a turban, turning around to address a procession of what may be grandchildren. Her bulk fills the whole stairway. Many of us smile, as if the size and loudness and innocent importance of this old woman were being offered to us, as encouragement.

A man sitting by himself, further down the car with his back to the window, looks at me, smiling. His face reminds me of the face on some movie star of a past era. Outdated good looks, a willed and conscious, yet easily defeated, charm. Dana Andrews. Somebody like that. I have an unpleasant impression of mustard-coloured clothes.

He does not come and sit beside me, but keeps looking at me from time to time. When I get up and leave the car I feel him watching. I wonder if he will follow me. What if he does? I haven't time for him, not now, I can't spare him attention. I used to be ready for almost any man. When I was in my teens, and later too, when I was a young wife. Any man looking at me in a crowd, any teacher letting his eyes pause on me in a classroom, a stranger at a party, might be transformed, some time when I was alone, into the lover I was always searching for – somebody passionate, intelligent, brutal, kind – and made to play opposite me in those simple satisfactory, explosive scenes everybody knows about. Later on, a few years married, I took steps to solidify fantasies. At parties, with my push-up brassiere, my tousled Italian cut, my black dress with the shoestring straps, I kept on the lookout for some man to fall in love with me, involve me in a volcanic affair. That did happen, more or less. You see it is not so simple, not so plain a case as my grieving now, my sure sense of betrayal, would lead anybody to believe. No. Men have left marks on me which I did not have to worry about hiding from Hugh, since there are parts of my body at which he has never looked. I have lied as well as I have been lied to. Men have expressed ravenous appreciation of my nipples and my appendix scar and the moles on my back and have also said to me, as it is proper for them to do, 'Now don't make too big a thing of this,' and even, 'I really do love my wife.' After a while I gave up on this sort of thing and went secretly to see a psychiatrist who led me to understand that I had been trying to get Hugh's attention. He suggested I get it instead by kindness, artfulness, and sexiness around the house. I was not able to argue with him, nor could I share his optimism. He seemed to me to have a poor grasp on Hugh's character, assuming that certain refusals were simply the result of not having been properly asked. To me they seemed basic, absolute. I could not imagine what tactics could alter them. But he was shrewd enough. He said he assumed I wanted to stay with my husband. He was right; I could not think, I could not bear to think, of an alternative.

The train stops at Field, just inside the British Columbia border. I get off and walk beside the tracks, in a hot wind.

'Nice to get off the train for a bit, isn't it?'

I almost fail to recognize him. He is short, as I believe those handsome movie stars often were, too. His clothes really are mustard-coloured. That is, the jacket and pants are; his open shirt is red, his shoes burgundy. He has the voice of somebody whose dealings bring him into daily and dependent contact with the public.

'I hope you don't mind me asking. Are you a Leo?'

'No.'

'I asked you because I'm an Aries. An Aries can usually

recognize a Leo. Those signs are sympathetic ones to each other.'

'I'm sorry.'

'I thought you looked like you would be an interesting person to talk to.'

I go and shut myself into my roomette and read my magazine, down to the ads for liquor and men's shoes. But I feel sorry. Probably he meant nothing more than he said. I am an interesting person to talk to. The reason is that I will listen to anything. It may be because of those articles in magazines I used to read as a teen-ager (when any title with the word popularity in it could both chill and compel me), urging the development of this receptive social art. I don't mean to do it. But face to face with anyone who has a conviction, a delusion – which most people have – or only a long procession of dim experience to share, I feel something like amazement, enough to paralyse me. You ought to get up and walk away, Hugh says, that's what I would do.

'Asking you were you a Leo, that was just for something to say. What I wanted to ask you was different but I didn't know how to put it. As soon as I saw you I knew I'd seen you before.'

'Oh, I don't think so. I don't think you have.'

'I believe that we lead more than one life.'

Diverse experience, many lives in one, is that what he means? Perhaps he is about to justify unfaithfulness to his wife, if he has a wife.

'I believe it. I have been born before and I have died before. It's true.'

You see? I say to Hugh, already starting a story for him, about this man, in my mind. *They always find me.*

'Did you ever hear of the Rosicrucians?'

'Are they the ones who advertise about the mastery of life?'

Irony may be wasted but he can detect flippancy. The boring reproachfulness of the convert hardens his tone.

'Six years ago I saw one of those ads. I was in a bad way. My marriage had broke up. I was drinking more than was good for me. But that wasn't all the trouble. You know? That wasn't the real trouble. I just used to sit and think, why am I here anyway. Like religion – I'd given all that up. I couldn't tell if there was such a thing as a soul. But if not, what the hell? You know what I mean?

'Then I wrote in and got some of their literature and started going to their meetings. First time I went, I was scared it was going to be a bunch of nuts. I didn't know what to expect, you know? What a shock I got when I saw the kind of people there. Influential people. Wealthy people. Professional people. All cultured and educated top-drawer people. This is not crackpot stuff. It is known, scientifically proven.'

I don't dispute.

'One hundred and forty-four years. That is the span from the start of one life to the next. So if you or I dies at, say, seventy, that's what – seventy-four years, seventy-four years to the start of the next life when our soul is born again.'

'Do you remember?'

'From the one life to the next, you mean? Well, you know yourself, the ordinary person doesn't remember a thing. But once your mind is opened up, once you know what is going on, why, then you start to remember. Only one life I myself know about for sure. In Spain and in Mexico. I was one of the conquistadors. You know the conquistadors?'

'Yes.'

'A funny thing, I always knew I could ride horseback. I never did, you know, city kid, we never had any money. Never was on a horse. Just the same I knew. Then at a meeting a couple of years ago, Rosicrucian conference in the Hotel Vancouver, a fellow came up to me, older man, he was from California, and he says, *You were there. You were one of them*, he says. I didn't know what he was talking about. *In Spain*, he says. *We were together.* He said I was one of the ones that went out to Mexico and he was one of the ones that stayed behind. He knew my face. And you want to know the strangest thing of all? Just as he was bending over to speak to me, I had got the impression that he was wearing a hat. Which he wasn't. You know the plumed kind of hat. And I got the impression his hair was dark and long, instead of grey and short. All before he ever said a word of this to me. Isn't that a remarkable thing?'

Yes. A remarkable thing. But I had heard things before. I have heard from people who regularly see astral bodies floating around just under the ceiling, people who rule all their days by astrology, who have changed their names and moved to new addresses so that the numerical values of the new letters will bless them. These are the ideas people live with in this world. And I can see why.

'What do you want to bet you were there too?'

'In Spain?'

'In Spain. I thought as soon as I saw you. You were a Spanish lady. You probably stayed behind, too. That explains what I see. When I look at you – and I don't mean any offence, you're a very attractive woman – I see you younger than you are now. That is probably because when I left you behind in Spain you were only twenty, twenty-one years old. And I never saw you again in that life. You don't mind me saying that?'

'No. No. It's very pleasant, really, to be seen like that.'

'I always knew, you know, there has to be something more to life. I'm not a materialistic person. Not by nature. That's why I'm not much of a success. I'm a real estate salesman. But I guess I don't give it the attention you've got to give it, if you want to be a success. It doesn't matter. I've got nobody but myself.'

Me too. I've got nobody but myself. And can't think what to do. I can't think what to do with this man except to make him into a story for Hugh, a curiosity, a joke for Hugh. Hugh wants life seen that way, he cherishes a dry tone. Bare feelings he must pass over, like bare flesh.

'Do you love me, do you love Margaret, do you love us both?'

'I don't know.'

He was reading a magazine. He reads whenever I speak to him. He said those words in a bored, exhausted, barely audible voice. Blood from a stone.

'Will I divorce you, do you want to marry her?'

'I don't know.'

Margaret approached on the subject managed to turn the conversation to some ceramic mugs she had just bought us, as a present, and to hope that I would not throw them out, in my rage, because she, Margaret, would find them useful should she ever move in. Hugh smiled to hear that, he was grateful. If we make jokes we can all survive. I wonder.

The happiest moment in our marriage I have no trouble deciding on. It was in Northern Michigan, on a trip when the children were small. A shoddy carnival, under grey skies. They rode on a miniature train. We wandered off together and stopped in front of a cage with a chicken in it. A sign said that this chicken could play the piano. I said that I wanted to hear it play the piano, and Hugh dropped a dime. What happened was that when the dime dropped, a trap door opened, a kernel of corn descended on the keys of the toy piano, and the chicken, pecking at the corn, produced a tinny note. I was shocked and called it a fraud; for some reason I had believed the sign. I had believed that the chicken would actually *play the piano*. But it was Hugh's act, his dropping the dime, such uncharacteristic frivolity, that seemed so amazing, an avowal of love, more than anything he did or said at any other time, any high point of need or satisfaction. That act was like something startling and temporary – a very small bird, say, with rare colours – sitting close by, in a corner of your vision, that you dare not look at openly. In that moment our kindness to each other was quite unclouded, not tactical, our struggles seemed unreal. A gate had opened, very likely. But we did not get past.

The unhappiest moment I could never tell you. All our fights blend into each other and are in fact re-enactments of the same fight, in which we punish each other – I with words, Hugh with silence – for being each other. We never needed any more than that.

He is the one person I would not mind seeing suffer. I would not mind seeing him drawn out, beads of pain on

his face, so that I could say, *Now you know, don't you, now you
see.* Yes. In his extremest pain I would show him my little,
satisfied, withdrawing smile. I would show it.

'When I came to understand about this it was like I had
been given a fresh start.'

People believe in fresh starts, nowadays. Right up to the
end of their lives. It has to be allowed. To start again with
a new person, your old selves known only to yourself;
nobody can stop anyone from doing that. Generous people
throw the doors open and provide blessings. Why not? It
will happen anyway.

The train is beyond Revelstoke, in the gradually
diminishing mountains. The coffee car is empty and
has been empty for some time, except for me and the
Rosicrucian. The waiters have cleaned up.

'I must go back.'

He does not try to stop me.

'It's been a great pleasure talking to you and I hope you
don't think I'm crazy.'

'No. No, I don't.'

He takes several pamphlets from his inside pocket. 'You
might want to look at these if you find the time.'

I thank him.

He rises, he even bows to me slightly, with a Spanish
dignity.

I walked into the Vancouver station alone, carrying my
suitcase. The Rosicrucian has disappeared somewhere, he
has vanished as if I had invented him. Perhaps he did not
come as far as Vancouver, perhaps he got off at one of the
Fraser Valley towns, in the chilly early morning.

Nobody to meet me, nobody knew I was coming. Part of the interior of the station appears to be boarded up, closed off. Even now, one of the two times in the day when there is sure to be some activity in it, this place looks cavernous, deserted.

Twenty-one years ago Hugh met me here, at this time in the morning. A noisy crowded place then. I had come west to marry him. He was carrying flowers which he dropped when he saw me. Less self-possessed in those days, though not more communicative. Red-faced, comically severe-looking, full of emotion which he bore staunchly, like a private affliction. When I touched him, he would never loosen. I could feel the stiff cords in his neck. He would shut his eyes and proceed, by himself. He may have foreseen things; the embroidered dresses, the enthusiasms, the infidelities. And I was not often ready to be kind. Annoyed to see the flowers drop, wishing to be greeted in other than comicbook style, dismayed to face his innocence which seemed even greater than my own, I did not mind letting him see a corner of my dissatisfaction. There are layers on layers in this marriage, mistakes in timing, wrongs on wrongs, nobody could get to the bottom of it.

But we went straight to each other; we grabbed hold and hung on. We crushed the retrieved unappreciated flowers, we clung like people surfacing, miraculously rescued. And not for the last time. That could happen again; it could happen again and again. And it would always be the same mistake.

Aooh.

A cry fills the railway station, a real cry, coming from outside myself. I can see that other people have stopped, have heard it too. The cry is like that of an invader, full of terrible grievances. People look towards the open doors, towards Hastings Street, as if they expect vengeance to come rushing in on them. But now it can be seen that the cry comes from one old man, from an old man who has been sitting with other old men on a bench at one end of the station. There used to be several benches; now there is just one, with old men sitting on it, no more noticed than old newspapers. The old man has risen to his feet to let out this cry, which is more a cry of rage, of conscious rage and terrorization, than a cry of pain. As the cry fades out he half turns, staggers, tries to hang onto the air with fully raised arms and open fingers, falls, and lies on the floor, twitching. The other old men sitting on the bench do not bend over to help him. Not one of them has risen, in fact they hardly look at him, but continue reading the papers or staring at their feet. The twitching stops.

He is dead, I know it. A man in a dark suit, some manager or official, comes out to inspect him. Some people continue with their baggage as if not a thing has happened. They do not look in that direction. Others like me approach the place where the old man is lying, and then stop; approach and stop, as if he were giving out some dangerous kind of ray.

'Must've been his heart.'

'Stroke.'

'Is he gone?'

'Sure. See the guy putting his coat.'

The official stands now in his shirt sleeves. His jacket will have to go to the cleaners. I turn away with difficulty, I walk towards the station entrance. It seems as if I should not leave, as if the cry of the man dying, now dead, is still demanding something of me, but I cannot think what it is. By that cry Hugh, and Margaret, and the Rosicrucian, and I, everybody alive, is pushed back. What we say and feel no longer rings true, it is slightly beside the point. As if we were all wound up a long time ago and were spinning out of control, whirring, making noises, but at a touch could stop, and see each other for the first time, harmless and still. This is a message; I really believe it is; but I don't see how I can deliver it.

WINTER WIND

From my grandmother's bedroom window you could look across the CPR tracks to a wide stretch of the Wawanash River, meandering in reeds. All frozen now, all ice and untracked snow. Even on stormy days the clouds might break before supper time, and then there was a fierce red sunset. Like Siberia, my grandmother said, offended, you would think we were living on the edge of the wilderness. It was all farms, of course, and tame bush, no wilderness at all, but winter buried the fence posts.

The storm started before noon, when we were in Chemistry, and we watched its progress hopefully, looking forward to something disruptive, to blocked roads and short supplies, and bedding down in school corridors. I imagined myself liberated by a crisis-charged atmosphere, aided by a power failure and candlelight and stirring songs offered against the roar of the wind, blanketed down with Mr Harmer, a junior teacher whose eye I often tried to catch in Assembly, comforted by his embrace at first merely warming and comradely, which might yet turn, in all the darkness and confusion – candle by this time blown out – to something more urgent and personal. Things did not get that far. But we were dismissed early, the school buses set out with their lights on in the middle of the afternoon. Usually I took the Whitechurch bus to the first corner west of town, and walked from there, three-quarters of a mile or so, to our house at the edge of the bush. This night, as two or three times a winter, I went to stay at my grandmother's house, in town.

The hallway of this house was all wood, polished, fragrant, smooth, cozy as the inside of a nutshell. A yellow lamp was on in the dining room. I did my homework – something I never bothered with, at home, because there was no place or time for it – on the dining-room table, after Aunt Madge had spread a newspaper to protect the cloth. Aunt Madge was my great-aunt, my grandmother's sister, they were widows.

Aunt Madge was ironing (they ironed everything, down to underwear and potholders) and my grandmother was making a carrot pudding for supper. Lovely smells. Compare this to the scene at home. The only warm room there was the kitchen; we had a wood stove. My brother brought in wood, and left tracks of dirty snow on the linoleum: I swore at him. Dirt and chaos threatened all the time. My mother often had to lie down on the couch, and tell her grievances. I argued with her whenever possible, and she said my heart would be broken when I had children of my own. We were selling eggs at this time, and everywhere there were baskets of eggs with bits of straw and feathers and hen-dirt stuck to them, waiting to be cleaned. I believed that a smell of hencoops came into the house on boots and clothes and you could not get rid of it.

In the dining room I could look up at two dark oil paintings. They had been done by another sister of my grandmother's, who had died in early middle age. One showed a cottage by a stream and one a dog with a bird in its mouth. My mother had pointed out that the bird was too big, in comparison with the dog.

'Well it was not Tina's mistake, then,' my grandmother said. 'It was copied from a calendar.'

'She was talented but she gave it up when she got married,' said Aunt Madge approvingly.

There was also in the room a photograph of my grandmother and Aunt Madge, with their parents and this sister who had died, and another sister who had married a Catholic, so that it seemed almost as bad as if she died, though peace was made later on. I did not bother to look at this photograph, except in a passing way, but after my grandmother's death and Aunt Madge's removal to a nursing-home (where she lives yet, lives on and on, unrecognizable, unrecognizing, completely divested of herself, dried up like a little monkey, past all memory and maybe past bewilderment, free), I salvaged it, and have taken it with me wherever I go.

The parents are seated. The mother firm and unsmiling, in a black silk dress, hair scanty and centre-parted, eyes bulging and faded. The father handsome still, bearded, hand-on-knee, patriarchal. A bit of Irish acting here, a relishing of the part, which he might as well relish since he cannot now escape it? When young he was popular in taverns; even after his children were born he had the name of a drinker, a great celebrator. But he gave up those ways, he turned his back on his friends and brought his family here, to take up land in the newly opened Huron Tract. This photograph was the sign and record of his achievement: respectability, moderate prosperity, mollified wife in a black silk dress, the well-turned-out tall daughters.

Though as a matter of fact their dresses look frightful; flouncy and countrified. All except Aunt Madge's; a tight, simple, high-necked affair, black with some sparkle about it, perhaps of jet. She wears it with a sense of style, tilts her head a little to the side, smiles without embarrassment at the camera. She was a notable seamstress, and would have made her own dress, understanding what suited her. But it is likely she made her sisters' dresses also, and what are we to make of that? My grandmother is done up in something with floppy sleeves and a wide velvet collar, and a sort of vest with crisscrossed velvet trim; something seems askew at the waist. She wears this outfit with no authority and indeed with a shamefaced, flushed, half-grinning and half-desperate apology. She looks a great tomboy, her mop of hair rolled up but sliding forward, in danger of falling down. But she wears a wedding ring; my father had been born. She was at that time the only one married; the eldest, also the tallest of the sisters.

At supper my grandmother said, 'How is your mother?' and at once my spirits dropped.

'All right.'

She was not all right, she never would be. She had a slowly progressive, incurable disease.

'The poor thing,' Aunt Madge said.

'I have a terrible time understanding her on the phone,' my grandmother said. 'It just seems the worse her voice gets, the more she wants to talk.'

My mother's vocal cords were partly paralysed. Sometimes I would have to act as her interpreter, a job that made me wild with shame.

'I wouldn't wonder she gets lonely out there,' Aunt Madge said. 'The poor soul.'

'It would not make any difference where she was,' my grandmother said, 'if people cannot understand her.'

My grandmother wanted then a report on our household routine. Had we got the washing done, had we got the washing dried, had we got the ironing done? The baking? My father's socks mended? She wished to be of help. She would make biscuits and muffins, a pie (did we have a pie?); bring the mending and she would do it. The ironing too. She would go out to our place for a day, to help, as soon as the roads were clear. I was embarrassed to think we needed help, and I especially tried to ward off the visits. Before my grandmother came I would be obliged to try to clean the house, reorganize the cupboards as much as possible, shove certain disgraces – a roasting-pan I had never got around to scrubbing, a basket of torn clothes I had told her were already mended – under the sink or the beds. But I never cleaned thoroughly enough, my reorganization proved to be haphazard, the disgraces came unfailingly to light, and it was clear how we failed, how disastrously we fell short of that ideal of order and cleanliness, household decency, which I as much as anybody else believed in. Believing in it was not enough. And it was not just for myself but for my mother that I had to feel shame.

'Your mother isn't well, she cannot get around to things,' said my grandmother, in a voice that indicated doubt as to how much would have been gotten around to, in any case.

I tried to present good reports. In the old days, when such things were sometimes true, I would say that my mother had made some pickled beets, or that she was busy ripping worn-out sheets down the middle and sewing the outer edges together, to make them last longer. My grandmother perceived the effort, and registered the transparent falsity of this picture (false even if its details were true); she said, well, is she really?

'She's painting the kitchen cupboards,' I said. It was not a lie. My mother was painting our cupboards yellow and on each of the drawers and doors she was painting some decoration; flowers or fish or a sailboat or even a flag. Although her hands and arms trembled she could control the brush sufficiently for a short time. So these designs were not so badly done. Just the same there was something crude and glaring about them, something that seemed to reflect the stiffness and intensity of the stage of the disease my mother had now got into. I did not mention them at all to my grandmother, knowing that she was going to find them extremely bizarre and upsetting. My grandmother and Aunt Madge believed, as most people do, that houses should be made to look as much as possible like other people's houses. Some of the ideas my mother had conceived and carried out could not help but make me see the sense in this conformity.

Also, the paint, the brushes, the turpentine, were left for me to clean up, since my mother always worked till she was exhausted, then stretched out groaning on the couch.

'There,' said my grandmother with annoyance and satisfaction, 'she will get herself involved in something like that, which she ought to know will wear her out, and she will not be able to do any of the things that have to be done. She will be painting the cupboards when she would be better off getting your father's dinner.'

Truer words were never spoken.

After supper I went out, in spite of the weather. A blizzard in town hardly seemed like a blizzard to me; so much was blocked out by the houses and the buildings. I met my friend Betty Gosley, another country girl who was staying in town with her married sister. We were pleased and rather excited to be in town, to be able to *go out* like this into some kind of evening life, not just the dark and cold and rushing storms that wrapped our houses in the country. Here were the streets leading into one another, the lights evenly spaced, a human design that had taken root and was working. People were curling at the curling rink, skating at the Arena, watching the show at the Lyceum Theatre, shooting pool in the poolroom, sitting around in two cafés. From most of these activities we were barred by age or sex or lack of money, but we could walk around, we could drink lemon Cokes – the cheapest thing – in the Blue Owl Café, watching who came in, talking with a girl we knew who worked there. Betty and I were not exactly at the centre of power, and we spent a lot of time, like nonentities at court, discussing the affairs of those more powerful and fortunate, speculating on the ups and downs of their careers, judging harshly of their morals. We told each other that we would not for a million dollars go out with certain boys, the truth being that we would have dissolved in happiness if these boys had even called us by name. We talked about which girls might be pregnant. (The winter following this, Betty Gosley herself became pregnant, by a neighbouring farmer with a speech impediment and a purebred dairy herd, whom she had never so much as mentioned to me; she then withdrew, abashed and proud, into the privileged life of married women, and could talk of nothing but kitchen showers, linens, baby clothes, morning sickness, which made me both envious and appalled.)

We walked past the house where Mr Harmer lived. His were the upstairs windows. The lights were on. What did he do in the evenings? He did not take advantage of the entertainment offered in town, was not to be found at the movies or the hockey games. He was not really very popular. And this was why I had chosen him. I liked to think I had a special taste. His pale fine hair, his soft moustache, his narrow shoulders in his worn, tweed, leather-patched jacket, the waspish words which were his classroom substitute for physical force. Once I had talked to him – it was the only time I had talked to him – in the town library. He had recommended to me a novel about Welsh coal miners, which I did not like. There was no sex in it, only strikes and unions, and men.

Walking past his house, loitering under his windows, with Betty Gosley, I did not show my interest in him in any straightforward way but instead made scornful jokes about him, called him a sissy and a hermit, accused him of shameful private practices which kept him home evenings. Betty joined in this speculation but did not really understand why it had to be so wild or go on so long. Then to keep her interest up I began to tease her, I pretended to believe she was in love with him. I said I had seen him looking up her skirt going up the stairs. I said I was going to throw a snowball at the wall between his windows, call him down for her. She was entertained at first by this fantasy, but before long she grew cold and bewildered and cranky, and headed back towards the main street by herself, forcing me to follow.

And all this wildness, crudity, hilarity, was as far as possible from my private dreams, which were of most tender meetings, chaste embraces melting into holy passion, harmony shadowed by the inevitable parting, high romantic love.

Aunt Madge had been happily married. The happiness of her marriage was remembered and commented on, even in that community where it is usually thought much better to leave such things unsaid. (Even today, if you ask how somebody is, the answer will often be that they are doing well, have bought two cars, have bought a dishwasher, and this way of answering is only partly based on simple, natural, poverty-bred materialism; it comes also from a superstitious kind of delicacy, which skirts even words like *happy, frightened, sad.*)

Aunt Madge's husband had been a leisurely sort of farmer, with political interests; he was opinionated, stubborn, entertaining. There were never any children, to dilute her feeling for him. She took joy in his company. She would never refuse an invitation to go to town with him, to go for a drive with him, even though she took her life in her hands every time she got into his car. He was a terrible driver, and in his later years half-blind. She would never shame him, by learning how to drive, herself. Her support of him was perfect. She could have been held up as an example, an ideal wife, except that she gave no impression of sacrifice, of resignations, of doing one's duty, such as is looked for in ideals. She was light-hearted, impudent sometimes, so she was not particularly respected for her love, but held to be lucky, or half-dotty, whichever you liked. After his death she was not really interested in her life; she looked on it as a waiting period – she believed firmly and literally in Heaven – but she had been too well brought up to give way to moping.

My grandmother's marriage had been another matter. The story was that she had married my grandfather while still in love with, though very angry at, another man. My mother told me this. She loved stories, particularly those full of tragedy and renunciation and queer turns of fate. Aunt Madge and my grandmother, of course, never mentioned anything about it. But as I grew up I found that everybody seemed to know it. The other man remained in the district, as most people did. He farmed, and married three times. He was a cousin of both my grandfather and my grandmother, and so was often in their house, as they were in his. Before he proposed to his third wife – this was what my mother told me – he came to see my grandmother. She came out of her kitchen and rode up and down the lane in his buggy with him, for anybody to see. Did he ask her advice? Her permission? My mother strongly believed that he had asked her to run away with him. I wonder. They would both have been around fifty years old at that time. Where could they have run to? Besides, they were Presbyterians. No one ever accused them of misbehaviour. Proximity, impossibility, renunciation. That does make for an enduring kind of love. And I believe that would be my grandmother's choice, that self-glorifying dangerous self-denying passion, never satisfied, never risked, to last a lifetime. Not admitted to, either, except perhaps that one time, one or two times, under circumstances of great stress. *We must never speak of this again.*

My grandfather was not a man to complain. He had a taste of solitude, he had married rather late, he had chosen another man's offended sweetheart, for reasons he did not divulge to anybody. In the wintertime he finished his chores early, doing everything thoroughly and efficiently. Then he read. He read books on economics and history. He studied Esperanto. He read his way several times through solid shelves of Victorian novels. He did not discuss what he read. His opinions, unlike his brother-in-law's, were not made public. His demands on life, his expectations of other people, seemed to be so slight there was never any possibility of disappointing him. Whether my grandmother had disappointed him, privately, and so thoroughly that any offers he might have made had been withdrawn, nobody could know.

And how is anybody to know, I think as I put this down, how am I to know what I claim to know? I have used these people, not all of them, but some of them, before. I have tricked them out and altered them and shaped them any way at all, to suit my purposes. I am not doing that now, I am being as careful as I can, but I stop and wonder, I feel compunction. Though I am only doing in a large and public way what has always been done, what my mother did, and other people did, who mentioned to me my grandmother's story. Even in that close-mouthed place, stories were being made. People carried their stories around with them. My grandmother carried hers, and nobody ever spoke of it to her face.

But that only takes care of the facts. I have said other things. I have said that my grandmother would choose a certain kind of love. I have implied that she would be stubbornly, secretly, destructively romantic. Nothing she ever said to me, or in my hearing, would bear this out. Yet I have not invented it, I really believe it. Without any proof I believe it, and so I must believe that we get messages another way, that we have connections that cannot be investigated, but have to be relied on.

This turned out to be a wild heavy storm, lasting a week. But on the third afternoon, sitting in school, I looked out and saw that the wind had apparently died, there was no snow blowing any more, there was even a break in the clouds. I thought at once, and with relief, that I would be able to go home that night. Home always looked a great deal better, after a couple of nights at my grandmother's. It was a place where I did not have to watch too closely what I said and did. My mother objected to things, but in a way I had the upper hand of her. After all, it was I who heated tubs of water on the stove and hauled the washing machine from the porch and did the washing, once a week; I who scrubbed the floor, and with an ill grace made her endless cups of tea. So I could say *shit* when I emptied the dustpan into the stove and some dirt went on the lid; I could say that I meant to have lovers and use birth control and never have any children (actually I wanted to make an enviable marriage, both safe and passionate, and I had pictured the nightgown I would wear when my lover-husband came to visit me for the first time in the maternity ward); I could say that there was nothing wrong with writing about sex in books and also that there was no such thing as a dirty word. The loud argumentative scandalous person I was at home had not much more to do with my real self than the discreet unrevealing person I was in my grandmother's house, but judging both as roles it can be seen that the first had more scope. I did not get tired of it so easily, in fact I did not get tired of it at all.

And comfort palls. The ironed sheets, the lovely eiderdown, the jasmine soap. I would give it all up for the moment in order to be able to drop my coat where I chose, leave the room without having to say where I was going, read with my feet in the oven, if I liked.

After school I went around to my grandmother's house to tell them that I was going home. By this time the wind had begun to blow again. I knew the roads would be drifted, the storm was not really over. But I wanted more than ever to go home. When I opened the door and smelled the pies baking – winter apples – and heard the two old voices greet me (Aunt Madge would always call out, 'Now, whoever can *this* be?' as she had done when I was a little girl), I thought that I could not bear any more of it – the tidiness, the courtesies, the waiting. All their time was waiting time. Wait for the mail, wait for supper, wait for bed. You might imagine that my mother's time was waiting time, but it was not. Lying on the couch, sick and crippled, she was still full of outrageous plans and fantasies, demands that could not be met, fights that could be picked; she kept herself going. At home there was always confusion and necessity. Eggs to be cleaned, wood to be brought in, the fire to be kept going, food to be prepared, mess to be cleaned away. I was always hurrying and remembering and forgetting, and then I would sit down after supper in the middle of everything, waiting for the dishwater to heat on the stove, and get lost in my library book.

There was a difference too in books read at home and at my grandmother's. At my grandmother's, books could not quite get out. Some atmosphere of the place pushed them back, contained them, dimmed them. There was not room. At home, in spite of all that was going on, there was room for everything.

'I won't be here for supper,' I said. 'I'm going home.'

I had taken off my things and sat down to have tea. My grandmother was making it.

'You can't ever set out in this,' she said confidently. 'Are you worrying about the work? Are you afraid they can't get on without you?'

'No, but I better get home. It's not blowing hard. The ploughs have been out.'

'On the highway, maybe. I never heard yet of a plough getting down your road.'

The place where we lived, like so much else, was a mistake.

'She's afraid of my pie crust, that's what it is,' cried Aunt

Madge in mock distress. 'She's just plain running away from my pie.'

'That may be it,' I said.

'You eat a piece before you go. It won't take long to cool.'

'She isn't going,' my grandmother said, still lightly. 'She isn't walking out into that storm.'

'It isn't a *storm*,' I said, looking for help towards the window, which showed solid white.

My grandmother put her cup down, rattling it on the saucer. 'All right. Go then. Just go. Go if you want to. Go and get frozen to death.'

I had never heard my grandmother lose control before. I had never imagined that she could. It seems strange to me now, but the fact is that I had never heard anything like plain hurt or anger in her voice, or seen it on her face. Everything had been indirect, calmly expressed. Her judgements had seemed remote, full of traditional authority, not personal. The abdication here was what amazed me. There were tears in her voice, and when I looked at her there were tears in her eyes and then pouring down her face. She was weeping, she was furious and weeping.

'Never mind then. You just go. Go and get yourself frozen to death like what happened to poor Susie Heferman.'

'Oh, dear,' said Aunt Madge. 'That's true. That's true.'

'Poor Susan living all alone,' my grandmother said, addressing me as if that were my fault.

'It was out on our old line, dear,' said Aunt Madge comfortingly. 'You wouldn't know who we mean. Susie Heferman that was married to Gershom Bell. Mrs Gershom Bell. Susie Heferman to us. We went to school with her.'

'And Gershom died last year and both her daughters are married and away,' my grandmother said, wiping her eyes and her nose with a fresh handkerchief from her sleeve, composing herself somewhat, but not ceasing to look at me angrily. 'Poor Susan had to go out by herself to milk the cows. She would keep on her cows and go on by herself. She went out last night and she should have tied the clothesline to the door but she didn't, and on the way back she lost her path, and they found her this noon.'

'Alex Beattie phoned us,' Aunt Madge said. 'He was one of the ones found her. He was upset.'

'Was she dead?' I said foolishly.

'They cannot thaw you back to life,' my grandmother said, 'after you have been lying in a snowbank overnight in this weather.' She had stopped crying.

'And think of poor Susie there just trying to get from the stable to the house,' Aunt Madge said. 'She shouldn't have hung on to her cows. She thought she could manage. And she had the bad leg. I bet that give out on her.'

'That's terrible,' I said. 'I won't go home.'

'You go if you like,' my grandmother said at once.

'No. I'll stay.'

'You never know what can happen to a person,' said Aunt Madge. She wept too, but more naturally than my grandmother. With her it was just a comfortable bit of leakage round the eyes, it seemed to do good. 'Who would have thought that would be the end of Susie, she was more my age than your grandmother's and what a girl for dances, she used to say she'd ride twenty miles to an open cutter for a good dance. We traded dresses once, we did it for a joke. If we had ever known then what would happen now!'

'Nobody knows. What would be the use of it?' my grandmother said.

I ate a large supper. No more mention was made of Susie Heferman.

I understand various things now, though my understanding them is not of much use to anybody. I understand that Aunt Madge could feel sympathy for my mother because Aunt Madge must have seen my mother, even before her illness, as an afflicted person. Anything that was exceptional she could see, simply, as affliction. But my grandmother would have to see an example. My grandmother had schooled herself, watched herself, learned what to do and say; she had understood the importance of acceptance, had yearned for it, had achieved it, had known there was a possibility of not achieving it. Aunt Madge had never known that. My grandmother could feel endangered by my mother, could perhaps even understand – at some level she would always have to deny – those efforts of my mother's that she successfully, and never quite openly, ridiculed and blamed.

I understand that my grandmother wept angrily for Susie Heferman and also for herself, that she knew how I longed for home, and why. She knew and did not understand how this had happened or how it could have been different or how she herself, once so baffled and struggling, had become another old woman whom people deceived and placated and were anxious to get away from.

MEMORIAL

Eileen woke up in full daylight to see June standing beside the bed holding a tray. On the tray was a mug of coffee, cream and sugar, slices of homemade whole-wheat toast.

'Oh, Lord. That's what I was going to do for you.'

'What was?'

'Bring you coffee in bed. I was awake earlier. I was just waiting. I was waiting till it got a little more light.'

Eileen did not say that she had been awake all night, or almost all night, aware of the firmness of the mattress, the smoothness of the sheets, and herself as a foreign and uncalled-for object on top of them.

'How can you live without a watch?' said June, and set the tray down. 'It's just as well you didn't get up and try anything. You couldn't have worked the grinder.'

Indeed Eileen had forgotten. They ground their own coffee. They got two or three kinds of beans from an import store downtown, and produced their own blend.

'Anyway I had to get up,' June said. 'There's an incredible lot of things to do.'

'I can help.'

'Help me now by drinking your coffee and staying put while I get some of the thundering herd out of the way.'

She meant the children, that was what she always called them. The same now. The same bright offhand tone. She was already dressed, in orange pants and an embroidered Mexican blouse of unbleached cotton. She looked entirely as usual, her sandy hair pulled back and held with an elastic band, long wispy bangs, loose on her forehead. The same look of quivering eagerness, bossiness, busyness, both touching and infuriating. Missionary wife. Ruddy skin, a rough texture to her cheeks and neck. Bereavement had heightened her colour, if anything.

Eileen saw that she had been naive to have expected a change. She had thought June's body might have loosened, in her grief, that her voice might have grown uncertain, or been silenced. But last night when they embraced, at the airport, she felt her sister's body humming as always with its separate power; she heard June's voice break through her own beginning consolations with edgy insistence, almost triumphing.

'It's so windy, did you have a horrible flight?'

June sent the younger children off to school. June and Ewart had seven children – that is, seven counting Douglas. The first five were boys. Then they had adopted two girls, of Indian or part-Indian blood. The youngest was still in kindergarten. Douglas had been seventeen.

Eileen could hear June talking on the phone.

'I don't want their feelings repressed but I don't want them artificially stimulated, either. Do you see what I mean? Yes. That's their normal environment. I think they're better off. But I want them to have an opportunity to express their grief. If they want to express their grief. Yes. Exactly. Yes. Thank you. Thanks so much.'

Then she phoned to arrange for a coffee-maker.

'I knew at the time I should have bought a fifty-cup model and not the thirty. I always end up doing this. Oh, no. No, it's all arranged. No, I'd *rather*. Thanks tons.'

Following this she phoned several people and asked if they had rides to the funeral, or memorial service, as it was being called. She phoned up other people and asked if they would mind providing rides for the people who were having difficulties; then she phoned the first people back and told them when and where they could be picked up. Eileen was up by this time, dressing, going back and forth to the bathroom. From the recreation room, downstairs, she heard rock music, turned unusually, perhaps deferentially, low. The older children must be down there. She wondered where Ewart was. She had the impression that not all these arrangements June was making were really necessary, or that, at least, it was not necessary for June to make them. Surely people could have figured out their rides for themselves. She found that she disliked even the tone of June's voice on the telephone. *Good morning, hi! Hi, it's June!* Such a cheerful buoyant matter-of-fact voice, and wasn't there in this very buoyancy some challenge, some lively insistence on control? Could it be said that June wished for admiration? Well, why not? If it will help. If anything will help.

Nevertheless Eileen disliked this tone, she was discouraged by it.

In the kitchen she washed her mug and plate. They were the only dishes in sight. The kitchen, at a quarter past nine in the morning, was shining like the kitchen in an ad. The dishes were all in the dishwasher, that was where they were. Eileen had forgotten about the dishwasher. She herself lived in an old house, a rented house in another city; she lived alone because she was divorced and her only child, her daughter, was wandering around Europe. She did not know how to operate a dishwasher.

She had left the crusts of her toast but now she ate them, because it was too difficult to figure out which garbage they should go into. It would take her a day here, at least, to get things straight. She had learned last night there was a new and complicated system of garbage division, to do with recycling. 'I will have to get around to doing that too,' Eileen had said, and June said, 'But *don't you?*'

Compared to June, she did live irresponsibly. Eileen had to see this, she had to admit it. Her lazy garbage all thrown together, her cupboards under their surface tidiness bursting with chaos. Once she and June had had a confrontation about brown paper bags. Eileen, saving paper bags, stuffed them into a drawer. June folded them and smoothed them flat and was about to file them tightly against each other so that the drawer's capacity was greatly increased and the bags were easier to remove. Both sisters laughed angrily.

'I mean it's *easier*,' said June. 'It's always easier. Actually in the end you save yourself time.'

'You're compulsive,' said Eileen, who would try when desperate to turn June's own language against her, using it flippantly and high handedly. 'Order is an anal perversion. I'm surprised at you.'

But she did try. In June's kitchen she tried all the time to remember the order, the always logical, though unexpected, classifications. She always made a mistake. When Ewart discovered one of her mistakes, something out of place, he would tap her on the arm with a look of apology and complicity, no words, shift whatever it was with a furtive flourish to wherever it ought to be. It was from this pantomime of his, this kindness and anxiety on her behalf, that Eileen understood how far all this was from being a joke, how deep and true June's outrage must be. In June's and Ewart's house she felt all the time the weight of the world of objects, their serious demands, the distinctions she had disregarded. There was a morality here of buying and use, a morality of consumerism. Eileen had never had any money, so she was able to be spendthrift, slipshod, content. June and Ewart, having such a great deal of money, bought and used each thing with a sense of responsibility which was not just a responsibility to themselves to own the best, the most efficient, durable, honest, things that were to be had, but a responsibility, as they would have said, to society. People who did not read *Consumer Reports* probably seemed the same to them as people who did not bother to vote.

The things they had the most difficulty buying were the things which serve no purpose but which are necessary to any house – pictures, ornaments. They had solved this finally by choosing Eskimo prints and carvings, Indian wall hangings, ash trays, and bowls, and some grey porous-looking pots made by a former convict now being sponsored as a potter by the Unitarian Church. All these things had an edge of moral value, and were decoratively acceptable besides. A pair of Kwakiutl masks – heavy stylized threat, dead ferocity – hung on the fireplace wall, receiving a good deal of admiration. What are such things doing in a living room, Eileen wanted to ask. She discovered in herself these days an unattractive finickiness about some things, about clothes, for instance, and decoration. A wish to avoid fraud, not to appropriate serious things for trivial uses, not to mock things by making them into fashions. A doomed wish. She herself offended. And Ewart and June did not mean to mock, they truly admired Indian art, they said, 'Isn't that fierce? Isn't it fantastic?' In Eileen's own living room were some dim watercolours of flowers, an accidental collection of secondhand furniture, and who was to say that this shabbiness, this avoidance of style, was not in its way quite as bad an affectation as a display of Kwakiutl masks, pocked fertility goddesses?

Ewart came in from the garage, wearing work pants and shirt. His hair had grown down to his earlobes. 'Would you like to see my Japanese garden?' he said to Eileen. 'I was just out giving the shrubs a bit of attention. You can't take your eyes off them when they're getting started.'

His voice was cheerful, but she caught in his vicinity a smell of bad, sad, sleepless breath, masked not vanquished by mouthwash.

'Of course I'd like.'

She followed him through the garage, and outside. It was a mild cloudy February day. 'It might be sunny yet,' Ewart said. He bent back the wet branches for her, he warned her where the slope of the great lawn was slippery, he was as usual a kind and worried host. Wealth had made him courteous beyond all normal requirements, reticent, conciliatory, mysterious. When June first met him, at university – both she and Eileen had gone to their local university on scholarships – he seemed to have no friends. June went after him with the same badgering, comforting zeal she later showed towards African students, drug addicts, people in jail, Indian children. She took him to parties, where he early found his role as drink-server, host- and hostess-helper, neighbour- and occasionally police-mollifier, holder of heads of people being sick in the bathroom, confidant of girls whose boy friends were being mean to them. June said she was showing him life. She considered him deprived, handicapped, his name and his money marking him just as sadly, in her view, as a mulberry splotch on the face, a club foot. Nobody thought she meant to marry him. Nor did she think so. It took a while for her to see the possibilities, Eileen believed. She did bring him home, but that was all in her programme of showing him life.

Eileen and June and their mother still lived then in the upstairs of a house behind a barbershop, on Becker Street. The rooms were dark, but had compensation. A fresh, soapy, masculine smell, from the barbershop. At night a rosy flash entering the front room from the café on the corner. Their mother had cataracts on both eyes. She lay on the chesterfield – she was stately, even lying down – and issued demands. She wanted glasses of water, pills, cups of tea; she wanted blankets removed and tucked in, her hair combed and braided. She also wanted radio stations phoned up and reproved for the use of slangy, vulgar, ungrammatical language; she wanted complaints delivered to the barbershop and the grocery store; she wished old friends or acquaintances to be contacted and given reports on her deteriorating health, and asked why they had not been to see her. June brought Ewart and made him sit and listen. By majoring in psychology June had tried to get round the problem of their mother, just as Eileen had tried to do by the study of English literature. June had been more successful. Eileen was gratified by the high incidence of crazy mothers in books, but failed to put this discovery to any use. June, on the other hand, was able to present their mother to her friends with no apologies but plenty of prior explanation and post-discussion. She made people feel *privileged*. Ewart had to listen to a long, melancholy, garbled and untrue story about how their family was related to Arthur Meighen, former Prime Minister of Canada. June told him he was getting a firsthand look at the delusions fostered in people of a certain temperament by a no-exit socioeconomic situation. (She was learning by leaps and bounds the language that would serve her well for the rest of her life.) Eileen could not help but be impressed by this unexpected reaping of advantages, this sudden objectivity.

'It's easier for me of course because I'm the second child,' June told her, and anyone else who might be listening. 'I was released from guilt,' she said, 'it was all piled onto Eileen.' Under the kind but hard scrutiny of those Psychology, Sociology majors, Eileen, gloomy enough by that time anyway as a graduate student, saw herself moving guilt-crippled, unaware; dragging her irrelevant, mistaken courses in Literature, her disagreeable lover (Howie, that was, the man she later married and divorced); blundering like a bat in daylight. Astonishing how in one year June was able to shed her teen-age plumpness, her fumbling for words, her innocence, dependency, confusion and gratitude. Who would have thought she had a loud clear voice waiting, a flushed bony face and nervous hurrying body waiting to be revealed, as well as all that certainty? Only a couple of years before, she had written poetry, she had read the books Eileen was reading, she had seemed to have some vague idea of fashioning herself after her older sister. Not a chance.

Which was foresighted of her, of course. Eileen had married Howie, the cranky journalist who had left her with a little girl to support. June had married Ewart and set about establishing their life. While Eileen's life took shape any way at all, blown apart by crises, deflected by pleasures, June's life was built, planned, lived deliberately, *filled*. There was a lack of drifting and moping. Occasions were made the most of.

Was this another occasion?

'This one Douglas helped me put in last week,' said Ewart, displaying to her a low bristly shrub. He used his son's name exactly as June did, casually yet emphatically. Natural, unacknowledged delicacy and hesitancy made his emphasis less troubling than hers. He went on to talk about Japanese gardens. He told her that, at one time, in Japan, precise regulations had been laid down concerning the height of stepping-stones. For the Emperor they were six inches high, and so on down to common folk and women who walked on stones of an inch and a half. He was putting in water.

'The sound of water in the Japanese garden is quite as important as the sight of it. It's going to fall over here, you see. It will be like a miniature waterfall, bisected by this rock. Everything is to scale. That's how you get the extraordinary effect. If you look at it and you're not looking at anything else – well, after a while it begins to seem like a real waterfall, a real landscape.'

He talked about the arrangements for bringing in this water, the system of underground pipes. He had always such detailed, minute knowledge about his current projects, such firm enthusiasm. He always seemed to know more than even somebody who had made such things his life's work would need to know. Perhaps it was because he himself did not really have a life's work, he did not need to earn his living.

An occasion, why not? An occasion to display, to air, to test those values that we live by. Ewart and June did live by values, they would tell you so. *Why not?* thought Eileen, listening to the discourse on pipes, and, when that was exhausted, to a discourse on shrubs. She preferred, did she, to see the fact of a death set up whole and unavoidable, in front of everybody's eyes? Without religion, that could not be done. That is, it could not be done. And suppose her daughter, suppose Margot? She had thought of that at once, as soon as she heard, relief and terror peculiarly alternating. It was as if Douglas, by attracting lightning, had given everyone else's child a breath of safety, at the same time reminding that lightning was there. Margot, who might at any moment be getting into a leaky boat, an about-to-be-hijacked plane, a bus with faulty brakes, might be entering a building where bombs had been set by terrorists, Margot ran more risk than Douglas living at home. And yet.

He had been killed in a car accident. The three other boys with him had not been much hurt.

A chunky boy. On the plane, Eileen had tried to get a clear picture of him. His fair hair was worn long, held with a band at the back of his neck, like his mother's. But he did not share the preoccupations of the long-haired of his own generation. Altered states of consciousness, transcendental perception, were no concern of his. He attached himself stubbornly to temporal, material, scientific interests, to moonflights, sports (as a spectator), and even to the stock market. He was like his father in his dogged, perhaps passionate, amassing and treasuring and reciting of detail. He enjoyed explaining. He had few friends. He walked around the house with a reserved and dictatorial air, drinking diet Coke. Ewart and June had always filled the weekends, the holidays, with family activities. They owned a sailboat. They went mountain-climbing and cave-exploring. They skied and skated and recently they had bought ten-speed bicycles. Eileen supposed that Douglas took part in all this, he could hardly avoid it; but his stodgy figure, his sedentary style, raised doubts as to how heartfelt, how thoroughgoing, such participation might be. He had gone to the experimental school which depended so largely on his parents' financial support. The freedom insisted on there, the efforts on behalf of creativity, might not have been congenial to him. Eileen could only suspect.

Douglas himself would not have indicated. He was not, he had not been, romantic enough to see himself as the rebel, the sceptic, in this orthodoxy.

His father squatted down to touch the shrubs, showing her the different kinds of needles, speaking of their complicated requirements, of soil analysis, water, nourishment. He gave his attention. He was not a sexually attractive man. Why not? His large sad butt, his vulnerable priggish look from the rear? Once June had told Eileen that she and Ewart had gone to some pornographic movies, with other couples from what was called a Growth Group, in the Unitarian Church. They were interested in exploring new stimuli. Eileen had told this to people, about her sister, she had made an example and a joke about it. Now she thought that her laughter had been beside the point. Not because it was unkind, as she had guiltily thought at the time, but because it was uncomprehending. This earnestness was no joke. Here was a system of digestion which found everything to its purposes. It stuck at nothing. Japanese gardens, pornographic movies, accidental death. All of them accepted, chewed and altered, assimilated, destroyed.

After the Memorial Service the house was full of June's and Ewart's friends and neighbours and the friends of their teen-aged children. The teen-agers were downstairs in the recreation room, in front of the floor-to-ceiling stone fireplace. Many of them claimed to be friends of Douglas. Perhaps they were. They came with guitars, recorders, candles. One girl came wrapped in a quilt. 'Is this where they're having the Memorial Party?' she asked at the door, in her soft radiance. Others wore fringed shawls, flimsy trailing dresses. They looked not so different from their elders as they might have wished. Downstairs they lit the candles; they had only that light, and the fire. They burned incense. They sang and played their instruments. The incense odour, rising, had an edge of marijuana.

'Their way of saying good-bye to Douglas,' said a long-haired, ravaged-looking woman, also shawl-wrapped, leaning over the banister. 'It's very lovely, really, it's very moving.'

But would Douglas have cared for it, for the Memorial Party? He would not have said. He would have stayed with it a while, anyway, out of politeness; then he might have gone to his room with the market section of the paper.

'They've got a joint or two down there, smells like,' said a man coming up behind this woman, and Eileen knew from the way the woman did not answer, from the closing of her face and her whole self, that it must be her husband. Unlike his wife, he had come conservatively dressed, he looked as men used to look at funerals. Such couples were common nowadays – husband responsible, respectable, vulnerable, only slightly longer hair and timid sideburns, tie and clean cuffs, a faintly apologetic or ridiculous air of real, though deplorable, money and power; wife careless, making-up-less, anything but matronly, trailing the garments of exotic poverty. Occasionally there was a couple who were the mirror-opposite of these – wife coifed and pastel-suited and button-earringed, husband in an embroidered velvet vest, amulets and crosses twinkling among the hairs of his chest.

This husband and Eileen moved into the living room, which was full of just such people. Shawls and caftans, printed cotton from India, jeans, expensive tailoring. It would not have been difficult, even two or three years ago, to tell the rich friends of Ewart and June, their neighbours, from the Unitarians, the Growth Group friends. Now it was impossible. Some of these people were probably both.

Ewart moved among them offering drinks. June was in the dining room, beside the table with the coffee and sandwiches. Sausage rolls, asparagus rolls. She had found some time to make those. Her clothing was lovely – a long hand-woven orange and gold dress and matching stole, thick and rough, Mexican or Spanish. Her silver-green eyelids were a surprise and a mistake, the only hint of something hectic, unsure.

'Are you all right?' she said to her sister. 'I haven't been able to take you round and introduce you to people, I'm just letting you fend for yourself.'

'I'm all right,' Eileen said. 'I'm drinking.'

She had given up asking what she could do to help. She had given up looking for things to do. The kitchen, the dining room, were full of women who knew where everything was kept, but they had hardly any more luck than she. June had forestalled all of them. Everything was thought of, everything was done.

The walls, the high, sloping ceiling of the living room were of warm wood; the carpet and the curtains were heavy, creamy, soft. Eileen drank vodka. The curtains were not drawn shut, and she saw them all in their splendid, confusing costumes (herself too, betraying her own sterner judgements, in a dark blue caftan embroidered with silver threads), moving, drinking, talking, against the late afternoon, the early evening. Against the rainy dark she saw them all so bright and sheltered. She saw the carpet of lights which was the city, the strip of blackness which was the water.

'Do you know where you are?' the husband said to her. 'You're up on the side of Hollyburn mountain. That's Point Grey over there.' He made her move closer to the window so that he could point out in the opposite direction the Lions Gate Bridge, a distant tiara of moving lights.

'Stupendous view,' he said.

Eileen agreed.

He was a neighbour, he told her, he had built a house a little further up the mountain. Like many rich people he seemed to be full of a sincere and puzzled, almost heavy-hearted, hope that he had got what he should.

'We used to have a house in North Van,' he said. 'And I wasn't sure for a long time we were right to give it up. I wasn't sure I would like this view as much. We used to look out and see the slope of this mountain, right where we are now, and the bridge and the city, and on a clear day we could see Vancouver Island. Looking westerly you get the sunsets. Magnificent. But now I'm just as much in love with this, too, I wouldn't ever want to go back.'

'Do you always like views?' said Eileen.

'Always like views?' he repeated, and showed by his bent head, his tolerant eyebrows, that he was waiting to be charmed.

'Well suppose you're in a low mood, you know, you might be feeling in a very low mood and you get up and here spread out before you is this magnificent view. All the time, you can't get away from it. Don't you ever feel not up to it?'

'Not up to it?'

'Guilty,' said Eileen, persistently though regretfully. 'That you're not in a better mood? That you're not more – worthy of this beautiful view?' She took a large drink, wishing of course that she had never started any of this.

'But as soon as I see the beautiful view,' said the man triumphantly, 'then I couldn't be in a low mood any more. That view does more for me than a couple of drinks. More than the stuff they've got downstairs. Besides, I don't believe in being in a low mood. Life's too short.'

Saying this reminded him that they were not at a party, after all.

'Life's too short. There's no rhyme or reason to the things that happen. Is there? Your sister's magnificent. Ewart too.'

Eileen went down the hall to the guest room, carrying a fresh strong drink. She passed the door of the room where the small children were playing. The children of friends, playing with June's small adopted daughters. They were playing Fish. She stood and watched them. She felt intimidated somehow by the Indian children, she felt on trial before them. Of course that was when June was there; she could feel June listening, watching – quivering, it seemed, with her keenness to detect failures of attitude. Who would believe now that June, as well as Eileen, had gone around the house talking a singsong pidgin English based on the speech of the Chinese couple at the Becker Street Groceteria? Eileen watched the smooth brown faces of the Indian children. What were they – June's badges, her trophies? She could not see them, only June.

She closed the door of the guest room, she lay in the

dark. Crossing her ankles, pushing the pillow up behind her head, still holding the glass but letting it rest on her stomach. She had come to the point she always came to in June's house. Douglas made no difference, death made no difference. She was becoming paralysed, she could not hold her own. From this house her life, her choices (if indeed there were any), she herself, did not make a favourable or even coherent impression. It had to be admitted that she lived haphazardly, she had wasted too much time, she did few things well. Never mind how all this looked when she was away from here, how she made it into funny stories for friends. Moreover, she had not been able to help.

On the plane she had thought that she would make tea biscuits. As if that would be possible, in June's kitchen.

The news that their father was dead, in the War, had come for some reason in a phone call, at ten or eleven o'clock at night. Their mother had made tea biscuits and tea, and got Eileen up to share them. Not June, she was too little. They had jam. Eileen was greedy but apprehensive. Their mother who was most of the time a dangerous person, full of mysterious hurts, unnameable grievances, seemed to have abandoned her usual position, to have turned neutral, undemanding, and, of all things, *shy*. She did not tell her news. (She would wake them in the morning with a long white face, an unwelcome kiss, a prepared voice. *Daddy is dead*.) Years later Eileen had tried to talk to June about this vigil with the biscuits, the revelation of their mother as someone frail and still; almost, almost – the thing they most hoped for then – an ordinary woman. June said she had worked through all that.

'Years ago, and in Gestalt too. I *really* did it in Gestalt. I worked it all out and finished with it.'

I have not worked through anything, Eileen thought. And further: *I do not believe things are there to be worked through.*

People die; they suffer, they die. Their mother had died of ordinary pneumonia, after all that craziness. Illness and accidents. They ought to be respected, not explained. Words are all shameful. They ought to crumble in shame.

The words from *The Prophet*, read at the Memorial Service that afternoon, had offended Eileen. Such fraud, she thought, such insolence. Unintentional – offered in fact with the modern equivalent of piety – but that was no excuse. Now in drunk reflection she saw that no words would have been any better. *Now in sure and certain hope . . .* No fraud in the words but what fraud now in saying them. Silence the only possible thing.

At one time she and June had been worth more consideration than they were now. At one time they had been less offensive. Was that not so? Ewart too, the neighbours too, the Unitarians too. At one time we could all be trusted to know what we meant, but not now, although we all mean well. June has been in Growth Groups, she has learned Yoga, she has looked into Transcendental Meditation; she has been naked, with others, in a warm place on an expensive island. As for Eileen, she has read a great deal, and knows how to be offended by all kinds of cheapness. You would think they would be better off than their mother was. But something is wrong just the same. The only thing that we can hope for is that we lapse now and then into reality, thinks Eileen, and falls asleep for a few seconds, to wake up scared, fingers tightening on the glass.

Almost spilled it. The rug, the spread. She drank all that was left and set the glass on the bedside table and almost at once fell asleep.

She woke still drunk, not knowing the time. The house was quiet. She got up, thought she must change into nightclothes. First she went to the bathroom, wearing her dark blue caftan, and then into the kitchen to look at the electric clock. The kitchen light was on. It was only a quarter past eleven.

She drank a full glass of water, which she knew from experience would reduce, or if she was lucky entirely eliminate, her morning headache. She went out the side door to the garage, thinking that she would stand there out of the rain and breathe fresh air. The door was up. Wavering, she felt her way along the wall past coiled garden hose and tools hung on nails. She heard someone coming but was not worried. She was too drunk. She did not care who it was or what they thought of her, finding her here.

It was Ewart. He had the watering can.

'June?' he said. 'June? Eileen. I didn't see how it could be June. She took two sleeping pills.'

'What are you doing,' said Eileen. Her voice was drunk, challenging but not really quarrelsome.

'Watering.'

'It's raining. Ewart you are a fool.'

'It's not raining any more.'

'It was earlier. I noticed when we were in the living room.'

'I had to water the new shrubs. They take an incredible amount of water at first. You can't depend on the rain being enough. Even for the first day.'

He was putting the can away. He came round the cars to her.

'Eileen. You better go in. You had a lot to drink. June looked in on you earlier. She said you were dead to the world.'

He was drunk too. She knew, not by his voice or by the way he moved, but by a certain weight, a density and stubbornness he had, standing in front of her.

'Eileen. You were crying. That's very kind of you.'

Not for Douglas, she had not been crying for Douglas.

'Eileen you know it's been a great help to June, having you here.'

'I haven't done anything. I wish I could do something.'

'Just having you here. June values you so much.'

'Does she?' said Eileen, not disbelievingly. How Ewart compelled politeness, even when they were both drunk.

'She is not able to express herself sometimes. She seems – you know, sometimes she seems a little – bossy. She is aware of it. But it is hard to change.'

'Eileen.' Ewart moved the two steps that brought him against her.

Eileen was a hospitable woman, particularly when drunk. This embrace did not exactly take her by surprise. It had been predicted, though she would be hard put to say how. Perhaps with Eileen – alone, wayward, astonishingly limp at times though brisk enough at others – such an embrace could always be predicted. And she permitted, she almost welcomed it, how could she extricate herself without gross unkindness? Even if this had not been in her plans, she could shift her expectations around enough to make room for it, thinking, as she usually thought at such moments, why not?

Women like this, women who think like this, are generally believed to be lackadaisical, purely wanting in spirit, dazed receptacles, pitiable. Other women express this opinion and men too, the very men in fact who have burrowed in them with every sign of gratitude and appreciation. Eileen knew this. She found it far from the fact. She supposed she was easily aroused. At the moment, not very much so; she did not anticipate great pleasure from her brother-in-law Ewart – who was now manoeuvring her, with more determination and adroitness than she would have expected, towards the back seat of the larger car – but she did more than suffer him. Nearly always she did more than that. She liked their faces at these times. She liked their seriousness – lovely devout and naked seriousness, attention to realities, their own realities.

Repetition of her name was all the speech she got from him. She had heard that before. What did Ewart mean by that name, what was Eileen to him? Women have a wonder. Pinned down not too comfortably on a car seat – one leg crooked and held against the back of the seat in danger of getting a cramp – they will still look for clues, and store things up in a hurry to be considered later. They have to believe that more is going on than seems to be going on; that is part of the trouble.

What Eileen meant to Ewart, she would tell herself later, was confusion. The opposite of June, wasn't that what she was? The natural thing for a man in pain to look for, who loves and fears his wife. The brief restorative dip. Eileen is aimless and irresponsible, she comes out of the same part of the world accidents come from. He lies in her to acknowledge, to yield – but temporarily, safely – to whatever has got his son, whatever cannot be spoken of in his house. So Eileen, with her fruitful background of reading, her nimble habit of analysis (material and direction different from June's, but the habit not so different, after all), can later explain and arrange it for herself. Not knowing, never knowing, if that is not all literary, fanciful. A woman's body. Before and during the act they seem to invest this body with certain individual powers, they will say its name in a way that indicates something particular, something unique, that is sought for. Afterwards it appears that they have changed their minds, they wish it understood that such bodies are interchangeable. Women's bodies.

Eileen was packing. She folded the wrinkled, stained caftan and put it at the bottom of her suitcase, in a hurry lest June, who had two or three times passed her door, should decide to come in. She and June were alone in the house. The children were all back at school today, and Ewart had driven over to town to get some piping for the water system. June was to drive Eileen to the airport.

June did come in. 'It's too bad you have to go so soon,' she said. 'I feel we haven't done anything for you. We haven't taken you anywhere. If you could stay a few days longer.'

'I didn't expect,' said Eileen. She was not appalled as she would have been the first day, not surprised. She knew that if she stayed a few days more June really would make an effort to show her the city, even though she had seen it before. She would be taken up the chairlift, driven through the parks, taken to look at totem poles.

'You must come for a real visit,' said June.

'I haven't helped you the way I meant to,' Eileen said. No sooner was that sentence out than it flung itself inside out and grinned at her. This was a day when there was nothing she could say that would work.

'I always pack more than I need.'

June sat on the bed. 'He was not killed in the accident, you know.'

'Not killed?'

'Not the actual crash. It couldn't have been too bad, really. Those other kids were just scratched up. He was dazed, probably. I think he was probably dazed. He climbed out of the car, they all did. The car was at a very strange angle on the roadbank. You see it had sort of climbed the bank and it was on its side, it must have been on its side, like this' – June set one hand, the fingers spread and slightly trembling, on top of the other – 'but on a corner, too, sort of – tilted. I don't really understand how it could have been. I try to picture it but I really can't. I mean I can't understand the angle it must have been at and how it could have been high enough. It fell on him. The car just – it fell on him, and he was killed. I don't know how he was standing. Or maybe he was not standing. You know, he may have – crawled out and been trying to get up. But I can't really understand how. Can you picture it?'

'No,' said Eileen.

'I can't either.'

'Who told you that?'

'One of the boys who – one of the other boys told his mother and she told me.'

'Maybe that was cruel.'

'Oh, no,' said June in a thoughtful voice. 'No. I don't think so. You do want to know.'

In the mirror over the dresser Eileen could see her sister's face, the downward profile, which was waiting, perhaps embarrassed, now that this offering had been made. Also her own face, surprising her with its wonderfully appropriate look of tactfulness and concern. She felt cold and tired, she wanted mostly to get away. It was an effort to put her hand out. Acts done without faith may restore faith. She believed, with whatever energy she could summon at the moment, she had to believe and hope that was true.

THE OTTAWA VALLEY

I think of my mother sometimes in department stores. I don't know why, I was never in one with her; their plentitude, their sober bustle, it seems to me, would have satisfied her. I think of her of course when I see somebody on the street who has Parkinson's disease, and more and more often lately when I look in the mirror. Also in Union Station, Toronto, because the first time I was there I was with her, and my little sister. It was one summer during the War, we waited between trains; we were going home with her, with my mother, to her old home in the Ottawa Valley.

A cousin she was planning to meet, for a between-trains visit, did not show up. 'She probably couldn't get away,' said my mother, sitting in a leather chair in the darkly panelled Ladies' Lounge, which is now boarded up. 'There was probably something to do that she couldn't leave to anybody else.' This cousin was a legal secretary, and she worked for a senior partner in what my mother always called, in her categorical way, 'the city's leading law firm.' Once she had come to visit us, wearing a large black hat and a black suit, her lips and nails like rubies. She did not bring her husband. He was an alcoholic. My mother always mentioned that her husband was an alcoholic, immediately after she had stated that she held an important job with the city's leading law firm. The two things were seen to balance each other, to be tied together in some inevitable and foreboding way. In the same way my mother would say of a family we knew that they had everything money could buy but their only son was an epileptic, or that the parents of the only person from our town who had become moderately famous, a pianist named Mary Renwick, had said that they would give all their daughter's fame for a pair of baby hands. *A pair of baby hands?* Luck was not without its shadow, in her universe.

My sister and I went out into the station which was like a street with its lighted shops and like a church with its high curved roof and great windows at each end. It was full of the thunder of trains hidden, it seemed, just behind the walls, and an amplified voice, luxuriant, powerful, reciting place names that could not quite be understood. I bought a movie magazine and my sister bought chocolate bars with the money we had been given. I was going to say to her, 'Give me a bite or I won't show you the way back,' but she was so undone by the grandeur of the place, or subdued by her dependence on me, that she broke off a piece without being asked.

Late in the afternoon we got on the Ottawa train. We were surrounded by soldiers. My sister had to sit on my mother's knee. A soldier sitting in front of us turned around and joked with me. He looked very much like Bob Hope. He asked me what town I came from, and then he said, 'Have they got the second storey on there yet?' in just the sharp, unsmiling, smart-alecky way that Bob Hope would have said it. I thought that maybe he really was Bob Hope, travelling around incognito in a soldier's uniform. That did not seem unlikely to me. Outside of my own town – this far outside it, at least – all the bright and famous people in the world seemed to be floating around free, ready to turn up anywhere.

Aunt Dodie met us at the station in the dark and drove us to her house, miles out in the country. She was small and sharp-faced and laughed at the end of every sentence. She drove an old square-topped car with a running board.

'Well, did Her Majesty show up to see you?'

She was referring to the legal secretary, who was in fact her sister. Aunt Dodie was not really our aunt at all but our mother's cousin. She and her sister did not speak.

'No, but she must have been busy,' said my mother neutrally.

'Oh, busy,' said Aunt Dodie. 'She's busy scraping the chicken dirt off her boots. Eh?' She drove fast, over washboard and potholes.

My mother waved at the blackness on either side of us. 'Children! Children, this is the Ottawa Valley!'

It was no valley. I looked for mountains, or at least hills, but in the morning all it was was fields and bush, and

Aunt Dodie outside the window holding a milk pail for a calf. The calf was butting its head into the pail so hard it slopped the milk out, and Aunt Dodie was laughing and scolding and hitting it, trying to make it slow down. She called it a bugger. 'Greedy little bugger!'

She was dressed in her milking outfit, which was many-layered and coloured and ragged and flopping like the clothes a beggar-woman might wear in a school play. A man's hat without a crown was shoved – for what purpose? – on her head.

My mother had not led me to believe we were related to people who dressed like that or who used the word bugger. 'I will not tolerate filth,' my mother always said. But apparently she tolerated Aunt Dodie. She said they had been like sisters, when they were growing up. (The legal secretary, Bernice, had been older and had left home early.) Then my mother usually said that Aunt Dodie had had a tragic life.

Aunt Dodie's house was bare. It was the poorest house I had ever been in, to stay. From this distance, our own house – which I had always thought poor, because we lived too far out of town to have a flush toilet or running water, and certainly we had no real touches of luxury, like Venetian blinds – looked very comfortably furnished, with its books and piano and good set of dishes and one rug that was bought, not made out of rags. In Aunt Dodie's front room there was one overstuffed chair and a magazine rack full of old Sunday school papers. Aunt Dodie lived off her cows. Her land was not worth farming. Every morning, after she finished milking and separating, she loaded the cans in the back of her pickup truck and drove seven miles to the cheese factory. She lived in dread of the milk inspector, who went around declaring cows tubercular, we understood, for no reason but spite, and to put poor farmers out of business. Big dairy interests paid him off, Aunt Dodie said.

The tragedy in her life was that she had been jilted. 'Did you know,' she said, 'that I was jilted?' My mother had said we were never to mention it, and there was Aunt Dodie in her own kitchen, washing the noon dishes, with me wiping and my sister putting away (my mother had to go and have her rest), saying 'jilted' proudly, as somebody would say, 'Did you know I had polio?' or some such bad important disease.

'I had my cake baked,' she said. 'I was in my wedding dress.'

'Was it satin?'

'No, it was a nice dark red merino wool, because of it being a late fall wedding. We had the minister here. All prepared. My Dad kept running out to the road to see if he could see him coming. It got dark, and I said, time to go out and do the milking! I pulled off my dress and I never put it back on. I gave it away. Lots of girls would've cried, but me, I laughed.'

My mother telling the same story said, 'When I went home two years after that, and I was staying with her, I used to wake up and hear her crying in the night. Night after night.'

> *There was I*
> *Waiting at the church,*
> *Waiting at the church,*

Waiting at the church.
And when I found
He'd left me in the lurch,
Oh, how it did upset me.

Aunt Dodie sang this at us, washing the dishes at her round table covered with scrubbed oilcloth. Her kitchen was as big as a house, with a back door and a front door; always a breeze blew through. She had a homemade icebox, such as I had never seen, with a big chunk of ice in it that she would haul in a child's wagon from the ice-house. The ice-house itself was remarkable, a roofed dugout where ice cut from the lake in winter lasted the summer, in sawdust.

'Of course it wasn't,' she said, 'in my case, it wasn't the church.'

Across the fields from Aunt Dodie on the next farm lived my mother's brother, Uncle James, and his wife, Aunt Lena, and their eight children. That was the house where my mother had grown up. It was a bigger house with more furniture but still unpainted outside, dark grey. The furniture was mostly high wooden beds, with feather ticks and dark carved headboards. Under the beds were pots not emptied every day. We visited there but Aunt Dodie did not come with us. She and Aunt Lena did not speak. But Aunt Lena did not speak much to anybody. She had been a sixteen-year-old girl straight out of the backwoods, said my mother and Aunt Dodie (which left you to wonder, where was this?), when Uncle James married her. At this time, she would have been married ten or twelve years. She was tall and straight, flat as a board front and back – even though she would bear her ninth child before Christmas – darkly freckled, with large dark slightly inflamed eyes, animal's eyes. All the children had got those, instead of Uncle James's mild blue ones.

'When your mother was dying,' said Aunt Dodie. 'Oh, I can hear her. Don't touch that towel! Use your own towel! Cancer, she thought you could catch it like the measles. She was that ignorant.'

'I can't forgive her.'

'And wouldn't let any of the kids go near her. I had to go over myself and give your mother her wash. I saw it all.'

'I can never forgive her.'

Aunt Lena was stiff all the time with what I now recognize as terror. She would not let her children swim in the lake for fear they would drown, she would not let them go tobogganing in winter for fear they would fall off the toboggan and break their necks, she would not let them learn to skate for fear they would break their legs and be crippled for life. She beat them all the time for fear they would grow up to be lazy, or liars, or clumsy people who broke things. They were not lazy but they broke things anyway; they were always darting and grabbing; and, of course, they were all liars, even the little ones, brilliant, instinctive liars who lied even when it was not necessary, just for the practice, and maybe the pleasure, of it. They were always telling and concealing, making and breaking alliances; they had the most delicate and ruthless political instincts. They howled when they were beaten. Pride was a luxury they had discarded long ago, or never considered. If you did not howl for Aunt Lena, when would she ever stop? Her arms were as long and strong as a man's, her face set in an expression of remote unanswerable fury. But five minutes, three minutes, afterwards, her children would have forgotten. With me, such a humiliation could last for weeks, or forever.

Uncle James kept the Irish accent my mother had lost and Aunt Dodie had halfway lost. His voice was lovely, saying the children's names. Mar-ie, Ron-ald, Ru-thie. So tenderly, comfortingly, reproachfully he said their names, as if the names, or the children themselves, were jokes played on him. But he never held them back from being beaten, never protested. You would think all this had nothing to do with him. You would think Aunt Lena had nothing to do with him.

The youngest child slept in the parents' bed until a new baby displaced it.

'He used to come over and see me,' Aunt Dodie said. 'We used to have some good laughs. He used to bring two, three of the kids but he quit that. I know why. They'd tell on him. Then he quit coming himself. She lays down the law. But he gets it back on her, doesn't he?'

Aunt Dodie did not get a daily paper, just the weekly that was published in the town where she had picked us up.

'There's a mention in here about Allen Durrand.'

'Allen Durrand?' said my mother doubtfully.

'Oh, he's a big Holstein man now. He married a West.'

'What's the mention?'

'It's the Conservation Association. I bet he wants to get nominated. I bet.'

She was in the rocker, with her boots off, laughing. My mother was sitting with her back against a porch post. They were cutting up yellow beans, to can.

'I was thinking about the time we gave him the lemonade,' Aunt Dodie said, and turned to me. 'He was just a French Canadian boy then, working here for a couple of weeks in the summer.'

'Only his name was French,' my mother said. 'He didn't even speak it.'

'You'd never know now. He turned his religion too, goes to St John's.'

'He was always intelligent.'

'You bet he is. Oh, intelligent. But we got him with the lemonade.

'You picture the hottest possible day in summer. Your mother and I didn't mind it so much, we could stay in the house. But Allen had to be in the mow. You see they were getting the hay in. My dad was bringing it in and Allen was spreading it out. I bet James was over helping too.'

'James was pitching on,' my mother said. 'Your dad was driving, and building the load.'

'And they put Allen in the mow. You've no idea what a mow is like on that kind of a day. It's a hell on earth. So we thought it would be a nice idea to take him some lemonade – No. I'm getting ahead of myself. I meant to tell about the overalls first.

'Allen had brought me these overalls to fix just when the men were sitting down to dinner. He had a heavy pair of old suit pants on, and a work shirt, must have been killing him, though the shirt I guess he took off when he got in the barn. But he must've wanted the overalls on because they'd be cooler, you know, the circulation. I forget what had to be fixed on them, just some little thing. He must have been suffering bad in those old pants just to bring himself to ask, because he was awful shy. He'd be – what, then?'

'Seventeen,' my mother said.

'And us two eighteen. It was the year before you went away to Normal. Yes. Well, I took and fixed his pants, just some little thing to do to them while you served up dinner. There I was sitting in the corner of the kitchen at the sewing machine when I had my inspiration, didn't I? I called you over. Pretended I was calling you to hold the material straight for me. So's you could see what I was doing. And neither one of us cracked a smile or dared look sideways at each other, did we?'

'No.'

'Because my inspiration was to sew up his fly!

'So then, you see, a little bit on in the afternoon, with them out to work again, we got the idea for the lemonade. We made two pailfuls. One we took out to the men working in the field; we yelled to them and set it under a tree. And the other we took up to the mow and offered it to him. We'd used up every lemon we had, and even so it was weak. I remember we had to put vinegar in. But he wouldn't've noticed. I never saw a person so thirsty in my life as him. He drank by the dipperful, and then he just tipped up the pail. Drank it all down. Us standing there watching. How did we keep a straight face?'

'I'll never know,' my mother said.

'Then we took the pail and made for the house and waited about two seconds before we came sneaking back. We hid ourselves up in the granary. That was like an oven, too. I don't know how we stood it. But we climbed up on the sacks of feed and each found ourselves a crack or knothole or something to look through. We knew the corner of the barn the men always peed in. They peed down the shovel if they were upstairs. Down in the stable I guess they peed in the gutter. And soon enough, soon enough, he starts strolling over in that direction. Dropped his fork and starts strolling over. Puts his hand up to himself as he went. Sweat running down our faces from the heat and the way we had to keep from laughing. Oh, the cruelty of it! First he was just going easy, wasn't he? Then thinking about it I guess the need gets stronger; he looked down wondering what was the matter, and soon he's fairly clawin' and yankin' every which way, trying all he can to get himself free. But I'd sewed him up good and strong. I wonder when it hit him, what'd been done?'

'Right then, I'd think. He was never stupid.'

'He never was. So he must've put it all together. The lemonade and all. The one thing I don't guess he ever thought of was us hid up in the granary. Or else would he've done what he did next?'

'He wouldn't have,' said my mother firmly.

'I don't know though. He might've been past caring. Eh? He just finally went past caring and gave up and ripped down his overalls altogether and let 'er fly. We had the full view.'

'He had his back to us.'

'He did not! When he shot away there wasn't a thing we couldn't see. He turned himself sideways.'

'I don't remember that.'

'Well, I do. I haven't seen so many similar sights that I can afford to forget.'

'Dodie!' said my mother, as if at this too-late point to issue a warning. (Another thing my mother quite often said was, 'I will never listen to smut.')

'Oh, you! You didn't run away yourself. Did you? Kept your eye to the knothole!'

My mother looked from me to Aunt Dodie and back with an unusual expression on her face: helplessness. I won't say she laughed. She just looked as if there was a point at which she might give up.

The onset is very slow and often years may pass before the patient or his family observe that he is becoming disabled. He shows slowly increasing bodily rigidity, associated with tremors of the head and limbs. There may be various tics, twitches, muscle spasms, and other involuntary movements. Salivation increases and drooling is common. Scientifically the disease is known as paralysis agitans. *It is also called Parkinson's disease or shaking palsy. Paralysis agitans affects first a single arm or leg, then the second limb on the same side and finally those on the other side. The face begins to lose its customary expressiveness and changes slowly or not at all with passing moods. The disease is typically one of elderly people, striking mostly persons in their sixties and seventies. No recoveries are recorded. Drugs are available to control the tremor and excess salivation. The benefits of these, however, are limited.* [Fishbein, Medical Encyclopedia.]

My mother, during this summer, would have been forty-one or forty-two years old, I think, somewhere around the age that I am now.

Just her left forearm trembled. The hand trembled more than the arm. The thumb knocked ceaselessly against the palm. She could, however, hide it in her fingers, and she could hold the arm still by stiffening it against her body.

Uncle James drank porter after supper. He let me taste it, black and bitter. Here was a new contradiction. 'Before I married your father,' my mother had told me, 'I asked him to promise me that he would never drink, and he never has.' But Uncle James her brother could drink without apologies.

On Saturday night we all went into town. My mother and my sister went in Aunt Dodie's car. I was with Uncle James and Aunt Lena and the children. The children claimed me. I was a little older than the oldest of them, and they treated me as if I were a trophy, someone for whose favour they could jostle and compete. So I was riding in their car, which was high and old and square-topped, like Aunt Dodie's. We were coming home, we had the windows rolled down for coolness, and unexpectedly Uncle James began to sing.

He had a fine voice of course, a fine sad, lingering voice. I can remember perfectly well the tune of the song he sang, and the sound of his voice rolling out the back windows, but I can remember only bits of the words, here and there, though I have often tried to remember more, because I liked the song so well.

As I was a-goen over Kil-i-kenny Mountain . . .

I think that was the way it started.
Then further along something about *pearly*, or *early* and

Some take delight in – various things, and finally the strong but sad-sounding line:

But I take delight in the water of the barley.

There was silence in the car while he was singing. The children were not squabbling and being hit, some of them were even falling asleep. Aunt Lena with the youngest on her knee was an unthreatening dark shape. The car bounced along as if it would go forever through a perfectly black night with its lights cutting a frail path; and there was a jack rabbit on the road, leaping out of our way, but nobody cried out to notice it, nobody broke the singing, its booming tender sadness.

But I take delight in THE WATER OF THE BARLEY

We got to church early, so that we could go and look at the graves. St John's was a white wooden church on the highway, with the graveyard behind it. We stopped at two stones, on which were written the words *Mother* and *Father.* Underneath in much smaller letters the names and dates of my mother's parents. Two flat stones, not very big, lying like paving stones in the clipped grass. I went off to look at things more interesting – urns and praying hands and angels in profile.

Soon my mother and Aunt Dodie came too.

'Who needs all this fancy folderol?' said Aunt Dodie, waving.

My sister, who was just learning to read, tried reading the inscriptions.

Until the Day Break

He is not Dead but Sleepeth

In Pacem

'What is *pacem?*'

'Latin,' said my mother approvingly.

'A lot of people put up these fancy stones and it is all show, they are still paying for them. Some of them still trying to pay for the plots and not even started on the stones. Look at that for instance.' Aunt Dodie pointed to a large cube of dark blue granite, flecked white like a cooking pot, balanced on one corner.

'How modern,' said my mother absently.

'That is Dave McColl's. Look at the size of it. And I know for a fact they told her if she didn't hurry up and pay something on the plot they were going to dig him up and pitch him out on the highway.'

'Is that Christian?' my mother wondered.

'Some people don't deserve Christian.'

I felt something slithering down from my waist and realized that the elastic of my underpants had broken. I caught my hands to my sides in time – I had no hips then to hold anything up – and said to my mother in an angry whisper, 'I have to have a safety pin.'

'What do you want a safety pin for?' said my mother, in a normal, or louder than normal, voice. She could always be relied upon to be obtuse at such moments.

I would not answer, but glared at her beseechingly, threateningly.

'I bet her panties bust,' Aunt Dodie laughed.

'Did they?' said my mother sternly, still not lowering her voice.

'Yes.'

'Well, take them off then,' said my mother.

'Not right here, though,' said Aunt Dodie. 'There is the Ladies.'

Behind St John's Church, as behind a country school, were two wooden toilets.

'Then I wouldn't have anything on,' I said to my mother, scandalized. I couldn't imagine walking into church in a blue taffeta dress and no pants. Rising to sing the hymns, sitting down, in *no pants*. The smooth cool boards of the pew and *no pants*.

Aunt Dodie was looking through her purse. 'I wish I had one to give you but I haven't. You just run and take them off and nobody's going to know the difference. Lucky there's no wind.'

I didn't move.

'Well I do have one pin,' said my mother doubtfully. 'But I can't take it out. My slip strap broke this morning when I was getting dressed and I put a pin in to hold it. But I can't take that out.'

My mother was wearing a soft grey dress covered with little flowers which looked as if they had been embroidered on, and a grey slip to match, because you could see through the material. Her hat was a dull rose colour, matching the colour of some of the flowers. Her gloves were almost the same rose and her shoes were white, with open toes. She had brought this whole outfit with her, had assembled it, probably, especially to wear when she walked into St John's

Church. She might have imagined a sunny morning, with St John's bell ringing, just as it was ringing now. She must have planned this and visualized it just as I now plan and visualize, sometimes, what I will wear to a party.

'I can't take it out for you or my slip will show.'

'People going in,' Aunt Dodie said.

'Go to the Ladies and take them off. If you won't do that, go sit in the car.'

I started for the car. I was halfway to the cemetery gate when my mother called my name. She marched ahead of me to the ladies' toilet, where without a word she reached inside the neck of her dress and brought out the pin. Turning my back – and not saying thank-you, because I was too deep in my own misfortune and too sure of my own rights – I fastened together the waistband of my pants. Then my mother walked ahead of me up the toilet path and around the side of the church. We were late, everybody had gone in. We had to wait while the choir, with the minister trailing, got themselves up the aisle at their religious pace.

> All things bright and beautiful,
> All creatures great and small,
> All things wise and wonderful,
> The Lord God made them all.

When the choir was in place and the minister had turned to face the congregation, my mother set out boldly to join Aunt Dodie and my sister in a pew near the front. I could see that the grey slip had slid down half an inch and was showing in a slovenly way at one side.

After the service my mother turned in the pew and spoke to people. People wanted to know my name and my sister's name and then they said, 'She does look like you.' 'No, maybe this one looks more like you'; or, 'I see your own mother in this one.' They asked how old we were and what grade I was in at school and whether my sister was going to school. They asked her when she was going to start and she said, 'I'm not,' which was laughed at and repeated. (My sister often made people laugh without meaning to; she had such a firm way of publicizing her misunderstandings. In this case it turned out that she really did think she was not going to school because the primary school near where we lived was being torn down, and nobody had told her she would go on a bus.)

Two or three people said to me, 'Guess who taught me when I went to school? Your Momma!'

'She never learned me much,' said a sweaty man, whose hand I could tell she did not want to shake, 'but she was the best-lookin' one I ever had!'

'Did my slip show?'

'How could it? You were standing in the pew.'

'When I was walking down the aisle, I wonder?'

'Nobody could see. They were all standing for the hymn.'

'They could have seen, though.'

'Only one thing surprises me. Why didn't Allen Durrand come over and say hello?'

'Was he there?'

'Didn't you see him? Over in the Wests' pew, under the window they put in for the father and mother.'

'I didn't see him. Was his wife?'

'Ah, you must have seen *her*! All in blue with a hat like a buggy wheel. She's very dressy. But not to be compared to you, today.'

Aunt Dodie herself was wearing a navy blue straw hat with some droopy cloth flowers, and a button-down-the-front slub rayon dress.

'Maybe he didn't know me. Or didn't see me.'

'He couldn't very well not have seen you.'

'Well.'

'And he's turned out such a good-looking man. That counts if you go into politics. And the height. You very seldom see a short man get elected.'

'What about Mackenzie King?'

'I meant around here. We wouldn't've elected *him*, from around here.'

'Your mother's had a little stroke. She says not, but I've seen too many like her.

'She's had a little one, and she might have another little one, and another, and another. Then someday she might have the big one. You'll have to learn to be the mother, then.

'Like me. My mother took sick when I was only ten. She died when I was fifteen. In between, what a time I had with her! She was all swollen up; what she had was dropsy. They came one time and took it out of her by the pailful.'

'Took what out?'

'*Fluid*.

'She sat up in her chair till she couldn't any more, she had to go to bed. She had to lie on her right side all the time to keep the fluid pressure off her heart. What a life.

She developed bedsores, she was in misery. So one day she said to me, Dodie, please, just turn me on my other side for just a little while, just for the relief. She begged me. I got hold of her and turned her – she was a weight! I turned her on her heart side, and the minute I did, she died.

'What are you crying about! I never meant to make you cry! Well you are a big baby, if you can't stand to hear about Life.'

Aunt Dodie laughed at me, to cheer me up. In her thin brown face her eyes were large and hot. She had a scarf around her head that day and looked like a gypsy woman, flashing malice and kindness at me, threatening to let out more secrets than I could stand.

'Did you have a stroke?' I said sullenly.

'What?'

'Aunt Dodie said you had a stroke.'

'Well, I didn't. I told her I didn't. The doctor says I didn't. She thinks she knows everything, Dodie does. She thinks she knows better than a doctor.'

'Are you going to have a stroke?'

'No. I have low blood pressure. That is just the opposite of what gives you strokes.'

'So, are you not going to get sick at all?' I said, pushing further. I was very much relieved that she had decided against strokes, and that I would not have to be the mother, and wash and wipe and feed her lying in bed, as Aunt Dodie had had to do with her mother. For I did feel it was she who decided, she gave her consent. As long as she lived, and through all the changes that happened to her, and after I had received the medical explanations of what was happening, I still felt secretly that she had given her consent. For her own purposes, I felt she did it: display, of a sort; revenge of a sort as well. More, that nobody could ever understand.

She did not answer me, but walked on ahead. We were going from Aunt Dodie's place to Uncle James's, following a path through the humpy cow pasture that made the trip shorter than going by the road.

'Is your arm going to stop shaking?' I pursued recklessly, stubbornly.

I demanded of her now, that she turn and promise me what I needed.

But she did not do it. For the first time she held out altogether against me. She went on as if she had not heard, her familiar bulk ahead of me turning strange, indifferent. She withdrew, she darkened in front of me, though all she did in fact was keep on walking along the path that she and Aunt Dodie had made when they were girls running back and forth to see each other; it was still there.

One night my mother and Aunt Dodie sat on the porch and recited poetry. How this started I forget; with one of them thinking of a quotation, likely, and the other one matching it. Uncle James was leaning against the railing, smoking. Because we were visiting, he had permitted himself to come.

'*How can a man die better,*' cried Aunt Dodie cheerfully,

> '*Than facing fearful odds,*
> *For the ashes of his fathers*
> *And the temples of his gods?*'

'And all day long the noise of battle rolled,' my mother declared,

> 'Among the mountains by the winter sea.'

> 'Not a drum was heard, not a funeral note,
> As his corpse to the ramparts we hurried. . . .'

> 'For I am going a long way
> To the island-valley of Avalon
> Where falls not hail, or rain, or any snow. . . .'

My mother's voice had taken on an embarrassing tremor, so I was glad when Aunt Dodie interrupted.

'Heavens, wasn't it all sad, the stuff they put in the old readers?'

'I don't remember a bit of it,' said Uncle James. 'Except –' and he recited without a break:

> 'Along the line of smoky hills
> The crimson forest stands
> And all day long the bluejay calls
> Throughout the autumn lands.'

'Good for you,' said Aunt Dodie, and she and my mother joined in, so they were all reciting together, and laughing at each other:

> 'Now by great marshes wrapped in mist,
> Or past some river's mouth,
> Throughout the long still autumn day
> Wild birds are flying south.'

'Though when you come to think of it, even that has kind of a sad ring,' Aunt Dodie said.

If I had been making a proper story out of this, I would have ended it, I think, with my mother not answering and going ahead of me across the pasture. That would have done. I didn't stop there, I suppose, because I wanted to find out more, remember more. I wanted to bring back all I could. Now I look at what I have done and it is like a series of snapshots, like the brownish snapshots with fancy borders that my parents' old camera used to take. In these snapshots Aunt Dodie and Uncle James and even Aunt Lena, even her children, come out clear enough. (All these people dead now except the children who have turned into decent friendly wage earners, not a criminal or as far as I know even a neurotic among them.) The problem, the only problem, is my mother. And she is the one of course that I am trying to get; it is to reach her that this whole journey has been undertaken. With what purpose? To mark her off, to describe, to illumine, to celebrate, to *get rid* of, her; and it did not work, for she looms too close, just as she always did. She is heavy as always, she weighs everything down, and yet she is indistinct, her edges melt and flow. Which means she has stuck to me as close as ever and refused to fall away, and I could go on, and on, applying what skills I have, using what tricks I know, and it would always be the same.

'She has a touch of genius'
Mail on Sunday

Born into the back streets of a small Canadian town, Rose battled
incessantly with her practical and shrewd stepmother, Flo, who
cowed her with tales of her own past and warnings of the
dangerous world outside. But Rose was ambitious – she won a
scholarship and left for Toronto where she married Patrick. She
was his Beggar Maid, 'meek and voluptuous, with her shy white
feet', and he was her knight, content to sit and adore her.

'A work of great brilliance and depth'
New Statesman

'Alice Munro captures a kaleidoscope of lights and depths...she
manages to reproduce the vibrant practice of life while
scrutinizing the workings of her own narrative art...an
exhilarating collection'
New York Times

Alice Munro

The Moons of Jupiter

'Witty, subtle, passionate'
New York Times

The characters who populate an Alice Munro story live and breathe.
Passions hopelessly conceived, affections betrayed, marriages made
and broken: the joys, fears, loves and awakenings of women echo
throughout these twelve unforgettable stories, laying bare the
unexceptional and yet inescapable pain of human contact.

'Only a few writers continue to create those full-bodied miniature
universes of the old school. Some of her short stories are so ample
and fulfilling that they feel like novels. They present whole
landscapes and cultures, whole families of characters'
Anne Tyler

VINTAGE BOOKS
London

Alice Munro

The Progress of Love

'Whatever it is that makes some writing come alive in every phrase and sentence, Alice Munro has it... I wouldn't willingly miss one of her stories'
Sunday Times

These dazzling and utterly satisfying stories explore varieties and degrees of love – filial, platonic, sexual, parental and imagined – in the lives of apparently ordinary folk. In fact, Munro's characters pulse with idiosyncratic life. Under the polished surface of these unsentimental dispatches from the small-town and rural front lies a strong undertow of violence and sexuality, repressed until something snaps, with extraordinary force in some of the stories, sadly and strangely in others.

'A writer of great sensitivity and delicacy'
Guardian

VINTAGE BOOKS
London

Alice Munro

Friend of My Youth

'The particular brilliance of Alice Munro is that in range and
depth her short stories are almost novels'
Daily Telegraph

A woman haunted by dreams of her dead mother. An adulterous
couple stepping over the line where the initial excitement ends
and the pain begins. A widow visiting a Scottish village in search
of her husband's past – and instead discovering unsettling truths
about a total stranger. The ten stories in this collection not only
astonish and delight but also convey the unspoken mysteries at
the heart of all human experience.

'Alice Munro's stories in *Friend of My Youth* are wonderful:
intricate, deep, full of absorbing and funny detail'
Independent on Sunday

VINTAGE BOOKS
London

Also available from Vintage

Alice Munro

Open Secrets

'*Open Secrets* is shocking and delightful and mysterious'
A. S. Byatt

Ranging from the 1850s through two world wars to the present,
and from Canada to Brisbane, the Balkans and the Somme, these
stories reveal the secrets of unconventional women who refuse to
be contained.

'A book that dazzles with its faith in language and life'
New York Times

'Alice Munro's stories are miraculous'
Lucy Hughes-Hallett, *Sunday Times*

VINTAGE BOOKS
London

Also available from Vintage

Alice Munro

Dear Life

'Deep and surprising and unsparing'
Guardian

Moments of change, chance encounters, the twist of fate that leads a person to a new way of thinking or being: the stories in *Dear Life* build to form a radiant, indelible portrait of just how dangerous and strange ordinary life can be.

'As rich and astonishing as anything she has ever done before'
New York Review of Books

'How lucky we are to have Munro herself and her subtle, intelligent and true work'
Financial Times

VINTAGE BOOKS
London

Alice Munro

Lying Under the Apple Tree

'Munro is still one of our most fearless explorers of the human being, as she descends, time and again, headlamp on full beam, pickaxe and butter-knife at the ready'
The Times

Spanning her last five collections and bringing together her finest work from the past fifteen years, this new selection of Alice Munro's stories infuses everyday lives with a wealth of nuance and insight. Beautifully observed and remarkably crafted, written with emotion and empathy, these stories are nothing short of perfection. A masterclass in the genre, from an author who deservedly lays claim to being one of the major fiction writers of our time.

'Munro is so good that one gropes for superlatives...(her) stories read like short novels; entire lives comprehended in a peripheral glimpse, an uncanny anticipation, a sudden intuition'

'Munro's artistry recalls the close attention and cool detachment of a psychoanalyst'
Times Literary Supplement

VINTAGE BOOKS
London